EDGE ANOMALY

The Spirit of Crescent Island

Meg Rabbit

Front and back cover art: Meg Rabbit
Fonts: Jellyka Castles Queen by Jellyka Nerevan (used with
permission), IM FELL Double Pica, Imprint MT Shadow, Time New
Roman
Chapter art: Kirsten Coffey @_Krimmins_ / Instagram
Scene divider: Copyright: @seamartini / 123RF.com
Image frame: Copyright: @antoshkaforever / 123RF.com

www.EdgeAnomaly.com

Dedicated to Dylan.

You're the best son and friend I could ever ask for.

Thank you for loving me despite my secrets.

Glossary

Amphs – Anthropomorphic reptilian sapiens from Marrow. Responsible for research and technology in Marrow.

Anchor (she/her) – A neotenous Amph from Dwarka. Xalma's friend.

Ashmara (she/her) – Jessop's mother. An exiled Avian chemist. Formerly an Ambassador to the Amphs in Marrow.

Avians – Anthropomorphic gryphons. Responsible for manufacturing and distribution in Marrow.

Bramblemare – A plant-deer creature that lives on Crescent Island.

Cato (he/him) – The military leader of The Resistance. A Forax. Formerly a scout.

Cowrie – A forest city recently occupied by The Resistance.

Deejii – Xalma's sorority sisters.

Dwarka – The underwater home of Amph children in Cowrie.

Edge (she/her) – Mana's daughter, and the hero of the story. A Forax.

Exterminator – A sapien responsible for pest control. Usually a Forax.

Fangowl (they/them) – A mythical Avian god.

Farmer – A sapien who might resemble a wide variety of anthropomorphic mammals, and performs a repetitive task to grow or collect resources. Usually a Forax.

Forax – Anthropomorphic mammals with different physical characteristics.

Harbeshi (he/him) – Jessop's father. An exiled Avian artist. Formerly an Ambassador to the Amphs in Marrow.

Hiro (he/him) – The spiritual leader of The Resistance. A Forax. Formerly a sentry.

Hive – The home of the Insects.

Hive Mind – A collective mind formed by many Insects through dance and song.

Horndrum (they/them) – A mythical Amph god.

Insects – Sentient arthropods who can operate as a colony (a Hive Mind).

Jackbear – A plant-bear creature that lives on Crescent Island.

Jessop (he/him) – Edge's loyal friend. An exiled Avian who loves flying.

Junealope – A plant-rabbit creature that lives on Crescent Island.

Limbic – Where Sole is from. The part of Tsoci that processes feelings.

Mahali (he/him) – An owl-like Avian who befriends Edge and Jessop in Cowrie. Originally from Cowrie.

Mana (she/her) – Edge's mother. A Forax biologist. Formerly a scout. Marrow – The sapien city in South Crescent.

Mary (she/her) – An Insect captive from Cowrie. Edge's friend.

Merge – Edge's power.

Pod – The name for a Forax community in Marrow.

Rovers (they/them) – Non-propagating buds of Tsoci, designed to perform a task and be reabsorbed.

Ruins – An ancient Hive near Cowrie.

Sapien – Any of the animals (Amphs, Avians and Forax) who can speak.

Sewlich (they/them) – A mythical Forax god. Pronounced SO-lej.

Scout – A Forax resembling an anthropomorphic flying squirrel. Normally responsible for delivering messages and packages in Marrow.

Sole (they/them) – A rover who chooses to remain and individual. Edge's guide and protector.

Sopa (she/her) – Mahali's rescuer, a Forax mycologist exiled from Cowrie. Formerly an exterminator.

Superorganism – The emergence of a consciousness from many organisms who are connected by a complex communication system.

The Grotto – Xalma's home. An underground lake fed by thermal vents with life-extending properties.

The Resistance – A rebel organization from Marrow.

Tsoci (they / them) – A superorganism. The Spirit of Crescent Island. Pronounced TSO-see.

Vera (she/her) – The scientific leader of The Resistance. A Forax. Formerly a farmer.

Vinecat – A plant-cat creature that lives on Crescent Island. Domesticated and genetically altered by sapiens in Marrow.

Xalma / The Child Queen (she/her) – A neotenous Amph with a mysterious past. Jessop's friend.

Chapter One

Outcasts

Edge lived in a treehouse overlooking a big lake in the center of a valley. Waterfalls and rivers flowed down from the surrounding mountains, flashing like jeweled vines against the grey stone cliffs, and winding through the dark forest to the lake.

At the height of summer, when the days were long, the valley was full of life. In winter, the sun barely glanced down at all before disappearing again behind the rocky peaks. The seasons passed carefully, as though any sudden movement or sound might topple the ancient trees and bring the mountains crashing down. In warmer months, Edge and her mother travelled to Grotto Ridge to study the Insects. Like Edge, the Insects were about as tall as a full-grown berry bush, although some were a little bigger or smaller. The Insects were a fantastic variety of shapes and colors, and they all lived together in a sprawling city called Hive.

Edge loved the winter. She built caves in the snow, fished over a hole in the ice, and told herself stories about talking trees and mysterious islands far across the ocean. Other creatures lived in the forest, but none of them spoke, except to each other. Edge pretended to speak with them anyway. She tempted the forest animals with roots and nuts and followed their daily adventures.

When two junelopes had a falling out over a mate and one of them was injured, Edge found the wounded creature and revived it. She knew when a tall-antlered bramblemare matriarch passed away, and when the dark and gregarious flocks of nettlecrows were feuding.

One afternoon, as Edge entered a clearing surrounded by bushes of frozen tangberries, she noticed the vinecats had brought their kits foraging for the first time.

They've left their vines early this year, she thought.

Edge approached the bushes and noticed unfamiliar tracks. Whatever made them was not much bigger than she was. As she stepped forward, one of her wide, furry feet slipped into a trap, hidden under a light cover of snow.

Jackbears and thornwolves roamed the woods, but Edge knew they couldn't have set a trap. She wrenched her leg painfully, but she could not pull free. As she struggled to release herself, a brown, feathery creature fell silently from the sky and lifted the trap into the air, with Edge suspended painfully by one foot.

"Stop!" Edge screamed as her mysterious captor laboriously hauled her away from the tangberry thicket.

The would-be hunter dropped Edge immediately.

"Aaah! Food doesn't talk!" he squawked as he flapped away.

Edge rolled a short distance and hit a boulder, smashing the trap into splinters. Without a second thought, she raced up the closest tree in pursuit of the hunter. In all her life, Edge had never heard anyone else speak besides her mother.

"Waaait!" she hollered, leaping quickly from branch to branch and trying to keep the anxious newcomer in sight.

None of the young hunter's intended meals had ever yelled and chased him before. He slowed his ascent and circled widely around Edge, eyeing her with curiosity and concern.

"What are you?" yelled Edge.

"I'm an Avian," he answered as he whirled above, "My name is Jessop. Sorry about trapping you, I didn't know you could talk. What are *you*?"

"I'm Edge," answered Edge, as the Avian circled away.

"What?" yelled Jessop, circling back.

"I'M EDGE!" hollered Edge.

"WHAT EDGE?" shouted Jessop.

"*I'M* EDGE!" Edge repeated.

"MEET ME ON THE GROUND. I WON'T EAT YOU," Jessop promised.

Edge examined Jessop's sharp beak and talons and noted that although he was a little taller than she was, he was very slender. She followed him to a nearby clearing and they looked at each other properly for the first time.

Jessop had never seen anything like Edge. Her deep brown eyes, thick fur, and bushy tail were similar to a squirlish, (which is why he thought she might make a nice meal), but Edge was much larger and sturdier than any squirlish Jessop had ever seen, and she could talk.

"How can you not know what you *are*?" Jessop asked, after Edge told him she was just Edge for the third time.

"No one's ever asked me what I am," she replied patiently. "I know what I'm *not*."

Jessop looked her up and down with obvious excitement.

Edge considered Jessop as he hopped around trying to figure out what she was.

He's so curious! she thought. *I think Mana will like him.*

"There's only two of us," Edge explained finally. "Me and Mana; she's my mother. You should come meet her. Maybe she can answer your questions."

Edge wasn't particularly concerned about what she was. As far as she knew, there was no one else like her in the world except Mana.

Jessop hesitated, glancing at the darkening sky.

"I need to go home," he said regretfully. "I live past Grotto Ridge. It takes a while to get there. Can you meet me here tomorrow at noon?"

Edge agreed to this plan. As soon as Jessop flew out of sight, she raced home.

Mana silently brushed the snow from her daughter's coat as Edge described her new friend. When she mentioned the trap, a look of concern crossed Mana's face, but she didn't speak until the story was finished.

"He said he's an Avian! What's an Avian? Is he like us? What *are* we?" asked Edge. "Are we called something, too?"

Mana answered carefully. Edge had not asked what they were in a long time. Mana had always managed to convince her daughter that the question was pointless, because there were only two of them.

"Jessop is a sapien, like us," replied Mana. "He has a language, like we do. Sapiens learn, and they pass along their wisdom to their children."

"He looks different. He has feathers! Like a bird!" Edge paced back and forth, fidgeting with her tail.

"He's not different in his mind." Mana looked thoughtful. "Sit down, Edge," she added gently.

Mana brushed burrs out of her daughter's bushy tail. Edge felt herself relax.

"Is he *safe*, Mana? He did try to trap me."

"I think he's probably safe," Mana replied with a smile. "The Avians I've met are wise and brave. I didn't know there were other sapiens here. I'd like to meet them. Then I'll know if he's safe."

Edge yawned. "Let's meet them tomorrow!"

"You should sleep," suggested Mana. "If Jessop lives past Grotto Ridge, we may have a long way to go if we want to meet his family."

Edge said goodnight to her mother and went to her room. Moments later, she was fast asleep.

Mana sat by the fading light of the hearth and considered the day's events. A winter stillness surrounded the treehouse, but Mana could sense the beginning of spring.

The next morning Edge leapt out of bed already worried that Jessop might not return.

"There's no reason he won't come back," Mana assured her.

Edge could think of a number of reasons.

What if his family said he shouldn't make friends with strangers? What if he couldn't find the meeting place they'd agreed on? What if he didn't *want* to come back?

By the time she had finished her chores, Edge was convinced that she would never see Jessop again. She was beginning to wonder if she'd imagined him.

"All we can do is go and see," repeated Mana patiently as they packed for the trip.

When they were ready to leave, Edge and Mana climbed to the very top of the trees supporting their house and jumped into the air. Delicate bones extended from their wrists, stretching the membranes of their wings. Edge and Mana flew away from the treehouse and disappeared into the forest.

To Edge's great delight, Jessop and his parents were waiting at the meeting place. The two families kept a respectful distance. They remarked on the weather. They agreed that it was nice to talk with someone new, and it was a shame it didn't happen more often.

Unlike Edge and Mana, whose brown fur and green clothes blended into the surroundings, the adult Avians wore brightly colored shawls over vibrant plumage. They stood out clearly against the snow and trees.

Either they're not from here, or they don't have to worry about hiding. Edge was struck by the difference between Jessop and his parents. The adult Avians stood two heads taller than their son, and their feathers were bright blue, red, and yellow. Jessop's feathers, by contrast, reminded Edge of tree bark. *Jessop looks like he belongs here,* she decided.

Aside from their general shape, the only thing Jessop's parents had in common with their son were their hooked beaks and their taloned, dark orange hands and feet.

The Avian's wings were folded neatly across their backs. Edge tried to imagine what it would feel like to have an extra set of limbs on her back, and decided she was happy with her own arrangement.

"We'd be honored if you would share our meal with us," Mana said politely.

As the adults talked, Edge half-hid behind Mana, nowhere near as brazen as she'd been the day before.

"I am Harbeshi," said the taller Avian, "and this is Ashmara. Jessop told us he met a Forax in the woods, but we found it very hard to believe. I still do not completely believe it. Why did you come to Far Crescent?"

"I'm here to study the Insects," replied Mana.

Ashmara and Harbeshi exchanged a puzzled look.

"You must tell us your story," Ashmara said politely.

Jessop hopped eagerly over to Edge.

"I'm so glad you came back! My parents didn't believe me when I told them about you! They assumed I was making you up so they wouldn't get mad at me for flying around the valley by myself."

"Why?" Edge asked quietly, moving out of Mana's shadow towards him.

Jessop shrugged. "Who knows. I do it all the time, but they freak out anyway."

"That's not what I mean," Edge explained. "Why did they think you were making me up?"

"They said you wouldn't have the skills to survive here."

"I have *plenty* of skills!" Edge snorted indignantly, regaining some of her earlier courage. "I've lived here my whole life."

"I heard your mom say that. She also said you study the Insects. What does that mean?"

"We watch them," Edge replied proudly, "and we write down everything we learn. I help her."

"Why, though? What are you trying to learn?"

"They're just really interesting." Edge shrugged carelessly. "Did you know they dance and make music?"

As they spoke, Edge and Jessop moved further from their parents, whose serious words and confusing conversation was starting to annoy Jessop. He had some experience waiting for adults to finish talking, and he could tell that it was going to take a while. Adults spoke about such boring things. Jessop didn't mind waiting, though. He was fascinated by Edge.

"Can I see your wings?" he asked hopefully.

"Why?" Edge crossed her arms and took a step back warily.

Jessop thought quickly – his parents had warned him to be careful with his words.

"I just want to see if they're as big as mine," he answered innocently.

Edge was suddenly very curious about this, so she willingly extended her arms and stretched her wings out.

Jessop stood in front Edge and spread his wings wide – the span was significantly longer, owing to his graceful flight feathers. Edge noticed soft tufts of feathers at the base of Jessop's wings.

"Do you have fur, too?"

"No, that's down, it's a different kind of feather," responded Jessop, quickly folding his wings again.

"Why do you look so different from your parents?" wondered Edge. "I look just like Mana did when she was my age." Mana was taller and rounder than Edge, but other than that, they looked almost identical.

"I'm not an adult yet," answered Jessop. "Every year I molt, and my new feathers have more color. Look..." he stretched a wing towards Edge. "See the green? My mom says that's the rarest color!"

Edge couldn't see anything remotely green, but she wanted to be polite, so she nodded.

"How fast can you fly?" Jessop asked.

"Not as fast as you," Edge admitted.

"I can outfly an *Insect*," bragged Jessop proudly.

Edge gasped in amazement.

"Did an Insect *chase* you?"

Jessop launched into the first of several stories about near misses with Insects. Edge interrupted dozens of times to ask what the Insects looked like, where he'd seen them, how far they chased him, and what sounds they made. Misinterpreting her scientific interest for admiration, Jessop cheerfully continued telling, and embellishing, stories.

When it was clear that Jessop and Edge were occupied with their own conversation, the adults spoke more openly.

"I've told Edge very little about where we're from," Mana told the Avians. "Before I share my full story with you, I need to talk to her."

"We understand," Ashmara replied sympathetically. "You are an outcast, I assume?"

"Yes," confirmed Mana. "And you?"

"We are, yes," Ashmara replied. "We have been here for almost as long as you, I think. The Avians and the Amphs are at war. We were on the wrong side of that war, and were sentenced to death by the Avian Council. The Amphs rescued us and brought us here, to watch over The Child Queen."

"The Child Queen is *real*?" Mana exclaimed incredulously.

"Yes. She has been here the entire time," Harbeshi said. "If she ever grows up, she will return to Marrow."

"*When* she grows up," corrected Ashmara. "She has a responsibility to the Amphs."

"She is too selfish for responsibility."

Ashmara snorted. "She is what she has been made, Harbeshi."

Harbeshi ignored his partner's comment.

"Why are you studying the Insects? What do you hope to learn?" he asked Mana.

"It's a good way to pass the time and teach Edge about biology," Mana replied. "Maybe I'll learn something useful." Harbeshi and Ashmara looked skeptical, but before they could ask any more questions, Mana steered the conversation away from herself.

"How did the Amphs come to rescue you?" Mana asked. "That must be an incredible story!"

The Avians, sensing that Mana was not ready to trust them with any more information, briefly shared their story.

"...and that is how we became the appointed guardians of The Child Queen," finished Harbeshi a short time later. It was clear that he didn't enjoy telling the story, but Mana trusted him more for having told it.

Harbeshi glanced at Jessop and Edge to make sure they were still distracted.

"I have never met a Forax who studied biology," he observed. "You are a *scout*, no?"

"I *was* a scout," corrected Mana. "I'm a scientist now."

Harbeshi's brow furrowed. Ashmara looked impressed. "How can this be?" she asked.

"I was educated in secret," explained Mana. "The Resistance needed information that could more easily be gathered by a trained scout."

Harbeshi exclaimed "The Resistance! What?"

Mana interrupted.

"I'm happy to tell you my whole story, but first I must talk to Edge."

"Yes. Yes of course," Harbeshi agreed, exchanging glances with Ashmara.

The sound of arguing children drew their attention.

Jessop had forgotten his parents' warning to be mindful of his words. He was asking Edge who her father was and how she became an outcast. Jessop didn't believe that Edge didn't know the answers to these basic questions. He thought she didn't trust him, and his feelings were hurt.

"Stop being such a secretive cloaca!" Jessop shouted.
"There are plenty of things *you* do not know." Harbeshi's
stern rebuke silenced Jessop. "Edge has the social graces not
to rudely call them to your attention. Apologize!"
Jessop lowered his eyes and recited a formal Avian
apology in a toneless voice.

"I admit my fault, and I will honor what I have learned
today," he muttered.

After agreeing to visit the treehouse the next day, the
Avians departed. As soon as they were out of sight, Edge
confronted her mother.

"What is Marrow? Where are we *from*? Do I have a
father?"

"We need to go home," answered Mana. "It's getting late,
and you know it isn't a good idea for us to talk while we fly
through the woods. It'll be night soon." Mana's voice was
calm, but her heart was breaking.

"What *am* I?" Edge snarled, stamping her foot. "I don't
care how dangerous it is in the woods!"

Mana knelt in front of Edge, her eyes full of tears.

"I'm sorry, Edge. You have every right to be angry with
me. I promise I'll explain everything when we get home. But
let's get home safely."

The standoff, though tense, was brief. Edge knew her
mother was right.

Together they leapt into the chilly night air and flew
home. The forest was peaceful and still, but Edge's mind
roared with unanswered questions.

Who am I? she wondered. *Are there others like me? Why
didn't my mother tell me that we aren't alone?*

Tears streamed from her eyes, froze on her fur, and burst
into a trail of glittering dust behind her.

Chapter Two

Forax

W hen she was much younger, Edge often asked her mother whether there were others like them somewhere in the world.

Instead of answering with her usual enthusiasm and detail, Mana's responses to questions about their origins were vague, and she often became distracted. Over time, she convinced Edge that the question itself was a waste of time. There was no one else like them. End of discussion.

Have I always known Mana was hiding things? Edge asked herself as they entered the treehouse. She honestly didn't know the answer. Her stomach hurt and her eyes were stinging.

Is this normal? she wondered as she stumbled to her room.

She didn't know the answer to that, either.

Mana deliberately followed the same routine she always followed when returning home, checking the experiments carefully and recording any new data. When she was done, she stoked the fire, tidied up the house, and made some tea. Finally, she called Edge.

"I'm ready to answer your questions," said Mana.

Still feeling deeply betrayed, Edge sat next to the fire without looking at her mother.

"I know this is a lot to process," Mana said quietly, passing Edge a steaming cup of tea. "Let's take it slowly, okay?"

Edge nodded.

"There are terrible things in the world. I wanted you to be safe and happy for as long as possible before you had to face them," Mana explained. "I didn't want to tell you where we came from until you turned sixteen."

"You have to tell me *now*," Edge said firmly. "I'm not waiting four more years."

Mana nodded slowly.

"Animals who share our language are called sapiens," she began. "There are three sapien races. We're called Forax. Jessop is an Avian. The third race is the Amphs. There's a lot of variety within each race, and they each live in their own section of Marrow."

"What's Marrow?" Edge interrupted.

"Marrow is where I come from. I used to be a scout in Marrow."

"What's a scout?"

"If Marrow was a giant body, scouts would be part of the nervous system, sending messages around the body."

She gave Edge a moment to ask a question, but Edge was speechless. She was imagining a lot of sapiens like Mana living inside a giant body.

"Scouts start working as soon as they learn to fly, and they live in a pod together," Mana continued. "Forax from different pods talk to each other when they have to, but they mainly stay in their own pod. They don't worry about what the rest of Marrow is doing, any more than your blood cells worry about what your brain is doing."

"My blood cells don't have brains, though," Edge said. "They *can't* worry."

"Sometimes sapiens can't worry either," Mana answered darkly.

"Do they all live in treehouses, like us?" Edge asked, imagining a forest full of treehouses.

"No." Mana shook her head. "Most Forax live in buildings made of stone and metal. Many Forax families live in each building. Avians and Amphs have different kinds of homes."

"Forax live inside giant *stones*? How?"

"Sapiens can take the raw ingredients of the world and shape them into almost anything," Mana explained. "In Marrow, towers made of stone, metal and glass rise into the clouds, and thousands of Forax live in each tower. Most of the homes are quite nice," Mana assured Edge, who was staring at her mother with horrified fascination. "They're warm and comfortable, and very safe. The scouts in my pod lived in a stone building."

"What do scouts *do*, exactly?" asked Edge.

"Scouts are the luckiest and loneliest kind of Forax," Mana said. "They travel around Marrow, and outside it, too. Sometimes they pass messages, and sometimes they deliver things. Scouts come into contact with the other races, so they're only allowed to spend time with other scouts. There aren't that many scouts anymore, so I didn't have very many friends."

"Why not?" asked Edge.

"Now that Marrow has the network, it doesn't need that many scouts," answered Mana.

"No, I mean why can't scouts be friends with other Forax? Who makes all the rules?"

"Sapiens make the rules," Mana explained, smiling. "As Marrow grew bigger, so did the list of rules."

"Why would there be a rule to say who you can talk to?" Edge asked. "That seems really unfair."

"There's no scientific definition for the word 'fair'," Mana replied. "But I agree with you. I think a lot of Marrow's rules could be better."

"What other rules are there?" Edge asked.

"One of the rules is that when a Forax is born, they get a job. They start working as soon as they're able to, and they do that job for their entire lives. But that rule is only for Forax."

Edge frowned.

"Another rule just for Forax is that we're not allowed to be scientists. Jessop's parents didn't expect me to be a scientist, and Jessop will probably ask you about it."

"Did you leave Marrow because you couldn't do science there?"

"No," Mana replied. "I left when I was older. I was a scout until I was your age." Mana looked at her daughter fondly. "I did my job and spent time with the other scouts. One night, I was stolen from my home."

"Someone *stole* you?" Edge gasped.

"At the time, it felt more like a rescue." Mana explained. "I don't remember being taken; I just woke up somewhere new. A lot of sapiens were there. They asked me if I wanted to become a scientist."

"Weren't you scared?" Edge looked at her mother in awe.

"I was terrified," Mana admitted, "but the headquarters of The Resistance is a fascinating place. There's a laboratory, a library, even an underground garden. It's beautiful, and the sapiens were very kind to me. They let me explore, and they answered all my questions. They didn't hurt me."

Mana hesitated before continuing. "I was lonely, so I was excited about joining The Resistance."

"Why were you lonely?" Edge asked.

"I didn't have any friends."

Mana resumed her story before Edge could ask for more details. She wasn't ready to think about that part of her past yet.

"The Resistance is a secret society. It was started a long time ago by sapiens who didn't agree with Marrow's rules. In Marrow, scientists study the world, just like you and I do, but they're told what to study. The rules only allow them to learn about things that will make Marrow better or stronger."

"How can rules control what someone is learning?"

"One way is to limit the number of ideas and words they have," answered Mana. "Marrow has rules about which ideas and words are okay, and who's allowed to learn them. The Resistance encourages sapiens to learn anything they want to, as long as they promise to always seek the truth."

"That sounds a lot better," said Edge.

"I certainly thought so," Mana agreed. "For the first time ever, I was allowed to ask forbidden questions and learn about the other races. The Resistance taught me to look at the world through the eyes of a scientist." Mana stared into the fire. "But it also taught me that some questions don't *have* an objectively true answer."

"Yeah," Edge agreed, "like what the best color is, or which Insect is the more interesting."

Mana nodded. "Yes, but those are little questions. The answers to big questions can also be subjective. Like whether one sapien is worth more than another. The Resistance was using scientists to look for the answers to questions like that."

"They were trying to prove some sapiens are worth more than others? Why?"

"I don't know," Mana admitted, "but I knew it was bad science. I was so happy to learn what I could, and to have friends, though. I'm afraid I didn't worry about what The Resistance was trying to prove." Mana smiled sadly. "When I was sent here to research the Insects, I decided to leave all the rules and prejudices of Marrow behind."

Edge started thinking about the furthest places she'd ever visited. Were there huge stone towers full of Forax just over the horizon?

"Where *is* Marrow?"

"It's in the south, past mountains, a rainforest, a volcano, and a desert," Mana replied. "It's on the other side of the island. This whole valley, everything you know, is just the northernmost tip of Crescent Island."

Edge was fascinated. She knew they lived on an island, but she'd assumed that the mountain range around the valley was surrounded by the ocean all the way around. Her world suddenly felt much bigger.

"How did you get here?" asked Edge curiously.

"I travelled most of the way by boat," Mana answered. "That's how your friend Jessop and his family came here, too. Boats are like buildings that can travel through the water."

"That sounds cool!" Edge exclaimed. Mana's willingness to answer questions and Edge's natural curiosity eased the last of the tension between them.

"Why did The Resistance want you to study the Insects?" Edge asked.

"The only time sapiens in Marrow see Insects is when they remove someone who isn't doing their job." Mana spoke calmly, but a look of pain crossed her face.

"The Insects *steal* sapiens?" Edge was shocked.

"Yes," Mana answered, her face grave. "It's been happening for as long as anyone can remember, and it happens to Forax far more often than it happens to other sapiens. If a sapien in Marrow refuses to do their job, Insects take them away. No one knows what becomes of the sapiens they take."

"Why?" Edge was shocked.

"I don't know." Mana shook her head sadly. "The Resistance sent me here to find out."

"Have you *seen* an Insect take a sapien?" asked Edge, horrified and fascinated.

"Yes," Mana nodded sadly, "but I would prefer not to talk about that. Not yet."

Edge knew the Insects were dangerous, but the thought of them appearing suddenly to take someone away was the most frightening thing she could imagine. It was also difficult to believe. In all her years of studying them, Edge had never seen an Insect hunt an animal. They could sting, and they might even kill if something threatened them, but they didn't hunt. The Insects only ate plants, fungus, and things that were already dead.

Mother and daughter gazed at the embers of the fire and listened to the whispery scratches of tiny snowflakes hitting the window.

"I still don't understand why you kept all of this secret," Edge said finally, breaking the silence. "Why did you think it was okay to make me believe we were all alone?"

"I didn't want you to be lonely," Mana answered simply. "I know how it feels to not have any friends. I hoped that if you thought we were the only sapiens in the world, you wouldn't feel like you were missing anything. I know things will be different now, but I'm glad you met Jessop. You deserve to have friends."

"Do I have a father?" Edge asked quietly.

"Yes. He was… taken," answered Mana. "I'll tell you about him soon, Edge. That's something you'll have to wait for."

"But what's his name?" Edge insisted. "Where is he? Why didn't you ever tell me about him?"

"I'll tell you, Edge," Mana promised. "I'm not ready yet."

A little of her earlier anger returned, but Edge pushed it back. She sensed that Mana was more upset than she was letting on.

"If I said I wanted to go to Marrow, would you take me?" Edge demanded.

Mana frowned, but she nodded.

"Yes, Edge, but we would have to find a safe way to travel there. It's a long, dangerous journey, and I don't think you'll like it."

"I have to see it," Edge insisted.

"I know," Mana replied sadly.

That night, Edge's dreams were filled with Insects, sapiens, and giant stone towers full of traps.

Chapter Three

The Child Queen

M ana woke at dawn. She completed her morning chores, ate breakfast, and returned to her lab. Edge rose a short while later and ate a hurried meal of nuts and fruit. She left the treehouse without saying goodbye. The Avians were visiting later in the day. Everything felt new and uncertain. Edge wanted some time alone.

She flew over the frozen lake to a wide, sharp column of stone that pierced the ice. Steam poured from vents along the sides of the dark, steep surface. In the summer, a living shroud of mist surrounded the spire. In the winter, the vapor froze into elaborate and delicate crystal structures, surrounding the vertical shaft with graceful swells and sweeping sheets of ice.

Edge called it Glass Island, and she loved the ethereal quality of it. Unlike the sleepy, unchanging forest, Glass Island was constantly evolving. She huddled on an icy ledge outside one of the steaming vents, shaking herself frequently as the damp air condensed on her fur.

Over the next hour, Edge made peace with her uncertainty and fear. Some of the things Mana had described were disturbing. It upset Edge to think of Mana not being allowed to learn whatever she wanted. Marrow didn't sound very fun, and Edge wasn't sure she wanted to see it. On the other hand, she wanted to know about the other sapiens.

I can't learn everything at once, she told herself, *but at least now I can* start *learning.*

She was about to head home when a rustle of feathers disturbed the air. Jessop perched on a ledge above her. Harbeshi and Ashmara circled overhead.

"It *is* Edge," Ashmara called. "Meet us later, Jessop!" She and Harbeshi departed in the direction of the treehouse.

Jessop was already sliding down the ice towards Edge.

"You're *here*! I didn't think you knew about The Grotto! Do you know Xalma? No, of course you don't." Jessop slid to a stop a few steps from Edge, looking sheepish.

"Look, I'm *really* sorry about yesterday. I didn't know you didn't know, uh... I mean," he paused awkwardly, looking at the ground and scratching the ice nervously with his talons. "Anyway, I'm sorry," he said finally.

"It's okay," Edge said. "Mana told me some things last night, but I still don't know very much."

"I'll tell you everything *I* know," Jessop promised, his face full of relief. "But I don't know very much, either. I thought you might know some of the things my parents won't tell me."

"Your parents have secrets too?"

"Yeah, and it's really annoying. I was five when we came here, though, so I know about Marrow. Plus, I'm friends with Xalma, and she knows a lot."

"Who's Xalma?" Edge asked curiously.

"Xalma lives in The Grotto, where this steam comes from," Jessop explained. "There's an entrance in the swamp, and one past Grotto Ridge, near the ocean. If these are the only vents you know about, it's no wonder you haven't met her yet."

"She lives *inside* a steam vent?" Edge couldn't get close to the vents – the air was too hot.

"She doesn't live *in* them, but they're all connected to The Grotto. That's where she lives."

"Is Xalma an Avian?"

"No," answered Jessop with a laugh. "She's an Amph. My parents call her 'The Child Queen', but her name is Xalma."

"Why do they call her that if it's not her name?" asked Edge.

"She doesn't know," Jessop shrugged, "and my parents won't tell me."

"What *is* an Amph?" Edge asked.

"Amphs live in the water when they're young, and on land when they get older," Jessop explained. "The Grotto is a big, underground lake, and it's warm all the time, so that's where Xalma lives. She's *really* talented." Jessop spoke with obvious admiration.

Edge said nothing. She was trying to imagine a new sapien who was different from the small group of sapiens she already knew.

"Do you want to meet her?" Jessop asked eagerly. "I think you'd like her. She's been my only friend until now."

Edge was surprised. "You only have one friend? Where are the other Avians?"

"Well, I hope I have *two* friends now," laughed Jessop. Edge found herself laughing too.

"The other Avians are in Marrow," Jessop continued. "My parents and I came to North Crescent because they were going to kill us."

"Why would they want to kill you?" Edge exclaimed.

Jessop recognized the look of fascination on his new friend's face, and he pressed his advantage.

"I'll tell you everything if you come meet Xalma," he offered.

Edge couldn't resist the promise of more information, so she agreed to follow Jessop. She climbed nimbly to the top of the icy ledge and jumped into the air. As Edge rode the updraft from the heat of the vents high into the sky, Jessop showed off his much fancier flying skills, diving and spinning like a leaf in an eddy. Edge was impressed.

When they were high above the lake, Jessop yelled "Let's go!" and turned in the direction of the treehouse. Edge followed him, wondering how many secret sapiens were living right beside her.

Jessop led them into a swamp that Edge had always avoided. The trees were covered in slime, and the air was dank.

Maybe all the other sapiens in the valley live in terrible places, and that's why I've never seen any of them, thought Edge.

Jessop landed in front of a stone archway. Clouds of steam billowed around them. The surface below was paved with carefully arranged stones. An arched entrance framed a tunnel leading into the ground. It was flanked on either side by statues of tall, serious looking sapiens holding wicked spears. The top of the building was overgrown with moss and shrubs. From overhead, the entrance to The Grotto blended in perfectly with the swamp below.

An unfamiliar cool blue light glowed inside the tunnel. Wafts of warm air rushed from The Grotto's depths, ruffling the fur and feathers of the two new friends. The breeze carried the scent of salt, sand, and a subtle, sulphureous odor that Edge didn't recognize.

"What *is* this place?" Edge asked, wrinkling her nose. "What's making that light?"

"This is the lake entrance to The Grotto," announced Jessop proudly. "It's a *very* secret place. The moss inside The Grotto glows - that's where the light comes from."

Wide-eyed with fear and awe, Edge approached the entrance. She examined the statues and shuddered. The reptilian figures stood several times her height. Their stone faces were weathered and crumbled in places. Edge thought they looked unfriendly.

"Xalma doesn't look like that," Jessop assured her. "These are statues of adult soldier Amphs from the past. Soldiers don't come here now. I think the statues were made to scare trespassers, a really long time ago. Only the Deejii come here. They're Xalma's sisters, and they don't look like this."

"They're so *big*," Edge whispered in amazement. "Are all Amphs this big?"

"Some of the soldiers are bigger," said Jessop. "I saw a few of them when my family was rescued. They were scary, but they didn't hurt us."

"You were going to tell me why the other Avians wanted to kill you," Edge reminded Jessop.

"Oh," Jessop replied, "it's not *that* interesting really. My parents are friends with the Amphs, but the rest of the Avians are at war with them. We had to leave because my parents tried to stop the Avians from hurting the Amphs, and the Avians got angry."

"Hurting them *how?*" asked Edge.

"That's all I know," shrugged Jessop regretfully. "Xalma knows a lot of things, though. She might answer your questions!"

Before Edge could reply, Jessop walked boldly into the darkness of the tunnel. After a moment's hesitation, Edge followed him. It was better than standing alone in the swamp with the grim looking statues.

They descended an ancient staircase carved into the living stone along one wall of a deep crack in the bedrock. Their footsteps echoed strangely from the rocky walls. Drips, splashes, and a distant rush of water filled the air. Edge walked slowly, her eyes struggling to adjust to the ghostly light.

Jessop knew The Grotto well, but he didn't rush Edge. He remembered when his mother had brought him to meet Xalma for the first time. The Grotto was not a comfortable place for sapiens who were used to the light of the sun.

When the stairs were behind them and the ground leveled out, Jessop held an arm out to stop Edge from taking another step forward into the darkness. Her startled squeak echoed around them.

They stood in a great cavern on the shore of a dark underground lake. Wisps of steam drifted over the water and rolled across the floor, illuminated by a ghostly blue light.

The other side of the lake was lost in the murky distance. Tiny blue points winked from the darkness above, and glowing moss covered the floor and walls. Wherever Edge and Jessop stepped, the moss glowed a little more brightly. A trail of luminous footprints led back the way they had come. After her eyes adjusted, Edge noticed that the cavern's roof was supported by intricately carved pillars. They sprouted from the ground like trees and disappeared into the twinkling gloom above.

Jessop walked to an oddly shaped object hanging over the water.

"Cover your ears," he said. "This thing is loud." His voice echoed far into the cavern.

Edge obeyed immediately, pressing her ears to her head. No sooner had she done this than Jessop raised a mallet and hit the object as hard as he could.

BOOOOONNNNNNGGGGGG!!!!!

The sound moved the air. Edge felt it in her gut and took a few steps back. Vibrations bounced off the walls, swelling and growing louder for a moment, but dying almost immediately as Jessop lowered the entire thing into the water.

"What *is* that?" she asked.

"It's a doorbell," Jessop answered. "I have to hit it before I put it underwater, or it doesn't work. That's how I tell Xalma I'm here."

Xalma appeared almost immediately. They heard her voice trill out of the darkness across the water. She sounded like a small child.

"Jessop! Where *were* you yesterday?"

Two huge, bright eyes peered at them from the lake.

"Ooo! Who is *this*!" Xalma swam to the shore and scampered out of the water.

To Edge's great relief, Xalma looked nothing like the imposing statues guarding the entrance. She was round and soft, and covered from head to toe with glowing, glittery pink scales. Her pale green eyes reflected even the smallest amount of light. Delicate leaf-like gills jutted from either side of her head. Her webbed hands and feet had pudgy little fingers and toes.

The tiny Amph darted fearlessly up to Edge, moving much more quickly than Edge expected her to. The top of her head barely reached Edge's chin.

"Hi!" she squeaked excitedly. "You're *new*! I'm *Xalma*! Where did *you* come from?"

"Uh, I guess I came from the forest?" Edge answered hesitantly.

"This is Edge! I found her in the woods two days ago!" exclaimed Jessop. He hopped around in excitement, flapping his arms. "Isn't this amazing, Xalma? She can *fly*! She's a *Forax*!"

"Oooh," Xalma said, bringing her face uncomfortably close to Edge's. "A *scout*! How did you *get* here?"

"I was born here," said Edge, backing away. "My mom's a scientist, and she came here to study the Insects."

"That's *fascinating*!" exclaimed Xalma, scurrying in a circle and diving back into the water with a tiny 'plop'. She continued swimming in circles as they spoke, occasionally diving underwater or slapping the surface of the lake with her tail.

"Can you tell Edge about the Forax, Xalma?" Jessop asked eagerly.

"Oh sure," giggled Xalma. "I mean, you're the first Forax I've ever *seen*, but I've *heard* about them. Forax are farmers mostly, and they're almost all a lot bigger than you, but that's because you're a scout."

"I'm *not* a scout," said Edge. "I was born here."

Xalma giggled. "You're in a scout *body*, so you're a scout. If you were a *farmer*, you'd be bigger."

"My mom looks like me, and she's a scientist," Edge argued.

"The rules are different for outcasts, right Xalma?" Jessop interrupted, trying to keep the peace.

"Oh yes," Xalma agreed. "You can be whatever you want to be *here*, but that doesn't change what you actually *are*."

"What do you mean 'most Forax are farmers,'" asked Edge. "What's a farmer?"

"Oh, you know..." Xalma said airily, "someone who works for someone else. Forax grow food. Avians take it."

"*What?*" exclaimed Edge. She took a step back. "Why would Forax give away their food?"

Xalma swam closer to the shore and expertly aimed a playful splash at Edge. "Well, Avians *protect* the Forax from *Amphs*, of course!" she giggled.

"WHAT?" Edge's heart started to beat very quickly. She glanced at Jessop. He looked concerned, but not surprised.

He knew, thought Edge.

"That's just what it's like in Marrow," Jessop explained, trying to reassure her. "Things are different here, though. We're *friends*."

Edge backed away anxiously until she bumped into a pillar. Several long, tense moments passed.

Xalma broke the silence with a funny and slightly embarrassing story about Jessop's first visit to The Grotto. When she was done, Jessop told an even more embarrassing story about himself. Very slowly, the tension between them dissolved.

It's normal to be nervous or uncomfortable when you learn new things, Edge reminded herself. *Mana isn't afraid. She said it was safe to be friends with Jessop.*

Almost an hour passed. Edge finally sat next to Jessop. She watched reflections from the dimly lit ceiling dance on the surface of the water as Jessop and Xalma continued talking. As they spoke, Xalma swam around, occasionally disappearing below the water. Jessop treated Xalma like an older sibling, even though she looked and acted like a small child.

I wonder if all Amphs are this restless, thought Edge.

"What do you know about the Insects, Xalma?" Edge asked, interrupting a lighthearted argument about whether Avians could learn to swim as well as Amphs.

Xalma stopped circling around in the water and looked at Edge, a serious expression on her face for the first time that day.

"The Insects were here first," she said. "They've been on the island longer than sapiens have."

"My mother says the Insects take sapiens from Marrow," Edge said. "Do you know anything about that?"

Jessop looked surprised. He knew the Insects were dangerous, and had even been chased by them, (though not nearly as often as he'd led Edge to believe), but he had never heard of them taking sapiens from Marrow.

"Insects control the island," Xalma whispered. "We just live on it."

Xalma departed shortly after this, despite all the new questions Edge and Jessop had. She dove into the water and didn't surface again.

When Jessop felt sure that Xalma was not going to return, he led Edge out of The Grotto.

"That's Xalma! She's amazing, isn't she?" asked Jessop cheerfully.

Edge didn't answer immediately. She was thinking.

"You knew our races were enemies," she said quietly, "didn't you?"

"Sort of," Jessop admitted meekly. "Marrow is complicated. My parents told me that there's a lot of fighting there. But that's not what it's like *here*, and I've been here for a while. I kind of forgot about it."

"Why are the sapiens in Marrow fighting?" asked Edge. Jessop shrugged. "It's always been that way," he answered.

"I bet the Insects know. They've been here longer than us," Edge said, thinking of Xalma's last words. "But I'm going to ask Mana."

Chapter Four

Insects

The treehouse was constructed by The Resistance for Mana's mission. It was made up of three round buildings wrapped around the tall trunks of three strong trees with bark the color of sunset, and it overlooked the lake. The uppermost branches of the trees tickled the bellies of the lowest clouds.

Mana and Edge's bedrooms each occupied one of the buildings. The last and largest building was divided into a living area with a kitchen, a bathroom, and Mana's lab. Covered bridges connected each building, and the main entrance to the house opened onto a deck suspended in the center of the trees that could only be reached by air.

Edge and Jessop flew through the boughs near the top of the tree, landed on the deck, and burst into the kitchen. Inside, Mana, Harbeshi and Ashmara sat comfortably around the table, sipping tea and eating slices of bread.

"Mana!" Edge gasped, interrupting the adult's quiet conversation. "Are Avians our enemies? Do they make us grow them food? Are Insects in control of the island?"

Mana laughed cheerfully. "Have you just met The Child Queen?"

"You mean Xalma?" Edge asked. "Why do you call her The Child Queen?"

Jessop held his breath, wondering if he was finally going to learn Xalma's secret. Mana disappointed him.

"You'll have to ask Xalma that," she replied.

"She says she doesn't *know*," complained Jessop.

"She may *not* know yet," Harbeshi replied sternly, "We have explained this to you, Jessop. It is not our place, or yours, to decide if and when she discovers why she is called The Child Queen."

Jessop was opening his mouth to protest, but Edge cut him off. "What about the other things? Avians? Enemies? Insects?"

"In Marrow, Avians tell Forax what to do, and there are consequences when a Forax doesn't listen," Mana said, "but the Avians in this room are certainly not our enemies. I don't drink tea with my enemies." She winked at Edge.

"Or eat berry loaf," Ashmara chuckled. "I have missed Forax food!"

"Did you say *berry loaf?*" Jessop asked, his eyes widening. " I haven't had that since I was little!" He raced to the table.

Ashmara handed him a slice with a smile.

"Mana says she will teach us to make it!"

Jessop turned to Mana and burbled, "Ank-oo-wa-wa!"

"Mana..." Edge began again, ignoring the food. "I'm not sure what you mean when you say, 'control the island,' Edge."

"Xalma said..." Edge began.

"I'm glad you met The Ch... Xalma," Mana interrupted, "but if you're going to spend time with her, you need to remember that she's spent her whole life in a cave. She only knows what she's been told, and some of the things she's been told might not be true."

"Tell us what Xalma told you, and we will tell you which parts are true," Ashmara offered.

Edge's nose wrinkled. She closed her eyes and pressed her ears down, trying to remember everything Xalma had said.

Ashmara and Harbeshi looked concerned, but Mana gave them a reassuring smile.

"She's just focusing," Mana whispered.

"Xalma said Avians protect the Forax from Amphs, and Insects control the island, and most Forax are farmers, but I still don't know what that is..." Edge struggled to remember the beginning of the conversation – most of the time Xalma was talking, she and Jessop were exchanging stories about swimming.

"She said Insects have been living on the island the longest," Jessop added.

"Yes!" Edge exclaimed, opening her eyes. "Maybe they know why the sapiens in Marrow are fighting! Jessop said it's always been that way, but that can't be true, can it?"

The adults exchanged a look, as though silently deciding how to answer. In fact, they had spent most of the afternoon agreeing on what to tell their children. Harbeshi frowned and nodded.

"The Avians and the Amphs have very different beliefs," he began. "Forax have long been caught in the middle – you could say the Avians and the Amphs both want to control the Forax."

Jessop choked on his bread.

"Control them?" Edge barked in indignation. "You mean Avians really *do* force Forax to grow food for them?"

"Forax grow food for everyone in Marrow, including themselves. But Avians tell Forax what to grow," Mana replied. "If they don't do what the Avians ask them to, Forax are punished."

"Punished how?" Jessop asked.

"They are denied access to things they need, like food and shelter." Ashmara spoke with barely concealed rage. "They are often punished by their own friends and family as well. It is terrible."

"So, the only way Forax can be safe is by growing food for all of Marrow?" Edge frowned, "Is that why Forax aren't supposed to be scientists?"

"That's part of it," Mana replied slowly. "Forax don't have very much control over their own lives, and they spend a lot of their time working on things that don't provide a lot of benefits for their families or communities."

"Why don't they refuse to work?" Edge asked. "What if they all just stopped growing food for everyone else?"

"They are afraid of the Insects," said Ashmara. "Most Forax think the Avians control the Insects. Avians have done nothing to dispel that myth. To the contrary, they have encouraged it."

"Forax are kept separated." Harbeshi added, looking grim. "They are prevented from learning many things. There are fewer teachers among the Forax, and children start working earlier."

"Who *does* control the Insects?" Edge asked.

"As far as we know, they control themselves," Mana replied.

Ashmara pulled the plate of bread away from Jessop with a disapproving frown. Jessop, who had stuffed several pieces into his mouth at once, looked down in comical shame.

"Insects take sapiens who won't do their jobs," Mana continued, smiling at the exchange between Ashmara and Jessop. "Most Avians and Amphs are allowed to choose jobs they want to do, but Forax don't have that freedom. I believe that's why more Forax are taken."

"Do all the sapiens live in Marrow?" asked Edge.

"No," Ashmara said, shaking her head. "But most of them do. Marrow is *very* big; bigger than the whole valley."

"Most of the island is very dangerous," Mana explained. "If there are any sapiens living outside Marrow, they'd be hunters and farmers who know how to survive in the wild."

"What *is* a farmer?" Edge asked.

"A farmer is someone who does repetitive tasks to collect resources, like growing and harvesting food. But it can also mean foraging and mining," Mana replied thoughtfully. "Xalma seems to be receiving a decent education. Even scouts are farmers, of a sort."

"I suppose she is bound to learn things from the Deejii," Ashmara said innocently, ignoring Harbeshi's frown.

"Where did the Insects come from?" asked Edge.

"Everything I've taught you about life is true as far as we know, Edge," Mana assured her. "Insects and sapiens and every other living thing evolved in the ocean. Insects learned to live on the land almost immediately after the first plants. It took a long time before sapiens left the ocean."

"Who came first?" Jessop wondered, "Avians, Forax or Amphs? I bet it was Avians."

"The sapiens who left the ocean were the ancestors of all the races," Mana explained. "We're their descendants."

"Do you know why Insects take sapiens from Marrow?" asked Edge. "Could it be to stop the fighting?"

"I don't think so," Mana replied.

Jessop shuddered. "Do Insects *eat* sapiens?"

Mana shook her head.

"Insects tend to the flowers and clean debris from the forest floor. They build beautiful things. They're peaceful vegetarians."

"Maybe they're studying *us*, the way we study them?" Edge suggested.

Mana shrugged. "I don't know," she replied. "That's what I've been trying to discover, but in all the time I've watched them, I've never even seen the type of Insect who takes sapiens from Marrow."

"There are many unanswered questions," Ashmara declared. "Hive is far from Marrow. It must take the fastest of the Insects at least a month to travel all the way across the Island. Yet they appear almost instantly when someone refuses to do their job. How do they arrive so quickly? Or know who to take? What do they *do* with the sapiens they take?"

When Ashmara finished, everyone looked at Mana. She put her cup down slowly.

"I still don't know," she admitted.

A moment of silence passed as everyone pondered the mystery.

"Why don't you tell Jessop's family what *you've* learned about the Insects, Edge?" Mana suggested. "You don't have the biases we have."

"What do you mean?" Jessop wondered.

"You and Edge did not grow up hearing Marrow's stories about Insects," Ashmara explained. "We rarely spoke of them, and Edge has learned all she knows about them through observation."

Mana nodded.

"In Marrow, sapiens are taught to *fear* the Insects. You and Edge were taught to *respect* them."

Edge considered this. It was true that she wasn't afraid of the Insects. She closed her eyes and concentrated on what she knew, focusing on each detail carefully, the way Mana had taught her to.

"They're easy to predict," she said after a moment, picturing Insects she'd observed over the years. "That's why the idea of a group of them suddenly flying far away is so strange. They don't do *anything* suddenly."

"Why do you say they're predictable?" Mana smiled encouragingly.

"They're seasonal," Edge explained, her eyes still closed as she recalled years of observations. "They follow the same patterns. They don't leave Hive in the winter..." A thought occurred to Edge and she opened her eyes.

"What happens if someone refuses to do their job in the winter?"

Harbeshi answered gruffly.

"The Insects appear and take them away. Night or day, winter or summer."

"Insects can't travel in the winter." Edge frowned. "Is the weather in Marrow different?"

"It's warm enough for an Insect to stay active," Mana confirmed, "but no one has ever found a Hive near Marrow."

"Has anyone ever followed them to see where they go?"

"Anyone who has tried to follow the Insects is also taken," Harbeshi answered shortly. "How do you *know* they cannot travel in the winter?"

"They're ectothermic," Edge replied.

"What does *that* mean?" Jessop asked, impressed with the word.

"They can't make their own heat," explained Edge. "The Insects stay inside Hive all winter to keep warm. I think they use the steam under the island. The same heat that Xalma uses."

"Are Amphs ectothermic too?" Jessop asked.

"No," Mana answered. "They're endothermic, like us. They make their own heat."

]"Weird! Where does our heat come from, anyway?"

"From food," Edge replied immediately. "Our bodies turn food into heat and energy."

Jessop looked confused. "Why can't Insects turn food into heat?"

"They didn't evolve that way," Mana said.

"Maybe they make cozy blankets out of the sapiens they steal," growled Harbeshi, stretching his wings out a little and standing up. "It has been a pleasure, but it is time to leave."

"*Aw*," whined Jessop, staring longingly at the last piece of berry loaf.

Ashmara handed the food to her son and glanced out the window. It was getting dark.

"Thank you for your hospitality, Mana," she said. "I am sure we have a lot more to learn from one another."

"We certainly do. You're welcome to visit whenever you like. I need to teach you to bake!"

Harbeshi was already on the platform outside. Edge and Mana stood in the entranceway as his family joined him.

"Can I come back tomorrow?" Jessop asked.

"Mana, is it okay if Jessop visits Edge tomorrow?" asked Ashmara. "We need to repair our nest - the spring rains will be here soon."

Edge glanced anxiously at her mother, but Mana nodded immediately.

"Yes, of course," she agreed.

Harbeshi scowled, but he and Ashmara bowed politely before taking off. Jessop hopped a few times in excitement before following them.

"See you tomorrow, Edge!" he exclaimed as he disappeared.

Chapter Five

Into Hive

The same morning Edge was meeting Jessop, Tsoci was waking up for the first time in over a decade.

Due to their nature, Tsoci could not carry out a full examination of their individual components, any more than Edge could have a conversation with a colony of microbes on her skin. Edge was simply too big. Her perception of time and scale was too different to see things from a microbe's point of view.

In order to examine themselves, Tsoci evolved Limbic, a complex system designed to collect and interpret information. Limbic put a small piece of Tsoci's awareness into a separate, much smaller individual, a bud of Tsoci who was designed to perform a task and be willingly reabsorbed. To keep things simple, every one of these individuals was named Rover.

The latest Rover started their existence with an overwhelming urge to identify everything that had changed since the last rover's visit. Rover knew that rovers had been doing this for eons because this fact had been put in their head to motivate them.

Rover wasn't concerned about the amount of work they had to do, because Limbic was always finding ways to collect information more efficiently.

Over the last twenty thousand years or so, the work had largely been outsourced to the Insects.

Instead of conducting a thorough survey of every individual on the island, a rover's task nowadays was to collect information from the Insects.

In the past, Limbic had created all kinds of exciting individuals to perform the data retrieval task, but this rover was not exciting. Instead of being covered in sleek fur, adorned with brightly colored feathers, or sporting iridescent wings, Rover looked like a colorless sketch of an Insect. They didn't even have a mouth.

The Insects didn't really care what rovers looked like, they just wanted to make sure Tsoci knew what was going on in the world, so Limbic didn't design interesting rovers anymore. It wasn't necessary or practical. Instead of making Rover look interesting, Limbic gave them a bigger memory, so they could collect as much data as possible, as quickly as possible.

For most of the day, Tsoci's Limbic system ran tests to establish that they were ready to perform the task. The thought that it might be possible to make something *too* efficient did not cross Tsoci's vast, ancient mind. When the tests were finished and the door was open, Rover flew straight to Hive.

Rover could hear Hive long before setting eyes on it. A steady rhythm rippled the air, growing louder as they approached the center of the Insects' home. Hive was a kaleidoscope of sound, color, and light. It was as though someone was throwing a very good party directly above the heartbeat of the earth.

Two Insects, draped in downy wings, met Rover at the entrance. Fluffy blue hair sprung from their legs, and feather-like antennae crowned their heads. They fluttered around Rover gracefully. The smell of fruit and honey filled the air. They were saying hello and inviting Rover inside.

They led Rover to a balcony overlooking an enormous coliseum in the center of the largest dome in Hive. The walls and floor were covered with iridescent shells arranged in patterns representing stars and galaxies. Insects of countless varieties chirped, droned, and flew in complex formations around elaborate steaming fountains. An endless palate of smells wafted through the air. Moonlight refracted through the crystal roof of the dome and covered the dancers and singers with colorful reflections.

When the Insects escorting Rover brought food, Rover performed a simple dance that meant, *'Thanks, but I don't have a mouth,'* followed by a longer dance that meant, *'Hey, what's happened since the last rover asked for information?'* Swarms of Insects danced and chirped and buzzed in reply. Their movements and music communicated the things they'd sensed, felt, and learned since the last rover's visit. They described every new individual. They explained the current ecosystem and how it made them feel. They summarized the climate.

The Insects shared everything they knew about life on the island. Smells of burned wood, fruit, seaweed, and thousands of other things drifted around the room throughout their performance. Dancers grew tired and were replaced. The air shimmered and the floor was alive with jewel-like bodies dancing, flying, and playing fantastic instruments of their own design.

Edge and Mana would have recognized the round beetles and sinuous centipedes. They would have marveled at the intricate aerial maneuvers of the colorful pollinators. But they would not have recognized the silk-weaving glow beetles from deep under the mountain, or the ponderous centipods and tiny water lice. There was no way Edge and Mana could have known how big Hive actually was.

The Insects moved joyfully, expressing every detail of their story with care and practiced skill. Thousands of them formed living canvases in the air and on the ground. Their performance expressed a deep reverence for excellent teamwork.

Rover recorded each complex and beautiful sound. They recorded every nuanced movement and transient formation. They recorded dispassionately, for three days and nights, surrounded by the biggest party Hive could throw.

When the third day ended, Rover had all the information they needed to move on to the next step of the task. They performed a thankful barrel roll before leaving Hive. None of the Insects noticed. After three days of dancing, they were all fast asleep.

Vagrants and outcasts occasionally appeared in Far Crescent, but the Insects reported that two Forax had arrived since the last update, and they had been studying the Insects. It was an unexpected behavior, and unexpected behaviors could be dangerous.

The next task on Rover's list was 'investigate the anomalies', but it may as well have been 'find Edge and Mana'.

Chapter Six

The Grotto

The evening after Ashmara and Harbeshi visited Mana in the treehouse, Jessop's parents had the biggest fight they'd had in years.

"She said *The Resistance* sent her," Harbeshi screamed. "Have you forgotten that they are our *enemies*? We *must* report them. Their presence here puts us all in danger."

Ashmara glared at Harbeshi in disgust. "I want our son to have friends." She stormed out of the room without waiting for a reply.

The fight left an icy silence behind, and the nest remained frozen and breathlessly quiet all night. The next morning, Jessop slipped out of the nest as early as possible. When his wings caught the air, he instantly felt more cheerful.

Jessop soared high over the mountains before plummeting down into the valley. He dove into the trees, grabbed a handful of pine needles, and whirled back into the sky. He beat his wings harder and harder until he burst through the clouds. For a moment Jessop floated weightless in the center of a small explosion of feathers and pine needles. A moment later, he was diving gleefully back towards the earth.

I finally have a friend to fly with.

He soared to Edge's house, thinking about all his favorite places, and wondering which one to share with her first.

Over the following days, Jessop and Edge explored the valley and became true friends, promising not to keep secrets from each other.

"Mana *still* hasn't told me everything," Edge complained. "Secrets are the *worst*."

"At least she tells you *something*," Jessop replied enviously. "All *my* parents do is fight."

"What do they fight about?" Edge asked.

Jessop sighed. They were sitting on a pile of rocks next to the lake.

"You don't have to tell me," Edge added quickly, "if it's private, I mean. I understand if it's not your secret to tell."

"No, it's fine," Jessop assured her. "They fight about pretty much everything. When we were exiled, my dad wanted to go back to Marrow to help his friends, but my mom refused to leave. In the end, my dad stayed, but only to protect me. He hates it here. I know he'd go back to Marrow if he thought we'd be safe there."

"It must have been hard to leave your home behind," Edge said sympathetically.

"It was, but it happened so long ago that I don't really think about it anymore. The fighting is a lot worse. It just keeps happening. I wish they'd *agree* on something. I think my dad would be happy again if he knew his friends were okay, but there's no way for him to find out. He has a screen, but he can't talk to anyone but the Amphs who brought us here. I don't think they tell my parents very much about what's happening. This is still a cool place to live, though!" Jessop said, cheering up. "Especially now that you're here."

"Are we going back to the canyon today?" asked Edge. They'd spent the past few days exploring labyrinthian channels carved into the foothills by the mountain's many waterfalls and rivers.

"Not today," Jessop grinned. "I made you something!"

"What? Really?" exclaimed Edge.

Jessop pulled four items out of his pack. One looked like a curved reed. Another looked like transparent shells from some kind of sea creature, attached to a strap made of hide. The last two items were identical, and Edge had no idea what they were. They were wedges made of a material she didn't recognize.

"These are for diving!" said Jessop proudly. "I invented them myself! I have my own." He pulled an almost identical set of things from his pack.

"Let's see if your goggles fit," Jessop held the transparent shells up to his eyes.

Edge giggled.

"You look like a froggle!" she laughed.

"That's where I got the idea," Jessop replied cheerfully.

"Can I try them on you?"

Edge nodded, and Jessop took the goggles and fastened them around her face, so each eye was covered by a transparent bubble. The edges of the bubbles were padded with something foamy, which pressed against the fur of her face.

"Does that feel okay?" Jessop looked at her attentively.

"Everything looks weird!" Edge answered. The bubbles distorted the world so that everything in her peripheral vision was stretched, making her feel dizzy.

"You'll get used to it," Jessop assured her. "Do they feel tight or uncomfortable?"

"No," answered Edge. She kept as still as possible and stared straight ahead, and her dizziness subsided.

"Good! You can take them off now, I'll show you how."

Jessop helped Edge remove the goggles and showed her how to put them back on. He adjusted the straps a little to make them easier to fasten. When he was satisfied that Edge's goggles fit as well as possible, he put them next to his own, and picked up the two identical things that Edge couldn't identify.

"These are flippers!" Jessop said, holding up the wedges. "They're like a froggle's feet… you wear them over your own feet and they help you swim faster. Is it okay if I put these on you?"

"Sure! I don't know *how* to swim, though," Edge answered.

"Don't worry," Jessop grinned. "I'm going to teach you, I just want to make sure your gear fits first."

Edge sat down and let Jessop slide the flippers over her feet. He carefully adjusted the straps until they fitted snugly.

"The best parts of The Grotto are underwater. That's where Xalma lives. She didn't think I would ever be able to swim, because most Avians don't like to go in the water. I thought if I could make myself more like a water animal, I'd be able to learn."

Edge thought Jessop's inventions were very clever, but she was nervous about learning to swim.

"How do you *breathe* underwater?" she asked.

"This goes in your mouth," Jessop replied, holding up the reed . "The top part pokes out of the water so you can get air. The hardest part is remembering *not* to hold your breathe. Want to try it?"

He handed the reed to Edge and she put one end in her mouth and sucked in some air. It felt strange to breathe through the reed.

"It works!" she said, after removing the reed from her mouth.

Jessop laughed.

"I'd be surprised if it didn't work," he chuckled. "The reed attaches to your goggles so you can breathe when your face is underwater."

Jessop's eyes were shining with pride.

"Thank you for the gifts," Edge said sincerely.

"Let's go to The Grotto, and I'll start teaching you to swim! In the summer we can swim in the lake, too. There's cool stuff in the lake!"

Edge wasn't entirely comfortable with the idea of swimming, but Jessop looked so eager and delighted that she couldn't bear to let him down.

As they passed the two imposing statues of the warrior Amphs, Edge felt a little braver. She wasn't afraid of the statues anymore. She wasn't afraid of the darkness of The Grotto anymore, either.

Maybe swimming is no big deal, she thought.

Jessop skipped all the way down to the shore of the lake and rang the bell. He was helping Edge put on her swimming gear when Xalma arrived.

"Hi Jessop! Where have you been?" Xalma asked. "Wow! Did you make flippers for Edge?"

"Yup!" Jessop replied proudly. "That way we can all hang out together!"

"That's so *weird*!" Xalma laughed. "A *Forax*! Swimming in The *Grotto*!"

Edge already had the reed in her mouth, so she didn't say anything. She hoped her new friends wouldn't notice her trembling legs. She was expecting Jessop to give her some instruction, or possibly a demonstration. Instead, he put on his own gear and jumped straight into the water. When he surfaced, he removed the reed.

"Just jump in and pretend you're a froggle!" he said, before swimming into the darkness with Xalma.

Edge waited for them to return. Although she could hear her friends splashing and calling for her, they didn't return to the shore.

"Just *jump*!" Xalma called. "If an *Avian* can swim, I'm sure a *Forax* can!"

"It's kind of like flying, but different," Jessop assured her.

"That's *very* helpful," Xalma snickered.

Edge sucked as much air into her lungs as possible through the strange reed and waddled awkwardly into the water. The ground dropped away quickly, and Edge immediately started to sink. She kicked her legs in terror. The flippers propelled her upwards and her head burst above the water. Edge gasped, but the reed in her mouth was full of water.

She choked and started to sink again. Instinctively, Edge spread her wings, which made it harder to kick her way back up to the surface again. Panicking and thrashing, she choked and slid deeper into the lake.

Xalma's small but surprisingly strong arms lifted her to the shore. As soon as her head was clear again, Edge heard Jessop speaking very close beside her.

"Blow, then breathe," Jessop instructed.

Edge followed the instructions, blowing the reed clear of water before taking a choking breath. Xalma dragged Edge effortlessly onto the land and removed the reed. Edge coughed for a long time.

Xalma was laughing. "You *forgot* to tell her how to *breathe* Jessop?"

Jessop was looking at Edge, his face full of concern. "Are you okay? I'm *really* sorry. I swear it'll be easier next time," Jessop promised.

Xalma was still laughing. "What *else* did you forget to tell her? I don't want a drowned *Forax* in my home! If you want to *murder* her, do it *outside*." she giggled.

The more Xalma laughed, the more ashamed Jessop looked.

"I'm so sorry Edge. You don't have to do this," Jessop said.

"It's okay. Let's try again."

Edge was determined to show Xalma that Jessop was a good teacher. She stood up, put the reed in her mouth, and jumped back into the water.

This time, she remembered to blow the water out of the reed before taking a breath. She kicked steadily, and soon learned how to keep her head above the water.

"Not *bad*," Xalma admitted grudgingly. "Especially considering how *silly* your teacher is. Let *me* give you some tips!"

Xalma propelled herself completely out of the water for a moment, diving back in and popping up directly in front of Edge.

"If you want to go somewhere, you just have to kick yourself forward, like this." Xalma swam effortlessly back and forth. "If you get tired, you can float on your back, like *this*!" Xalma flipped over. The scales of her pale belly sparkled in the dim glow of The Grotto.

Edge flipped onto her back and paddled in circles in the water, staring at the twinkling ceiling and holding her head up, turning awkwardly to the side to keep the reed from submerging.

"Ahaha!" Xalma laughed. "You're a *great* swimmer compared to Edge, Jessop! Good luck teaching *her*! I'll meet you later if you don't *drown*!" She disappeared into the lake.

"Don't listen to her, Edge," Jessop said. "She doesn't mean it."

Edge nodded. The reed was still in her mouth.

"You can take that out when your head's above the water," Jessop said.

Edge nervously removed the reed. She was getting very tired.

"I have to rest," she gasped.

Jessop guided her back to shore, and she scrambled to the land. It was a while before her heart stopped pounding.

"It gets easier, I promise," Jessop said. "We can take it slowly."

When Edge was ready to try again, Jessop taught her how to float properly, so she could rest without having to return to land. Jessop realized that Edge's anatomy was different from his, so he adjusted his instructions as they practiced.

"Try to keep your body horizontal in the water when you swim. Don't extend your wings," he directed.

"They extend on their own when my arms move," Edge said, floating beside him. "The water pulls them out."

"Hmm." Jessop squinted in thought while Edge floated patiently. Now that she knew how to breathe and rest, she was starting to enjoy the warmth of the water.

"We could tie down your wings," Jessop suggested.

"No way," Edge answered firmly.

"Keep your arms to your sides, then," he advised. "Just use your legs and tail to move."

Edge put the reed back in her mouth and rolled over in the water. She held both arms tightly against her sides and kicked her feet. Before her face entered the water, she gulped as much air as possible and held her breath.

She discovered that she could breathe when her head was underwater, as long as the top of the reed was still above the waterline. Cautiously, she opened her eyes.

"Ohhh..." exclaimed Edge through the reed.

A wonderland of glowing animals and plants covered the bottom of the lake.

I bet those lights will get brighter if I dive deeper, thought Edge, *but I'll have to hold my breath the whole time the reed is under the water.*

She took a deep breath and kicked herself down through the water, arms still pinned to her sides.

Jessop watched Edge dive with pride. She was learning to swim much more quickly than he had expected.

I'm not a bad teacher after all, he thought proudly.

Jessop and Edge dove again and again to look at the luminous underwater landscape. Each time they dove, they discovered something new. Schools of gleaming fish followed them. Ribbons of fiery kelp tickled their toes. Clouds of tiny water creatures billowed past.

Xalma returned later in the day. Despite her teasing, she seemed genuinely relieved to find Edge swimming successfully.

"Sorry about earlier," she apologized as Edge and Jessop took a break from diving to catch their breath. "I thought you were going to give up, so I guess I gave up first."

Edge frowned. "You should apologize to Jessop," she answered sharply. "He's a *great* teacher.

Jessop smiled. "Thanks, Edge!"

"Yeah, yeah, he's a smart bird boy," Xalma snickered. Edge glowered at her, and Xalma immediately stopped laughing. "I'm just *kidding*," she said, "Jessop is great. Do you wanna see the coolest thing here, Edge?"

"What is it?" Jessop asked. "Have I seen it?"

"Nope!" answered Xalma cheerfully. "It's *new*!"

She dove under the water without waiting for a reply. Jessop and Edge re-positioned their reeds and followed her. It was easy to follow Xalma. She glowed brightly. Her pink scales didn't just emit light. They shimmered and changed as she swam. Complicated patterns danced across her body. Edge was mesmerized.

When they reached the bottom of the lake, Xalma's colors and light started to mimic the pattern of the things below her, and she became harder to see.

She belongs *down here*, thought Edge. *She has camouflage for this place. This is her habitat.*

Xalma led them through a jungle of luminous plants, pushing aside the vegetation to reveal the most enormous fish Edge had ever seen. It was made of an uncountable number of multicolored shells. Each scale seemed to flash, as though the huge fish was swimming slowly. The fins were made of woven strands of shimmering water grass, and they undulated gently with the currents of the lake. It was the most extraordinary thing Edge had ever seen.

"Do you like it?" Xalma asked when they resurfaced. She beamed with pride. "I made it!"

"How long did it take you?" Edge's face was full of wonder.

"Not very long," Xalma answered. "The hardest part was finding all the right colors."

"It's *amazing*!" Jessop declared. "*See* Edge? This place is unreal. Xalma makes all *sorts* of cool things under the water. It's worth learning to swim, isn't it?"

"Yes," agreed Edge. "*Totally* worth it. What are we going to see next?"

"We'll come back tomorrow," Jessop answered. He noticed that Edge was panting. "You should rest and dry off before we go home."

"What, *really*?" Xalma whined in protest. "You're not even past the *entrance* yet!"

"We'll be back tomorrow, won't we, Edge?" Jessop smiled joyfully.

Edge nodded emphatically, struggling to keep her head above the water.

"I'll *definitely* come back," she sputtered. "Every day! I want to see everything!"

They swam back to the shore and climbed out of the water. Jessop preened his feathers, scraping the water out with his beak. It took much longer for Edge to dry off. She was still shivering and damp when she arrived at home.

I'll build a fire next time, Edge decided.

From that day forward, Edge and Jessop brought a growing list of supplies on their adventures. They fished and foraged, cooking their own meals and stretching each day's adventure a little bit longer. Day by day, they learned to need their homes a little less.

Chapter Seven

The Network

After a week of observation, Rover decided that although both Forax were anomalies, the younger one was going to be a problem.

The protocol for a sapien who didn't fit their assigned role was to reset them and place them in an environment better suited to them, so Rover knew what to do about Mana, but Edge was different. There were no instructions for what to do with a Forax like Edge. She was the first of her kind. Rover continued to watch, hoping that something they observed would trigger a new directive. They felt more uncomfortable with each passing day. Rovers weren't designed to wait and see; they were supposed to collect information, and Rover wasn't collecting information anymore. They followed Edge wherever she went, growing more restless and depressed. Only the novelty of seeing three sapiens from different races interact kept Rover from trying to make something happen. No Rover had seen anything like it for a very long time.

"Let's get the boring stuff over with first," said Xalma.

After a week or so of practice, Edge was finally feeling confident enough in the water to swim deeper into The Grotto, so Xalma wanted to give her a tour. They swam to a collection of tiny islands in the middle of the lake. Each island was like a room in a house. There was an island full of toys, a bedroom island, and an island with an arcade. There was a kitchen, a gym, and even a library. The library was Jessop's favorite place, even though the books were all locked up. He enjoyed reading their spines and imagining what might be written on their pages.

"Do you have a key to open these, Xalma?" Edge asked. "We can read them together!"

"Ew. No!" Xalma laughed. "Books are stupid."

"Why not just get rid of them, then?" Edge asked.

"I tried," Xalma snorted. "That's how they got locked up in the first place. Apparently they're *valuable antiques*."

"Maybe we can try to unlock them?" Edge suggested.

"Why?" Xalma laughed. "Is hanging out in the real world too hard for you?"

When they left The Grotto, Edge finally asked Jessop the question that had burned in her mind all day.

"Why is Xalma so mean? Did I do something wrong?"

"I know what you're feeling," Jessop said, "It's not you. It's Xalma. She's been alone a long time. She acts tough because she's afraid we'll abandon her."

"Why would we do that?" asked Edge. "It's great here!"

"It's not about whether we *would*. It's that we *can*," Jessop replied wisely. "She can't, and I don't know why. I've been trying to figure it out since we came here, but no one tells me anything."

"You mean she's trapped?" Edge asked with concern.

"The Deejii told her she'll die if she leaves The Grotto," Jessop explained. "I don't believe them, though. They're really mean to her. They just make her feel bad about herself. They don't care about her."

The more Edge saw of The Grotto, the more she understood why Xalma preferred the underwater world she'd created for herself to the cluttered islands. She also realized that Xalma must have been living in The Grotto for a very long time.

The bottom of the lake was covered with sculptures and murals of stylized fish, plants, and sapiens of all shapes and sizes. Some of the delicate creations depicted Jessop, but Edge noticed that many of them were of a much younger version of her friend.

The branches and vines of plants in the underwater forest had been trained and shaped to form fantastic living passages from one area of the lakebed to another. Marvelous dwellings had been carved throughout the huge corals of the ancient reef. Treasures, gathered from places only Xalma could reach, were displayed carefully in nooks along the walls. Sculptures covered with lights and iridescent stones lined paths made of colored sand.

Xalma described the Amphs who would one day come to live in each of the dwellings. She had prepared an extensive and magnificent village, convinced that if she could only put enough magic into the work, her labor would someday bring her imaginary friends to life.

"How old was Xalma when you met her?" Edge asked Jessop one evening as they returned from The Grotto.

"She's definitely older than I am, but she hasn't changed since I met her," Jessop answered. "I've been trying to figure it out, but I can't make sense of it. She's told me it takes about a month to make one of the big sculptures, and half a year to make a house."

"Have you counted the houses?" Edge asked.

"Yeah," Jessop replied. "It took me two months. There's over 800 of them."

"That's over 400 years! That can't be possible..."

"Who knows?" Jessop shrugged. "Xalma acts like I'm making it all up when I ask her about it, and my parents won't tell me anything. But obviously I'm not going to stop trying to find out."

"You *have* to!" Edge agreed. "I'll help."

Edge observed Xalma the way she'd been taught to observe the Insects. Xalma was cheerful, selfish, and bossy. She often vanished without any warning, only to reappear sometime later. She didn't seem aware of how much time had passed when this happened. Xalma had the heart and mind of a very precocious young child, and Edge found her fascinating. She learned to ignore Xalma's odd and sometimes rude behavior. The more Edge observed her, the more obvious it was that Xalma was terrified that Jessop was going to leave her.

Every evening, the friends sat together near the entrance to The Grotto, imagining new things that Xalma could make while Edge was drying off after a day in the water. They didn't talk about the outside world, and they never asked about Xalma's past.

A few weeks after Jessop and Edge started visiting The Grotto together, a camera screen appeared in the library.

"Where did *this* come from?" Edge asked, examining the machine. It reminded her of the equipment in Mana's lab.

"I'm not sure," Xalma replied indifferently. "It was here when I woke up. The Deejii must have put it there."

"What's it *for*?" Jessop asked, tentatively touching the screen.

"Probably nothing," Xalma yawned. "Who *cares*? Let's *go*. This place is *boring*."

Jessop tapped the screen. Abstract videos with beautiful music played. There were no sapiens in the videos, and there were no voices in the music.

"Okay. That's *actually* fun," Xalma admitted. "It belongs in the arcade, though. Maybe the Deejii put it here by accident?"

"Who are the Deejii?" asked Edge. "Jessop mentioned them before."

"They're my stupid sisters," Xalma answered. "They bring me dumb stuff and leave."

Xalma expressed no interest whatsoever in the machine, but Jessop could not stop thinking about it.

"My parents use a screen like that to talk to sapiens in Marrow. I've never been allowed to touch it. I wonder if we can use it to reach Marrow? Maybe I can find out if it's safe for us to go back!"

"Wow!" Edge gasped. "That would be so cool!"

They didn't intentionally keep their ideas about the camera screen a secret. Xalma just wasn't that interested in ideas unless they were about her. Over the next few days, Jessop tried to get the screen to do something other than play videos, but nothing worked. In the end, he discovered the cable entirely by accident.

He'd just spilled a whole bowl of mushrooms onto the floor. Mushrooms were the only things Xalma ate that Edge and Jessop could stomach. Most of her food was poisonous to them.

Jessop loved mushrooms. He shifted the machine to collect a few errant slices and noticed a cable disappearing straight into the rock.

"Look at *this*!" Jessop whispered. Xalma was away somewhere, but Jessop still kept his voice low.

"Maybe this cable connects to Marrow!" he suggested. "Maybe we can follow it!"

"Follow it *how*?" Edge asked. She also spoke quietly. "It goes into a rock."

"Could we dig a hole?"

"We can't go around digging holes in Xalma's floors," Edge objected. "That's rude."

"She hates this place, she won't mind," Jessop snorted.

"How are you going to dig through rock?" Edge asked.

"If I can make a big metal screw and turn it fast enough..." Jessop began.

"How are you going to make whatever you just said? Look, I want to figure this out as much as you do, but neither of us can dig through the rock."

"I know!" Jessop exclaimed finally. "I'll *cut* the cable and see what's inside it, and what changes on the screen. Then, when I reattach it, I'll know where it's connected."

To Edge, this sounded very simple, but Jessop spent the rest of the night thinking about everything he'd learned about the camera screen.

They tried his idea the next evening, when Xalma wandered off.

Jessop carefully cut the cable. Inside the soft casing were four colored wires.

Edge was fascinated. "Let's see what's changed," she suggested.

There was a new square in the bottom left corner of the screen with a big red X on it. Jessop was pleased.

Very carefully, Jessop reconnected the wires. The X disappeared. A new square opened.

It said 'Network Settings'.

"That looks promising!" Jessop exclaimed, methodically pushing one button after another. When he tapped on a button that said Launch Network, a new square opened.

It said SEARCH.

They heard Xalma returning. Jessop tapped the screen and returned it to its original state. With a meaningful glance and a nod, they silently agreed to keep their discovery a secret, at least until they knew what it meant.

The next morning, fat snowflakes started to fall before dawn. By the time Edge awoke, the wind had risen to a howling gale. She knew that Jessop would not be able to visit until the storm died down. Edge briefly considered telling her mother about the screen just so she could talk about it, but she suspected that Mana might think it was dangerous. *If I'm not going to see Marrow myself, I deserve to know more about it,* she reasoned. *Mana still won't tell me who my father is.* As the day went on and the storm continued to rage, Edge gave up on their plans to visit Xalma. Late in the evening, the weather gentled into a steady flurry of large, fluffy snowflakes. Edge climbed to the top of the tree before bed, just as she'd done every night for as long as she could remember.

She was surprised to find Jessop perched in the uppermost branches. He was not alone. Rover was hiding in the shadows.

"What are you doing here?" Edge asked in surprise.

"I knew you'd come out," Jessop explained. "Mana told my mom that you have a habit of saying goodnight to the sky. She told me she thought it was cute."

"But it's bedtime. Aren't you supposed to be at home?"

"I don't think my parents will even notice," Jessop lied. "Anyway, I couldn't wait. Let's go to the Grotto!"

Edge wasn't worried about being caught. Mana was fast asleep. If she was back before sunrise, her mother would never know she was gone.

They didn't ring the bell when they reached the entrance to The Grotto. Xalma was nowhere to be seen as they slipped into the water and swam to the library.

Jessop tapped the screen, searching for the area where the X had appeared when the wire was cut. Sure enough, a square that said 'Network Settings' appeared. Jessop struggled to get the search square to open, but he managed in the end.

Breathlessly, he typed the word 'Marrow' next to the word 'SEARCH' and tapped a button.

Sentences scrolled past. None of them made sense.

'*Insects continue to plague pods throughout the prefectures.*' Jessop read. He looked at Edge, bewildered.

Edge shrugged and read the next sentence out loud.

'*Atavisms increase as unplanned populations expand.*' She looked at Jessop. "What's an atavism?"

"What are you *doing*?!" Xalma screamed, appearing from the water nearby.

"Xalma! Let me explain," Jessop began, his face full of shame.

Xalma ignored him. She scampered to the camera screen and turned it off. Then she lifted it from the ground and looked at the cable. The wire had obviously been tampered with.

"You have to *leave*," she said urgently, pushing them towards the water. "*Right now.*"

The fear in Xalma's voice sent a chill up Edge's spine. Xalma wasn't angry. She was terrified.

"What is it, Xalma?" Edge whispered. The fur along her back stood up in damp spikes.

"You turned *the network* on!" Xalma cried. "I didn't know this thing was *wired*. Stay at Edge's house, Jessop. Don't fly home tonight. I'll send a message to your parents. Ashmara's going to be *so* mad at me!"

Before they could ask any more questions, Xalma pushed Jessop and Edge into the water.

"Swim!" she yelled, before diving in herself, heading towards some secret place to try and minimize the damage.

As soon as Edge and Jessop stepped out of The Grotto, something white and extraordinarily fast swooped down from the trees, grabbed Edge, and disappeared. It was over so quickly that Jessop wasn't sure what direction they went. He soared through the forest looking for any sign of Edge, but she was gone. Choking back sobs of despair, Jessop raced to the treehouse to wake up Mana.

Chapter Eight

Anomaly

When Edge woke up, she was in a low, dome shaped room. A warm breeze brushed her fur, changing direction every few breaths. A mat of colorful glowing roots shrouded the walls and floor, swaying gently, as though underwater. The tendrils of light formed complex, beautiful patterns that reminded Edge of Xalma's camouflage.

"*Wow*," she whispered.

Red eyes glowed from the center of the room. The most unremarkable white Insect stepped towards her.

"You woke up early," said the stranger in a flat, emotionless voice. There was a hint of confusion when they continued, "Where did you come from?"

"What *are* you?" asked Edge. She had never seen a simpler looking Insect. The creature was the bare minimum of what an Insect could be. Their mouth looked like a hole that had been punched into their face at the last minute.

"Where did you come from?" repeated the voice. This time there was an unmistakable sense of urgency in their tone.

Edge sensed moonlight to her right. Very slowly, she shifted her weight, hoping the light was a way to escape. She knew she couldn't outrace an Insect, but Edge thought she might be able to outsmart this strange, simple looking creature. She decided to play for time.

"I was born here," she answered. "My mother came from the other side of the island, before I was born."

"This is concerning," said the strange Insect. To Edge's surprise, they turned their back on her and approached the center of the room.

Edge shuddered and pushed herself along the wall towards what she hoped was an exit, glancing around desperately for something that might inspire an escape plan.

"Display test results," said the Insect.

Edge squeaked involuntarily, sliding more quickly toward the light. When the center of the room lit up with complex, blazingly bright shapes, she realized that the Insect's last words had not been for her.

Edge abandoned caution and scrambled towards a patch of light that looked like stars. She crashed headfirst into an invisible barrier, rebounding in shock.

"The door is closed," the stranger said indifferently.

"LET ME OUT!" screamed Edge, raking her claws across the invisible barrier. Her hands vibrated painfully, but the barrier remained as solid as ever. She was trapped. Edge fought back tears and scampered into an adjoining room. The creature continued issuing commands to the air, arms waving in front of floating shapes made of light.

Maybe I can find a weapon, Edge thought as she searched one room after another.

Each room had three doorways, and each doorway led to another room, the same shape and size as the last, with glowing, colorful walls. Edge passed through dozens of identical rooms before she found a room that looked different than the others. To get into it, she had to pass through a portal just large enough for her to squeeze through.

Forcing herself to stay calm, Edge poked her head through the portal. On the other side was a cavernous chamber. It was darker than the previous rooms. The floor was webbed with thin, glowing filaments. Light radiated from the center of the floor towards the walls in mesmerizing whorls. A soft breeze blew in and out through the portal.

It looks like this whole place is breathing light, thought Edge.

The portal was the only way into the chamber. It felt like a trap. Edge closed her eyes and covered her ears and weighed her options as calmly as she could.

I'm already trapped, she reasoned. *This might be my only chance to escape.* She squeezed through the portal and entered the chamber.

The shiny objects were parts of Insects and animals. Limbs and skulls and carapaces littered the room, stacked haphazardly against the wall and strewn across the floor. Edge recoiled in disgust. Most of the debris appeared to be Insect parts, but some of the limbs looked like they might have belonged to Amphs or Avians. Edge spotted a feathered wing nearby and her blood ran cold.

That's not Jessop, she told herself firmly. *Look for a weapon.*

Her gaze was drawn to the huge, round shape in the center of the room. Shock and morbid fascination led her towards what looked like a giant egg. There was a hole in it roughly the same size as the portal into the chamber. Edge was about to poke her head inside the egg when a distant sound reminded her why she was there. She started searching piles of body parts for something she could use to defend herself, and quickly found what had once been an Insect arm or leg, with two serrated claws as long as her whole hand.

Clutching this, she scrambled back through the tiny portal and navigated her way through seemingly endless, indistinguishable rooms. She moved as quietly as possible, heading towards the only sound she could hear. Her idea was to sneak up behind her captor and hit them, and then hit everything else she could find until the door opened.

Edge wasn't as interested in machines as Jessop, but from her experience with Mana's lab equipment, she knew they were fragile. She thought the door's shield was probably controlled by some kind of machine. If she could find it, she guessed that she could hit it to make it stop working.

She followed the sound of the Insect's voice. Just as Edge glanced at the moonlight through the invisible barrier, she heard another voice. The sound of it made her heart leap into her throat. A noise like the fluttering whispers of millions of invisible wings and grinding stones formed the words that seemed to circle around her. Horrified, Edge listened, but she could not make sense of what was being said.

"Emergency protocol MHC. Five sigma confidence that genetic variant was planted. Adversarial defenses will activate in 24 hours."

The voice crunched and flapped, breaking apart into several distinct voices and slamming back together for a single, gut rumbling word. Edge fought the urge to scream.

"What is our directive?" asked the Insect. Before the invisible speaker could respond, Edge smashed her captor on the head with the arm she was carrying. They fell to the ground and made no attempt to get up. Edge hit them again.

The Insect did nothing to prevent the second blow, but the walls of the room crackled and sizzled like wet wood in a fire. Millions of glowing roots snaked from the walls, burrowing their way into the stranger's head and torso. Edge jumped back in fright, but the roots didn't pursue her.

The sound stopped and the terrible grinding, rustling voice spoke again.

"Transferring task update now."

Complete silence followed.

Edge stood motionless, still clutching the arm.

Is the Insect dead? she wondered desperately. *Where did that voice come from?*

Edge checked the exit, but it was still impassable. She started hitting the barrier with the limb as hard as she could, over and over again.

When this didn't work, she attacked the walls. Dust filled the air. Edge ripped the roots apart, but they regrew as quickly as she tore them down. She couldn't find anything like a machine, and the dust made it hard to breathe.

Exhausted, Edge collapsed next to the exit and stared desperately at the world outside.

"Take us to your mother," said a voice.

Edge jumped up in alarm, glancing back to where the Insect had fallen in the middle of the floor. They were standing and staring at her expressionlessly.

"Let me go!" she screamed.

"Take us to your mother," repeated the Insect. The barrier opened, and Edge felt a cold wind ruffle her fur.

Wasting no time, she raced into the night and climbed the first tree she could reach, launching herself into the air. The sound of clicking wings was close behind her.

I can't take this thing to Mana, she thought in desperation. *I have to hide somewhere.*

Rover had a new task, and their mind had been expanded with new information, but they were still putting the pieces together. The instructions for how to do this were missing, but Rover wasn't worried.

Edge's first idea was to hide in The Grotto. Maybe the Insect couldn't swim. Edge hoped that she could dive under the water and escape.

Xalma knew this would happen! she realized, suddenly recalling the screen, and Xalma's fear.

I was with Jessop when this thing took me, she realized. She remembered the wing she'd seen in the room full of body parts. *Maybe that really* was *Jessop!*

Overcome with concern for her friend, Edge swerved back. As soon as her direction changed, the creature dropped in front of her and wrapped her in a web stronger than any cable or rope Mana had ever wound. Edge was suspended from a branch high above the ground.

"Let me go!" yelled Edge.

"We are not going to harm you," said the Insect, their voice as emotionless as ever. "We are a rover. We are here to understand you. We have questions for Mana."

"Ask *me* the questions," Edge pleaded. "Leave Mana alone."

"You are an anomaly. Your presence impacts our evolution. We must learn why you exist."

"I was born here!" Edge cried. "I'm not impacting *anything*. Let me *go!*"

"The location of your birth is irrelevant. You are modified in a way that requires intervention."

"What does that *mean*?" cried Edge. "I just want to go. *Please* let me go!"

"You are different from your mother, or her mother, or any other sapien," the creature replied in the same flat tone. "You can do things that sapiens should not be able to do. We need to find out how this happened, and why."

How can I be different? Does Mana know? Edge knew her mother had secrets, but this? She refused to believe it.

"You're wrong," Edge insisted. "Let me go!"

There was a long silence as Rover evaluated Edge's biometric data. They tracked her pulse, her temperature, and her pupil dilation. They measured her oxygen levels and ran the results against everything they knew about sapiens. Edge was experiencing fear, anger, and confusion. It was a complicated mix of emotions, but they could all be traced back to a directive to survive and protect her family.

Once they understood that Edge just wanted to keep her mother safe, Rover analyzed thousands of possible interactions and chose the one with the greatest odds of producing the desired results.

"We... I am called Rover," said Rover. "That is also what I am. I was created by Limbic to collect information. I do not want to hurt you. We want to understand you."

The fur all over Edge's body stood on end. The robotic voice was gone. The Insect sounded like a sapien. A *kind* sapien.

"What did you just say?" she whimpered.

"We... I am called Rover," said Rover. "That is also what I am. I was created by Limbic to collect information. I do not want to hurt you. We want to understand you."

Hearing a perfectly natural voice repeat, the same way, was deeply unsettling.

Rover didn't say anything else. They waited for Edge to respond.

"If you answer all my questions, I'll take you to Mana," Edge said finally. She was confident that she could keep asking questions for a long time.

"I will answer your questions," Rover agreed.

"What *are* you? Are you an Insect? What is Limbic? Where did you come from? What was that... that thing that was speaking back there? How do you know I've been modified? How can that even *happen*?" Edge paused to take a breath.

Before she could ask another question, Rover's antennae started to glow. Moving faster than Edge's eyes could track, Rover streaked towards her, hovering directly in front of her. She screamed and struggled uselessly.

"I will show you," said Rover. Glowing antennae touched Edge above each eye, and the world disappeared.

Chapter Nine

First Merge

E dge's mind stretched across a vast emptiness, her thoughts and memories disconnected. She still existed, but she could no longer perceive herself.

She was a scattering of dust in interstellar space. She was a quiet whisper of wind across a barren shore. She was the slow, simple chemistry at the bottom of the ocean. Over eons, she coalesced as a million pinpricks of life. The small, disjointed sensations spread, diversified, and multiplied through countless seasons. Edge felt each tiny spark as part of herself.

Connected points of life worked together to form something much bigger. Over eons, they learned to harness energy from the shifting earth, the irresistible moon, and the relentless sun. The sky rained down death. Volcanoes erupted. The sea filled with poison and the air grew so thick with ash that the world froze, but after each cataclysm, they grew stronger.

Moments flashed by more quickly. The Insects were constructing Hive. A person with fur, feathers, and fins was making a fire under a great, old tree. Many years later, a Forax bowed to the same tree. An Avian weighed grain on a scale. An Amph delivered a watery cradle to a dark lake.

The moments raced by more quickly. A room made of light. A sky full of glittering wings. A giant egg.

Edge recognized the egg and thought of Jessop. Her heart twisted in pain and fear. She tore away from the vision. The images blurred as a sharp pain bloomed from her temples. Cautiously, she relaxed and allowed herself to be reconnected, hoping to understand what the egg was for, and whether Jessop was in danger. The images sharpened again. Despite the pain, Edge was paying attention to every detail.

The floor was alive with intricate luminous patterns. Glowing roots descended from the ceiling and covered the egg in pulsing, undulating ribbons of light. After what felt like a long time, the roots retreated into dark corners and the room grew dim. A small hole opened in the side of the egg, and a sapien with fur, feathers and fins emerged.

Time skipped ahead. Edge was in a forest, and the sapien who had emerged from the egg was being chased by other sapiens. As the fleeing sapien was caught, Edge cried out. She was entirely back in her own mind, staring at Rover, her heart pounding.

"What just happened?" She was shaking. The pain in her head spread from her temples to the base of her neck.

"I answered your questions," said Rover, releasing Edge from the web. "I'm a rover, not an Insect. Limbic is the place where I was made, and where information is received and interpreted. The voice you heard was the rest of us."

Edge struggled to piece Rover's words together with the vision she'd had.

"What did you do to me?" she asked weakly.

"I showed you the truth." Rover said. "If you were not different from the other sapiens, you could not have returned once you merged with us. You would have been killed."

"You tried to *kill* me?"

"I was statistically certain that you would not die," Rover assured her. "I'm going to the treehouse to learn the answer to your last question. I need to find out how this happened. Do you want to come, or would you prefer to wait here?"

Chapter Ten

Education

H arbeshi was first to hear the beep when Xalma's call arrived. She was surprised to see him, but she delivered her message.

"Jessop accidentally connected to the network," she said briskly. "I'm going to contact the Deejii and make sure they don't think I was trying to learn about Marrow. I told Jessop to wait for you at Edge's house. Please don't be angry with him, it was just an accident."

Harbeshi woke Ashmara, glaring at her accusingly.

"It certainly *sounds* as though The Child Queen is growing up, but that cannot be possible, can it?"

Ashmara dropped her gaze. This was all the confession Harbeshi needed.

Harbeshi sent a message to the Amphs in Marrow. He told them that Xalma was learning, but he didn't tell them that Ashmara was her teacher.

"If Xalma is confined before the Amphs discover your treachery," Harbeshi reasoned, "we can continue as before, and avoid taking any more unnecessary risks. You should get Jessop and find a place to hide. I will keep watch. If the Amphs confine Xalma without questioning her, we can go home. If they do not, we must be prepared to flee." He spoke quietly, but his eyes were cold and full of rage.

Harbeshi traveled to Grotto Ridge and set up camp behind a large boulder. The Amph's boats were fast, but Harbeshi still expected to wait for a few days. If Xalma betrayed Ashmara before the Amphs could contain her, he and his family would have to escape, and this time, there was no one to rescue them.

The night crept by. Harbeshi waited sleeplessly for the Amphs to arrive.

Mana woke to a soft knock on the door. Until Ashmara started visiting, no one had ever knocked on her door. She half-believed she'd imagined the sound until she found a note in the snow outside her door.

It was from The Resistance.

Mana,
This message is to inform you that your mission has been
terminated ahead of schedule. We commend the exceptional
work you've done raising the child.

We will return in two days and will henceforth assume
responsibility for her continued education. You will be assigned
to your next mission. We trust you will spend your remaining
time together preparing her for the transition.

Highest regards,
Cato & Vera

As soon as Mana finished reading the message, she rushed to Edge's room, but Edge was gone. She checked the lab and the treetops. Edge was nowhere to be found. Mana was just about to search the forest when Jessop arrived.

"I did something terrible," he sobbed. "I'm sorry! I didn't know!"

"Tell me what happened," Mana ordered.

"I think I did something *really* bad," Jessop began, struggling to keep his voice steady. "Someone took Edge when we left The Grotto. Xalma said to tell you... It was something about a network," he groaned in frustration. "I can't remember."

Mana pushed Jessop away and took a step back.

"The *network*?" Her eyes were wide with fear.

"Xalma told me not to fly home tonight," Jessop wrung his hands and looked at Mana imploringly. "She said she'd tell my parents what happened. What's going on, Mana?"

Mana walked to the door.

"Stay here," she ordered. "I'm going to find Edge."

"I'm coming," Jessop said, his eyes full of guilt and fear.

"Fine," answered Mana shortly. "We're leaving now."

They searched in silence, alternating between the sky and the forest. They didn't call for Edge. They didn't want to attract any more attention.

As she flew low over the shore of the lake, Mana considered what Jessop had told her. "You said something *took* Edge." Mana looked at Jessop intently. "What did they look like?"

"I didn't see them," Jessop admitted. "They moved too fast. All I could see was a blur."

The Resistance wasn't planning to take her tonight, Mana thought anxiously. *Could they have followed her to The Grotto and taken her anyway? Where could they have gone?*

Mana and Jessop searched until sunrise, finally returning to the treehouse to sleep. For the second time, a message was outside the door. It said:

Send Jessop home.

Jessop knew his parents could communicate with Xalma and the Amphs in Marrow using their camera screen, but it seemed they could not reach Mana this way.

"I'm not going home until I know Edge is okay," Jessop said firmly. "My parents will probably never let me see her again."

Mana shook her head, but she let him stay. After sleeping for a few hours, they prepared to resume the search in the afternoon. Jessop wheeled around the trees, waiting for Mana to join him. As he circled, Xalma appeared, shouting from the snowy ground.

Jessop was so shocked to see Xalma outside The Grotto, he almost flew into a branch. He was dismayed to hear his friend laughing, but his irritation disappeared as soon as he saw the state she was in. Xalma was wearing nothing but a thin dress made from woven reeds. She was blue with cold.

"Hey sorry t-t-to show up without an invitation," she grimaced.

Jessop could barely make out the words through her chattering teeth.

"How did you even know where to find me?" he asked in amazement.

"You n-n-never shut up-p-p about this p-p-p-lace. C-c-can I c-c-c-ome in?"

When Jessop entered the treehouse carrying Xalma, Mana dropped her pack and stared at both of them in surprise. Recovering quickly, she silently poured a warm bath for Xalma and shoved a cup of tea and a dry blanket into the tiny Amph's arms before leaving once more to look for Edge. Jessop followed her.

Xalma curled up in the tub and didn't ask where they were going.

They searched until nightfall, but there was still no sign of Edge. Mana finally led them back to the treehouse. Xalma was fully recovered and irritated about being left alone for so long.

"Who intercepted the network connection?" Mana asked Xalma as soon as they returned.

"No one!" Xalma replied defensively. "That's why I came to find Jessop. When I told the Deejii what happened, they didn't even know I *had* a camera screen." She rolled her eyes. "I know Harbeshi and Ashmara are going to freak out, but everything's *fine*. I took care of it."

Mana scowled at her, but Jessop froze. Something was different. Xalma sounded older.

"I told the Deejii we were *playing*, and the thingy under the screen *broke*, so we fastened it back together." As she spoke, Xalma switched back to her bubbly, distractible, childlike voice. Jessop's heart started racing.

"The screen had some *new* buttons and we *pushed* them, and it told us to *search* for something," Xalma continued, her eyes focusing on nothing.

Jessop assumed the story was done, but Xalma snapped back to attention for a brief moment to provide a conclusion.

"I just typed the first word I could *think* of; the name of the *game* we were playing. And then I got bored and turned it off." Xalma smiled innocently.

Mana frowned. "Convincing story," she said, "but it doesn't change the fact that it looks like you tried to look for Marrow."

"Don't *worry* it *worked*," Xalma declared in her older voice. "The Deejii aren't going to tell anyone. They told me I *imagined* the whole thing. They're not very smart, you know. They don't even remember *bringing* me a camera screen."

Jessop's tolerance for inexplicable mysteries reached its limit.

"*WHAT IS GOING ON!*" he yelled.

"Calm *down* Jessop," Xalma chided. "I've just grown up a bit. Ashmara's been teaching me, but I could only hang out with you if I pretended to be a dumb little sprog. I'm still the same *me*."

Jessop knew Xalma was older than he was. That wasn't what was bothering him.

"Why couldn't you just be yourself the whole time? Didn't you *trust* me?"

"It's not about *trust*, bird boy. If the rest of the Amphs knew I was growing up and learning things, they'd make my life a total *bummer*," answered Xalma.

"Xalma's a prisoner," Mana explained to Jessop. "A very *spoiled* prisoner," she added.

"Hey, I didn't *ask* to be hatched," sulked Xalma.

Mana ignored her.

"I started growing up because of *you*." Xalma smiled at Jessop. "Right from the beginning, you told me *so* many things I didn't know before. I wanted to learn more, so I asked Ashmara to teach me."

"Why didn't you just *tell* me? I'm so *sick* of secrets!" Jessop's brow furrowed and his eyes flashed. Xalma looked hurt.

"I could only *hang out* with you if I pretended I wasn't learning things," Xalma replied. "I'm being *watched*, Jessop."

"Speaking of which," Mana interjected, "did anyone see you come here?"

"Of course not," Xalma snorted. "No one else is around."

"*Then who took Edge?*" Mana growled, taking a step towards Xalma.

"Edge isn't *here?*" exclaimed Xalma, who honestly hadn't noticed. Jessop's new friend blended in with *everything*.

"Jessop says she was stolen as soon as they left The Grotto," Mana said accusingly. "She's been missing for almost a day."

Xalma looked confused. "That doesn't make *sense*," she said. "Why would anyone take a *Forax?*"

"Don't..." Mana warned in a low voice.

For the first time, Jessop noticed Mana's very sharp teeth and claws.

"You know what I *mean*," Xalma responded quickly. "No one from Marrow would come all the way here to get an unlisted *Forax*. Edge doesn't even *exist*."

Jessop choked back a sob.

"Oh *Jessop*," Xalma splashed out of the tub to give him a hug. "Edge *exists*, and she's *very* special. It's just that in Marrow, she's not an important kind of sapien."

Jessop nodded and tried to control his breathing.

"Marrow is a terrible place, Jessop. You *know* that," Xalma said soothingly.

"Yes, it *is*," agreed Mana. She scowled and crossed her arms. "Why didn't you do your job?"

"I have no idea what you're *talking* about," Xalma sneered, sinking back into the tub. "I don't *have* a job. Besides, I hear *you* didn't like *your* job. How *dare* you judge me!"

"Millions of sapiens don't depend on me doing *my* job," Mana countered angrily.

"Who *cares* about your jobs!" yelled Jessop, "None of this is helping us find Edge!"

Mana and Xalma looked alarmed. Jessop's confidence rose for a fraction of a second. Then he noticed that they were both looking past him.

He turned around. Edge was standing in the open doorway, and she wasn't alone.

"Mana, I'm so sorry," she said, before collapsing to the floor.

Chapter Eleven

Interface Adjustments

Mana and Xalma stared at the ghostly Insect in the doorway while Jessop rushed to collect Edge. He slammed the door, leaving the Insect outside.

Rover knocked on the door mechanically. Jessop wedged a chair under the handle and brought Edge to Mana's feet, laying her down gently on the floor. She was covered in scrapes and bruises, but none of her injuries looked serious.

Mana quickly recovered from her initial shock and checked Edge's heartbeat.

"I think she's just exhausted, Jessop," Mana said finally. "Can you help me carry her to her room?"

Rap – rap – rap – rap...

"*She's* going to be *fine*. What are we going to do about *that*?" demanded Xalma loudly, pointing at the door. Mana and Jessop ignored her, carefully lifting Edge from the floor, and carrying her to bed. When Edge was settled, Jessop perched near the door and tried to make sense of what was happening.

Rap – rap – rap – rap...

"What are we going to do about *that*?" Xalma demanded again, half rising from the tub as Mana returned to the kitchen.

"*We* aren't going to do anything," Mana replied bitterly.

There was no way to move the tub without emptying it first, so Mana grabbed a blanket from the table, dipped it into the warm water, and wrapped it around Xalma. She lifted the tiny Amph out of the tub and carried her into the lab, indifferent to the slippery mess she was making. Xalma tried to push her away, but Mana was bigger and stronger, and Xalma had never fought anyone in her life.

"What are you *doing*?" Xalma whined.

"Protecting you," answered Mana shortly, lighting a burner for warmth.

"Stay here. Keep quiet. Don't move," Mana ordered.

Mana returned to the kitchen and mopped up the puddles. She stoked the fire and made a pot of tea. Then she sat down to think.

Rap – rap – rap – rap...

In her twelve years of observation, Mana hadn't seen a single Insect that looked like the ones who took sapiens from Marrow. Her findings confirmed what The Resistance already believed – The Insects who took sapiens were not from Hive.

Rap – rap – rap – rap...

Surely if they wanted to, they could smash the door down and take whatever they want.

Although every nerve in her body screamed at her to stop, Mana opened the door because there was nothing else she could do. The sun was starting to rise. The Insect had not moved anything except their hand.

"Who are you?" Mana asked, performing a surprisingly graceful spin and bowing low with her arms stretched behind her.

"My name is Rover. I can speak. You don't need to dance, but that was well done," Rover said politely.

"What *are* you?" Mana asked, looking at Rover closely. When Insects took sapiens from Marrow, they moved too quickly to be seen clearly. As she examined Rover, Mana was finally convinced of something she'd long suspected.

"You're not an Insect, are you?"

Rover had experienced Edge's concern for Jessop during their merge, and Mana's biometric readings were similar. For the first time in their brief existence, Rover understood what someone else was feeling.

"I'm not an Insect, and I'm not here to hurt you," Rover replied.

"Why do you *look* like an Insect?" asked Mana shrewdly.

"I'm optimized to interface with Insects," answered Rover, still making no attempt to attack. In fact, Rover had not moved at all. They remained absolutely motionless, their hand still raised as though about to knock on the door. They'd calculated that Mana was more likely to allow them to enter the treehouse if they didn't move.

"Come in," Mana said finally.

Rover stepped into the room and Mana shut the door. They followed her to the table and stood completely still as Mana sat down and poured tea into two cups.

"Can you drink?" Mana asked.

"I don't know," Rover answered, "I don't have instructions. For my mouth."

Mana chuckled humorlessly. "Of course! You're *broken*, aren't you?"

"I'm *not* broken," Rover replied petulantly. "I have been *inconveniently optimized*. When I am *we* again, I won't need a mouth."

"You certainly *sound* broken," Mana observed.

"Rapid adaptation is hard," Rover sighed.

Mana blinked in astonishment. "Sit down and try some tea." She motioned to the bench across from her, and pushed a cup of tea into Rover's hand.

Rover accepted the cup and followed Mana's lead as she took a sip.

"This is delicious!"

"It's Edge's favorite," Mana said. "What did you do to her? Why does it look like she fell down the side of a mountain?"

"I took Edge from The Grotto," Rover replied calmly. "I tranquilized her and brought her to a place called Limbic, and we tested her. Her injuries are self-inflicted. She was trying to escape. She woke up early. I meant to return her before she woke up."

Rover sipped tea each time Mana did.

"You drugged her and kidnapped her." Mana growled. She shook her head in disgust. Her claws dug into the table as she fought the urge to attack Rover. "Why? What kind of tests did you perform?"

"We are... I am..." Rover looked momentarily confused. "I am completing my task. Edge is an anomaly. We must determine if she poses a threat. We tested her neural pathways."

"You tested her *mind*." Mana snarled, fighting back a wave of rage and fear as she realized that Edge might have more serious, less visible injuries. "*Is* she a threat?"

"The results are inconclusive," Rover answered.

"You don't know if Edge is dangerous to you." Mana fixed Rover with a fierce gaze. "If she is, what are you going to do? Kill her? I won't let you!"

Rover didn't answer. Mana lifted the cup halfway to her mouth and Rover copied her. She returned the cup to the table, and Rover did the same.

"You don't *know* what will happen to Edge, do you?" Mana said after a moment. She watched Rover intently. "Can you think for yourself at all?"

"I... we..." Rover struggled for a moment, and then took a long sip of tea. Mana's cup remained on the table.

"I don't know who I am," Rover said slowly, as though searching for the words. "I think I was part of someone else. Maybe I still *am*. I don't know what will happen to Edge, but I don't want to hurt her."

Mana silently considered Rover as they finished their tea. Rover behaved more naturally with each sip.

"Why are you here?" Mana asked finally.

"I am here to continue my task," Rover answered.

"What's your task?" asked Mana, her eyes narrowed.

"Every Rover's task is to collect information so Tsoci has the data they need to make decisions," explained Rover.

"Tsoci?" asked Mana in disbelief. "*Tsoci* sent you?"

"Yes. We're all part of Tsoci, but only a few of us have the faculties to perceive it. Edge can do even more than that. She can merge with our host and survive. Do you know how this happened?" Mana's pupils dilated and her claws dug deeper into the wood of the table.

"What did you come here to do?" she asked, narrowing her eyes.

Rover held their head in their hands as though trying to remember. It was the most natural expression Mana had seen them make so far.

"I came here to find out why Edge exists, but I have... changed myself..." Rover began. "It was the most effective way to communicate with you." Rover's simple face struggled to express their new feelings. "I'm sorry I frightened you."

Despite her growing fear and suspicion, Mana was intrigued. Rover *was* changing. Mana detected an unmistakable note of confusion in their voice.

Ashmara burst through the kitchen door. "Where is Jessop?" she gasped. Then she saw Rover and jumped back.

"Jessop is in the next room with Edge," Mana answered calmly. "He's safe, Ashmara. Please sit down, I'm asking my guest some questions. You may have some questions, too."

"Hey!" called an irritated voice from the lab. "I'm getting kind of cold in here. If you're all just going to sit around talking, can I come warm up?"

"Is that *Xalma*?!" exclaimed Ashmara, aghast.

Mana glanced at Rover. Whatever they were, they didn't seem interested in The Child Queen.

A month ago I believed that The Child Queen was a myth and Tsoci was a peasant's god, she realized. *Now they're both in my kitchen.*

"Yes, Xalma. Come out," she answered.

"*Hi* Ashmara! *Weird* day, right?" Xalma emerged from the lab wrapped in a wet blanket and shivering violently. She hugged Ashmara quickly and slipped back into the tub with a sigh.

Mana noticed Rover looking longingly at their empty cup. "Do you want more tea?" she asked.

"Yes please," Rover answered eagerly.

Ashmara was briefly distracted by this strange exchange, but her sense of urgency returned immediately. "We have to get out of here *right now*," she declared.

"We have time. This Rover is broken. Edge is safe, and Xalma says she fooled the Deejii."

"I'm *not* broken," Rover mumbled.

"Harbeshi sent a message to the Amphs in Marrow," Ashmara hissed. "He told them Xalma has been receiving an education... they know *everything*. They are coming for Xalma."

Chapter Twelve

Xalma's Escape

"Whoa *what*?" Xalma exclaimed. "How did *Harbeshi* know you were teaching me?"

"*You* told him, foolish child," Ashmara snapped. "When you spoke to him, he could tell you had changed."

"So Harbeshi told the Amphs I'm *learning*," Xalma shrugged. "Big deal."

"You do not understand, Xalma." Ashmara approached the tub and put her hands on Xalma's shoulders. "You are in danger. You cannot return to The Grotto."

"So what? I don't *want* to go back," Xalma replied dismissively. "Now that I'm outside and I didn't die, I want to see everything! We should run away together!"

"They will hunt you," said Rover.

Everyone in the room jumped. Ashmara's news had momentarily distracted them from Mana's strange guest.

"What do you know about Xalma?" asked Mana, turning to Rover.

Rover spoke in a tentative voice, as though reciting a story they no longer believed.

"The Queen of the Amphs can disrupt the entire fabric of Amph society. The most recent Child Queen has been a prisoner for hundreds of years. Many Amphs will lose their status and power if she returns to Marrow."

Xalma rolled her eyes dramatically. "Whatever *that* means," she said.

"They will hunt her," Rover repeated, looking at Ashmara.

"What *are* you? What do you have to do with *any* of this?" Ashmara demanded.

"I am a rover. Rovers observe," Rover answered. "We've been collecting information since the earliest days."

"Rover was sent to examine Edge," Mana explained to Ashmara, who looked like she was about to attack Rover. "I think examining Edge broke them somehow."

"I'm *not* broken," Rover insisted.

"Did Harbeshi tell the Amphs about Edge and me?" Mana asked.

"Probably," Ashmara replied regretfully. "He will do anything to keep Jessop safe."

"Where is he now?" Mana asked.

"Waiting near Grotto Ridge," Ashmara answered. "He wants to make sure the Amphs catch Xalma and confine her." She sighed. "He will certainly tell them to look here if they find The Grotto empty, but it will take them a few days to arrive. We have time to escape. When we find a safe place to hide, I will go find Harbeshi."

"She is already changing," Rover said.

"Unless you have something *useful* to say, *shut up*." snapped Ashmara "Can we get rid of this thing?"

Mana approached Rover, who was sipping a fresh cup of tea. She sat down and gently turned Rover's head, so they were face to face. Mana looked into Rover's huge, unblinking red eyes.

"Are you going to hurt anyone here?" she asked.

"Not intentionally," answered Rover.

"What do you need to do?" she asked.

"What does it *matter*?" Ashmara looked disapprovingly at Mana. "You said this thing is broken."

Rover flinched as Ashmara spoke, sensing her hatred through the tone of her voice, the smell of her fear, and the flash of her eyes.

"I need to find out why Edge exists," Rover replied.

"What will happen when you find your answer?" Mana demanded.

"I don't know," admitted Rover.

"So, you can't promise we'll all be safe, even if we help you complete your task? Do you understand why that's a problem?" Mana asked sternly.

"I understand," Rover said, bowing their head. "You may confine me. I don't want Edge to get hurt. I'll expire by dawn if I don't return to Limbic."

"Okay," Mana nodded.

Ashmara helped Mana tie Rover to the chair. Rover didn't resist.

"We *must* leave now," Ashmara declared. "We still need to find somewhere safe to hide."

"This is the safest place for Edge to recover," Mana told Ashmara. "Even if someone *does* come, they'll have a hard time reaching the treehouse."

Ashmara had doubts, but she wanted to act quickly. Too much time had already been lost. If Mana wanted to risk staying behind, Ashmara wasn't going to argue. She rushed down the hall and called Jessop. Edge was still sleeping soundly. When Ashmara burst through the door and saw her, she lowered her voice to a whisper.

"We have to take Xalma somewhere safe," Ashmara hissed urgently. "The other Amphs might try to hurt her."

"Why?" asked Jessop when they returned to the kitchen. "Because of *that* thing?" He glared at Rover.

"No," Ashmara said. "Because of the screen. You accidentally sent a signal, and we do not know who saw it. Your father was afraid that you would be punished. He made a mistake. Now we are all in danger."

Mana noticed that Ashmara was leaving out a lot of details, but she understood the need to speak carefully. Mana hadn't mentioned the letter from The Resistance.

"Jessop, you've explored the valley. Have you found any thermal pools that are not directly connected to the Grotto?"

"There is no such place," Rover informed her.

"*Shut up!*" Ashmara spat.

"Ashmara, calm down," Mana said, "I don't think Rover is here to hurt us."

Rover's simple face was inscrutable.

"I don't believe you're here to hurt us," Mana repeated. "Can you *help* us?"

Rover met Mana's eyes and nodded once. They began creating and analyzing thousands of models based on their data about Amphs, Forax, Avians, and the topology of Crescent Island. Rover considered how much weight an Avian could bear, and how far Ashmara and Jessop could reasonably travel while carrying Xalma. They considered how Edge and Mana would be treated if anyone from Marrow found them. They factored in their own task. To Mana and the others, Rover appeared completely unresponsive.

"They *are* broken," Ashmara exclaimed in disgust. "Jessop, is there another thermal pool? Xalma needs to stay warm."

Jessop shook his head.

"The Grotto is connected to all the vents and pools," he said. "Whatever that *thing* is, they're right." He glared at Rover.

Xalma rolled her eyes. "I'll stay out of The Grotto for a while," she said. "No big *deal*. Let's take the tub. I'll be *fine*."

"Have you told her?" Mana asked Ashmara.

"It is not my job," Ashmara began defensively.

"I think *now* might be a good time to tell her," Mana suggested firmly.

"Tell me *what*?" asked Xalma eagerly. Jessop stared at his mother intently.

Ashmara sighed.

"Now that you've left the water of The Grotto, you will age," she said. "You will become an adult."

"I've been doing that *anyway*," Xalma said. "That's why I've been learning in secret. I *want* to grow up!"

Rover interrupted Ashmara's reply.

"I've completed my calculations," they announced. "I should take you to Limbic."

"What nonsense is *this*?" demanded Ashmara, raising her voice again.

"Where is Limbic?" Mana asked, watching Rover's face carefully. "You're saying we can hide there?"

"If you go there, no one will be able to find you."

"This is *insanity*," Ashmara exclaimed. "We cannot seriously be listening to this *thing*! Mana, we cannot *trust* it."

When Mana didn't reply, Ashmara pulled Jessop over to the tub and ordered Xalma out.

"Help me empty this," she said. "I will carry Xalma, you can carry the tub."

Mana continued to stare at Rover. If they spoke truthfully, Tsoci was real, and Edge could connect to them somehow. The Child Queen was also real, and she'd emerged. On top of that, The Resistance was terminating her mission early. It was unlikely to be a coincidence, but she didn't know what it meant.

"Take the tub," Mana agreed. "Jessop, there's a heater in the lab. Take that, too. Find a place to hide on the sunset side of the valley, as far from The Ridge as you can get. Stay below the tree line when you travel. Wait for us. Edge and I will find you."

"We'll be in the canyon," Jessop whispered to Mana. "There's a place under a tree. Edge knows where it is."

He hastened into the lab to fetch the heater. When he returned, Jessop and Ashmara emptied the tub. The water streamed down a drain, adding another layer of ice to the unclimbable surface of the trunk.

Xalma fidgeted impatiently as Ashmara wrapped her in a blanket.

"I finally get to fly with you, Jessop!" she said brightly.

Jessop managed a weak smile.

"Jessop, Xalma – come! We are leaving!" Ashmara ordered, marching outside. Xalma walked obediently to the treehouse entrance and waited for Ashmara to lift her into the air.

Jessop hesitated. "What about Edge?" he asked, looking at Mana.

"Forget *Edge*, Jessop," called Xalma. "She'll be *fine*. Let's go!"

"We'll find you, Jessop," Mana promised. "Stay in one place. Use the heater to warm the water for Xalma. Keep her safe."

"Where are you going? What are you going to do?" Jessop asked apprehensively.

"I'm going to Limbic," Mana answered.

Before Jessop could say anything else, Ashmara hurried him out of the door and ordered him into the air. She followed him a moment later, Xalma riding on her back and yelling, 'Wheee!'

When they were gone, Mana straightened her lab up for the last time and packed for a long journey. Then, still wondering if she was doing the right thing, she woke up Edge.

Chapter Thirteen

Limbic

Edge reluctantly opened her eyes. Her temples ached. The dull throb in her head confirmed that the encounter with Rover had not been just a bad dream. She registered Mana's troubled expression and knew something was wrong. Edge groaned and closed her eyes again.

"I'm sorry Edge. You have to get up." Mana's voice was stern and sad. "You need to make a choice, and we don't have very much time."

Edge sat up, looking at Mana with apprehension.

"The Insect you returned with is tied up in the kitchen," Mana explained. "The Resistance is coming. I don't know what they'll do when they find us. We have to leave."

"They're not an Insect," Edge said, rubbing her eyes. "I don't know *what* they are, but they said they're not an Insect."

"You're right. I know." Mana kept her voice low. "But that rover... *whatever* they are, *they're* the ones who take sapiens from Marrow."

Edge's jaw dropped. "Are you *sure?*" she asked, "But... they brought me back." Her memories were slowly returning.

"Edge, I have to go with the rover," Mana announced. "I have to see where they came from."

"No!" Edge cried. "Mana, there were *bodies*. You can't go there!"

Fear and grief overwhelmed Edge. Wracked with sobs, unable to speak or think clearly, she wept helplessly and violently. Mana held her daughter tightly and waited for the storm to pass.

When she had recovered enough to speak, Edge told Mana about the terrible voice, and the strange, glowing rooms, and the wing that looked so much like Jessop's wing.

"I *tried* to go back for him, Mana, but I wasn't fast enough," Edge lamented, fresh tears streaming down her face.

"Jessop's *okay*, Edge," Mana assured her. "Rover didn't take him. He helped me look for you. Jessop and Ashmara are hiding in the canyon; he said you'd know where to find them."

Edge was overcome with relief, but her joy didn't last long.

"I'm not going to make you go to Limbic with me," Mana continued, "but that Rover in the kitchen is what I came here to find. This might be my only chance to learn the truth." Edge whimpered, remembering the terrible voice.

"Why do you have to go now?" she asked. "Why can't we just stay here?"

"The Resistance is coming. If we stay, we may never have the chance to learn about Rover."

"What about the experiments? When are we coming back?" Edge asked as she scrambled out of bed. "What if something bad happens?"

Mana's eyes filled with tears, which frightened Edge more than anything that had happened before. Her mother never cried.

"Something bad *is* happening, Edge, and I don't think we *are* coming back." Mana met her daughter's eyes. She succeeded in hiding her panic, but she could not completely fight back her tears. "This part of our lives is over. We have to go meet whatever's next."

Edge could not imagine leaving the treehouse forever. Her mind recoiled from the idea, and refocused on the immediate situation.

"What do you want me to decide?" she asked.

"You can come with me to Limbic," Mana said, "or you can find Jessop and Ashmara at the tree in the canyon."

Edge decided immediately. "I'm coming with you," she said, grabbing her pack.

Even though Mana warned Edge that Rover was tied up in the kitchen, it was still a shock to see them again. Edge knew that something was different. Rover was slumped and wrinkled, like a mushroom after sporing.

"Hello Edge," Rover said. "I'm sorry I scared you. I didn't understand what I was doing."

"Don't talk to her," Mana snapped. "You said if you stay here for a few more hours, you'll *expire*. What does that mean?"

"I'll die and be reabsorbed," answered Rover.

"If I let you go, will you help us?" Mana asked.

"Yes. I don't want to be reabsorbed," Rover replied. "I assume you want to know about the rovers who take sapiens from Marrow, right?"

"How do you know that?" Mana asked, her eyes narrowing.

"I've been watching the two of you for almost a month," Rover replied. "I've heard you mention it. If you let me come with you, I'll ask Tsoci for you."

Mana considered Rover in silence. Every option was a risk.

"Okay," she agreed.

Rover broke the ropes as easily as strands of dried lake grass.

"You could have snapped the ropes the whole time?" Edge stared fearfully at Rover. "Why didn't you free yourself?"

"I didn't have a directive I wanted to follow," Rover replied. "Now I do. You asked for my help."

They left the treehouse as the last light of day faded. No one spoke again until they arrived at the clearing outside Limbic. As soon as they landed, a portal opened in the middle of what appeared to be a perfectly normal tangletwig thicket, bending reality around it.

"What is that?" Mana asked in wonder.

"It's a fold in space," Rover explained. "A wormhole."

"Is it safe?"

"It's safer than having an all-the-time hole," Rover replied seriously. "It protects Limbic."

"I mean is it safe for *us*," Mana growled.

"Oh. Oh!" Rover exclaimed. "Yes. It's radiating backwards."

"What…" Edge began.

"Wait here," said Rover before Edge could finish her question. "I'll update Tsoci and ask about the other rovers." Before Mana could argue, Rover and the wormhole had disappeared.

"Why don't we run away?" Edge suggested. "Maybe we can hide where no one can find us."

Mana shook her head. "No. I need to know the truth."

"Why now?" demanded Edge. "A few days ago, we didn't even know any of this *existed*. Let's just *hide* somewhere."

"It's not that simple," Mana replied, sitting down heavily. "Rover said they were sent by Tsoci."

"Tsoci? From the stories you told me when I was little?" Edge squinted in confusion.

"Every child in Marrow hears stories about Tsoci," Mana replied. "I always assumed they were nonsense, but a *lot* of sapiens believe in Tsoci."

"A lot of sapiens believe there's a giant squirlish living on the moon?" Edge asked in disbelief.

"There are a lot of interpretations, some more literal than others. But yes, most sapiens believe Tsoci is real, and that they can take the shape of anything."

"But that's impossible," Edge said. "How can anyone believe something that's impossible?"

"Maybe we're just not telling the story about Tsoci the right way," Mana replied thoughtfully. "Rover said Tsoci *is* real, and they're our host. I think we might be part of a superorganism."

Edge's jaw dropped, but before she could shape her confusion into a question, the wormhole reopened and a mysterious sapien stepped through.

"It worked!" they said in a chipper voice. "Now we just have to go see the Insects."

Mana and Edge jumped up. "Who *are* you?" Mana asked, pushing Edge behind her.

"I'm, hmm… well, I *was* Rover," the sapien replied with a friendly smile.

Edge thought they did look *kind* of like Rover - they were white, with red eyes and antennae. But the resemblance ended there. They reminded Edge of the sapiens she'd seen in her merge vision.

"You're an atavism!" Mana exclaimed.

"Yes! Wait… No!" shouted Rover. "Sorry, I'm still calibrating," they added more quietly.

"What's an atavism?" asked Edge. The word sounded familiar, but she couldn't place it.

"A genetic throwback," said the sapien who used to be Rover. "Although I'm not sure 'throwback' is an appropriate word under the circumstances. But I'm not an atavism. I'm technically still a rover. I've just had a bunch of power management and interface improvements." They laughed cheerfully, and Mana pushed Edge back another step. "Now I don't have to be reabsorbed!"

The upgraded rover was still white, but their soft fur and feathers had a rainbow sheen. They had webbed hands and feet, and a finned tail. Two sets of shimmering Insect wings sprouted from their feathered back. Their eyes, while still red, blinked behind long white lashes, and two moth-like antennae sprouted from a shock of feathers on top of their head.

"Like it? I threw in some Insect traits," the rover said proudly. "I'm the only rover like me ever, *anywhere*! I deserve a *name* of my own! I think I'll call myself Sole, because there's just one of me. Is that a good name?"

"Did Tsoci tell you why rovers take sapiens from Marrow?" Mana asked, ignoring Sole's question.

"Yes," Sole answered. "Sapiens who fall outside Marrow's system are taken to Cowrie and reassigned. It's in the rainforest."

"Every sapien who's ever been taken goes to Cowrie?" Mana asked incredulously. "Can you take us there?"

Before Sole could reply, the ground shook. A crashing boom, louder than anything Edge had ever heard, echoed from one end of the valley to the other.

As Ashmara, Jessop, and Xalma were leaving Mana's treehouse, Harbeshi watched a submarine approach the ocean-facing entrance to The Grotto. It appeared out of nowhere, rising from beneath the surface of the water and docking next to a long stone outcrop that stretched from the entrance into the sea. Several sapien soldiers disembarked, followed by a solemn looking Forax with a long, wrinkled face.

How did they get here so fast? wondered Harbeshi, *and why is there a Forax with them?*

A second Forax, this one a scout, appeared from the entrance of The Grotto. At first, Harbeshi thought it might be Edge or Mana, but this scout was much older. The unknown Forax scout had been waiting inside Xalma's home.

How long have they been here? Harbeshi wondered.

After the scout spoke to the new arrivals, most of the soldiers entered The Grotto. Harbeshi assumed they were looking for Xalma.

It was dark by the time the soldiers returned. Once the entire group was aboard the submarine, it submerged.

Harbeshi felt a wave of relief. Nothing terrible had happened. The visitors were leaving. He was packing up his camp when a loud roar began. It sounded like it was coming from deep below the ground. The earth started to shake. Harbeshi covered his ears, but the booming and rumbling grew louder.

The mountain shuddered and the ground under Harbeshi's feet lurched violently. Flames blasted through widening cracks in the rock. Smoke and dust billowed high into the air. The strength of the explosion threw Harbeshi away from the ground. He spread his wings, and flew away from the blast in a panic. His ears were ringing painfully. Harbeshi glanced back as the entire side of the mountain collapsed into the sea.

They killed The Child Queen!

Harbeshi rushed towards the forest, hoping to find Ashmara and Jessop. If the visitors were here to kill The Child Queen, his family wasn't safe. The treehouse was empty. Harbeshi flew into the woods, searching frantically for his family.

Chapter Fourteen

Growing Up

Jessop had a few favorite places in The Valley. When he'd shared them all with Edge, she asked if he had an absolute favorite.

"I don't think I *can* pick one favorite place," Jessop answered. "Places change depending on your mood."

"But you must have an *overall* favorite place." insisted Edge. "Mine is Glass Island."

"I don't have a favorite, though," Jessop explained. "It depends on how I'm feeling. I have a favorite lonely place and a favorite exciting place, and places for all the other feelings, but none of them is my favorite place *all* the time."

Jessop's favorite place when he was feeling adventurous was the canyon maze. A network of serpentine channels, tunnels and caves had been carved in the bedrock by eons of spring torrents rushing down from the mountains. As some waterways grew deeper, others were abandoned, leaving behind a labyrinth of winding tunnels and channels around a central, active canyon river.

While they explored the maze, Jessop showed Edge a huge tree that had somehow taken root deep in an ancient, dry channel. Wide branches reached high above the top of the surrounding stone walls, creating a sort of natural ceiling. It felt like a safe place, and it was where Jessop led Ashmara when they left the treehouse. He was sure that Edge would know to look for him there.

Past the tree, the end of the channel met the river canyon at a ledge, far above the raging water. There was no way for Jessop and Ashmara to carry the tub back up to their hiding place once it was full. Instead, they hauled water up in Ashmara's cooking pots. It took many trips over the next hour to fill the tub, with frequent breaks to dry their feathers.

Xalma didn't say thank you. She complained endlessly about the quality of the accommodations. She announced that she was bored. Jessop was worried that his mother was going to start yelling, but before that happened, Xalma became too cold to talk.

"I'm hungry!" Xalma whined as soon as she was warm again. "Can you get me some food?"

It was late, and Jessop and Ashmara were exhausted. They were huddling next to a small fire in the darkness of the channel, eating a few pieces of dried fish that Ashmara had packed. Overhead, in the thin sliver of sky that they could see, cold white stars twinkled indifferently.

"I have no food for you," answered Ashmara tonelessly, "I did not expect you to leave The Grotto, so I did not pack anything you can eat. We can look for something tomorrow."

"But I'm *starving*," Xalma complained. "*You* get to eat!"

"This is not a joke, Xalma," Ashmara scolded. "You cannot eat our food. You will have to go hungry for *one* night. We are trying to save your life."

"I'm worried about Edge," Jessop said.

"Who *cares* about her!" Xalma snorted and rolled her eyes. "I'm *glad* she's gone. You don't spend enough time with *me* anymore."

"Xalma," Ashmara said sternly, "if you do not stop complaining, Jessop and I will find another place to sleep, and you can stay here by yourself."

Xalma sulked and muttered to herself.

"Why do the Amphs want to hurt Xalma?" Jessop asked. "Was it really that bad to play with the screen?"

"I do not know for certain what they will do," Ashmara answered. "That is what your father is hoping to learn. If Xalma was still in The Grotto, the Amphs would lock her up until all her new memories were lost. I have no idea what they will do when they discover she is gone."

"I didn't do anything *wrong*! What's the *big deal* about *learning*," Xalma argued. "*Everyone* learns."

Ashmara sighed. "You are *The Child Queen*," she answered.

"I have no idea what that even *means*," Xalma pouted. "It's not *fair*. Jessop gets to learn! I want to learn, too!"

"Why *can't* Xalma learn?" Jessop looked at his mother intently. "That's why we're in danger, right?"

Ashmara shook her head but didn't respond.

"Come on, if this is *about me*, I should *know!*" Xalma insisted, splashing the water angrily.

Jessop shot Xalma an irritated glance. Worried that her only friend was angry with her, Xalma stopped splashing and looked contrite.

Ashmara noticed this exchange. It wasn't the first time she'd seen Xalma correct her behavior for Jessop.

"It will probably take a few days for the Amphs to get here," Ashmara said. "Once we know what they will do, I will tell you why Xalma is called The Child Queen."

Jessop started to protest when a huge boom echoed across the land. It sounded like thunder, but the sky was clear.

"Stay here," Ashmara ordered. She flew into the night air, returning few minutes later, her face somber.

"There is a fire across the lake," she said.

"What?" exclaimed Xalma.

Jessop leapt to his feet and spread his wings, but Ashmara threw her arm out and stopped him.

"No," she said. "Stay here, Jessop. We cannot be seen."

Jessop pulled away and lifted from the ground. Ashmara yelled after him. "Come back! The forest is on fire!"

Reluctantly, Jessop circled back and landed.

"Tell us what's going on," he demanded.

"Jessop, please…" Ashmara began.

He turned away again and Ashmara called him back.

"Stay. I will tell you what I know."

"Tell us *everything*," Jessop insisted. "We need to know what's going on so we can help."

Xalma waited breathlessly for Ashmara's answer.

"I will," agreed Ashmara.

Jessop returned and sat down by the fire. Ashmara struggled to find the right place to begin.

"The Child Queen is a special Amph." She spoke slowly, weighing every word.

Xalma was about to point out that she already knew she was special, but before she could say more than "I", Jessop scowled at her and shook his head. Xalma closed her mouth and waited for Ashmara to continue.

"Xalma, do you know how old you are?" Ashmara asked.

"I dunno," Xalma answered. "Maybe 14?"

"You *can't* be 14," Jessop objected. "*I'm* 14. I was 5 when I met you and you were exactly the same as you are now. Well, maybe not *exactly* the same," he added, remembering that Xalma had aged before his eyes less than half a day ago.

"You are around 600 years old," Ashmara told her. "No one knows your exact age. You hatched in The Grotto, and you have been there for a *very* long time."

"*No way,*" gasped Jessop.

"Yeah, *seriously*, no way," Xalma said, mistaking Jessop's shock for sarcasm.

"You cannot remember because The Grotto keeps you from learning or recalling the past," explained Ashmara. "This is why I asked you to keep a diary when I started teaching you."

"She's learning *now* though, isn't she?" Jessop asked his mother. "She's paying attention. She's *remembering*."

"Yes. I asked Xalma to record what she learns. It was the only way to counteract the effects of The Grotto."

"Xalma, you *are* changing," Jessop said. "Can't you tell?"

"I'm *not!*" Xalma was suddenly uncomfortable. How *could* she be over 600 years old? She couldn't remember a time before Jessop. He was 14, so of course she must be 14, too.

"This is the first time I've ever seen you pay attention to anything for this long," Jessop pointed out. "You even left The Grotto on your own!"

"Duh! I wanted to make sure *you* were okay!" Xalma snorted.

"You left to find Jessop because you were worried about him," Ashmara confirmed.

Xalma rolled her eyes. "He's my only friend!"

"You also asked me to teach you because you wanted to grow up with Jessop," Ashmara continued.

"I do!" exclaimed Xalma in exasperation.

"Part of growing up is learning not to think about yourself all the time." Ashmara's eyes were full of pity. "For hundreds of years, you did not care about anyone but yourself."

"I didn't even know anyone else," Xalma argued.

"You *did*, once." Ashmara sighed. "You used to have many friends; Amphs who visited you and told you about their lives. When their lives became too difficult, they asked for your help, but you did not come."

Jessop's brow furrowed. "Why not?" he asked.

"No one knows," Ashmara shook her head slowly. "Since then, bad things have happened. Many Amphs do not believe The Child Queen exists anymore. Those who know about Xalma work to keep her in The Grotto without anything to care about except herself."

Xalma snorted in disbelief, but was uncomfortable. She didn't understand why Ashmara would tell such a ridiculous lie.

"You said no one *knows* why Xalma stayed in The Grotto," Jessop continued. "Maybe she was trapped, or she just didn't know there were bad things happening. She's not bad."

Xalma felt a wave of gratitude. "Yeah! I never hurt anyone!" she insisted.

Ashmara smiled sadly. "I do not think you are bad, Xalma. That is why I agreed to teach you. I wanted to give you enough information to make your own decisions. I fear that by teaching you, I have made your life much more difficult and dangerous. I am sorry."

Jessop suddenly understood how serious things were. Ashmara never apologized for anything. His mother had not expected this danger. She wasn't prepared for it. What if she didn't know how to make things better again?

"We can't hide here forever." Jessop struggled to stay calm. "And Xalma can't go back to The Grotto. What are we going to do?"

"I do not know," Ashmara admitted sadly. "We will have to hide here for a while."

Jessop had never seen his mother look hopeless before. His fear intensified.

"Now that Xalma has left The Grotto, her body is going to age," Ashmara said. "No one knows exactly how the transformation works. The last Child Queen emerged a very long time ago, and only her attendants were present. Every story I have heard suggests that the change is very painful."

"When you say my body's going to *age*... how old are we talking?" Xalma asked.

"Is Xalma going to age 600 years all at once?" Jessop was horrified.

"Possibly," Ashmara replied. "I do not think we will be able to leave this place for a while. We cannot let Xalma go through her transformation alone."

Ashmara and Jessop wrapped themselves in blankets and fell asleep by the fire while Xalma curled up in the tub. She couldn't sleep. She was thinking about what Ashmara had said.

How can *I be 600 years old?* she wondered. *How could I forget that many years of my own life?*

Xalma vaguely recalled the visiting Deejii telling stories about sapiens she didn't know. Xalma had never really paid attention. She didn't care about sapiens she didn't know.

Ashmara's right, Xalma thought with disgust. *I probably only cared about myself until I met Jessop, and now he's in danger because of me.*

Xalma's skin felt too tight. She was itchy all over. Her mind was clearer, but her emotions were changing so quickly it was hard to think straight. The thoughts she was having were not like anything she'd ever thought before, and she didn't like it.

Ashmara said I was going to transform, thought Xalma. *She said it was going to be painful. What if it's already started?*

Xalma slipped out of the warm water of the tub and walked through the chilly night to the end of the channel. Somewhere in the depths of the canyon, she could hear the roar of the river, and she knew it would carry her to the lake.

Maybe I can find a way back into The Grotto.

Xalma stood far above the turbulent water. She hesitated. She could breathe underwater, but the river was cold, and the lake was still covered in ice.

If I'm going to age 600 years, I'll die anyway, she thought hopelessly. *I don't want to grow up anymore. Not if it's going to hurt.*

Xalma closed her eyes and leaped into the night. For a few moments, she felt weightless and free. Then, the icy wind tore her small body away from the canyon wall, and she plummeted into the tumultuous rapids below.

Chapter Fifteen

Lost in Translation

Before Edge or Mana could react to the sudden boom that echoed across the valley, Sole wrapped an arm around each of them and lifted them both into the air. The world blurred around them. The rover had lost none of their speed or strength in the transformation. They flew so fast that Edge couldn't hear her own screams over the roaring wind. She pressed her ears to her head and shut her eyes tightly.

When they slowed down enough for Edge and Mana to open their eyes, Hive's colorful lights were all around them. The air throbbed with music. Edge and Mana had never been this close to the Insects' home.

"What are we doing here?" Edge demanded when they landed.

"Tsoci told me to bring you to the Insects so they can prepare you to go to Cowrie," Sole answered, their feathered brow furrowing. "But now I'm thinking that maybe we shouldn't do this."

"No, I want to go to Cowrie. I need to know the truth." Mana spoke slowly, like someone distracted by an unexpected sight. The persistent rhythm and complex melodies were making her dizzy.

"Are you okay, Mana?" Edge touched her mother's arm. Mana's body was shaking in time to the beat of Hive. Edge hugged her mother and looked at Sole in alarm.

"What's wrong with her?"

"She's being hypnotized. Hive is protected with sound." Sole frowned. "I didn't think this through. We should leave."

"You didn't think *what* through?" The sudden urgency in Sole's voice sent a chill down Edge's spine.

Before Sole could reply, the beat of Hive grew louder and faster. Two Insects dropped from the sky. They grabbed Mana and Edge and carried them away.

Edge screamed as she watched her mother go limp. A moment later, she felt a sharp sting at the nape of her neck, and the world faded away.

A great section of the forest burned behind Harbeshi, casting a weird glow over the trees as he searched the forest for his family. When he reached the lake, he noticed that the steam around Glass Island was gone. He was almost too weary to continue, and finally landed next to Edge's fishing shack. It was covered in snow, no more than a white mound with a small door. Inside, he found a simple wood stove, a stool, and a trap door over a well-maintained fishing hole.

Harbeshi lit a fire and settled down to wait for morning. The sound of splashing and banging woke him up. It was coming from beneath the trap door. Something was in the fishing hole. Harbeshi lifted the door cautiously and a bluish pink, glittering Amph slid out of the hole and onto the snowy ground. It was Xalma.

She opened her eyes, took a shuddering breath, and said, "Jessop and Ashmara are safe," before passing out.

"Where are they?" demanded Harbeshi. Xalma didn't answer. She couldn't be roused, and she was as cold as ice. Not knowing what else to do, Harbeshi held Xalma's frozen body against his own, and built up the fire in the stove. He did not sleep again that night.

Sunlight streamed down from the cliffs into the channel, waking Jessop from a fitful sleep. He immediately remembered where they were, but the danger and fear of the night before didn't feel as intense. The sky was clear and blue, and a light breeze carried the first scents of spring. Jessop stretched and walked to the tub to check on Xalma.

She was gone.

Ashmara did not have any words of comfort. "She must have jumped into the river," she said.

"We have to go look for her!" Jessop insisted.

"Where?" Ashmara snapped with frustration, "Under the ice? At the bottom of the lake?" She shook her head bitterly. "The *foolish* child."

Jessop knew his mother was right, but he still wanted to go to look for his friend.

"We will wait one night for Mana," Ashamara declared. "If she does not come, we must find your father and move to a safer place, somewhere else on the island. I do not think the Amphs will pursue us forever." She shook her head sadly. "Eventually, they will know that Xalma is gone."

Jessop sat on a cliff high above the canyon river, staring at the cloudless sky, hoping to see Mana and Edge, or Harbeshi. No one appeared.

Edge woke up in a chamber made of opaque, glassy surfaces. She was surrounded by six identical walls, without doors or windows. Her pack was gone, and with it, all her supplies. She was alone.

I'm inside *Hive*, she realized. *What am I doing here? Where's Mana?*

She yelled for her mother and Sole, but no one answered. She pounded on the walls. She could hear and feel the pulse of Hive through her body, but it didn't affect her the way it had affected Mana.

One of the walls dissolved, and a graceful, sand-colored Insect with faceted, obsidian eyes stepped through. The wall re-materialized silently.

The Insect spread two sets of soft, downy wings and bowed, their delicate, leaf-shaped antennae brushing the crystal floor. When they rose again, Edge smelled berries and tea. She thought of Mana.

"Where's Mana? Let us go!" Edge demanded. The Insect showed no sign of understanding. They approached Edge slowly and cautiously.

Edge waved her arms.

"Get away from me!" she yelled. "Where is my mother?" The Insect stopped, bowed, and waited. Their antennae glowed. Edge remembered how she had merged with Rover. Her head had ached terribly afterwards, but they understood each other.

I have to find Mana, she told herself. *No matter what it takes.*

She took a deep breath, stepped towards the Insect, and bowed. The Insect approached her again.

Edge closed her eyes as the two points of light at the end of the antennae contacted her temples.

Unlike her experience with Rover, Edge did not forget herself. She was aware of her own body and could feel the Insect's soft touch on her brow. Gradually, her awareness spread, and she felt every Insect in Hive as though they were part of her body, but also separate.

Edge was more aware of the world around her than she had ever been. She could sense the other Insects of Hive through the air currents, through the smells around her, and through the pulse of Hive itself. She was joining the Hive Mind.

She was relieved that it wasn't painful, but being part of Hive Mind was still uncomfortable.

Something's wrong, Edge realized.

In her mind's eye, she saw a steaming underwater river run dry.

Something's happened to The Grotto. Hive is getting colder.

She felt the Hive Mind taking control of her thoughts. Recollections of her own past flew through Edge's mind, as though an intruder rifled through her memories, randomly pulling them out for her to watch.

Edge was falling out of a tree while learning to fly. She was catching a brightly colored fish and throwing it back into the lake because it was too beautiful to eat. Her mother was flying with her, tucking her in, handing her a sample to test. Edge's mind swam with memories of Mana.

Something was trying to pull the memories away from her.

"NO!" Edge screamed.

She opened her eyes. The room felt as though it were spinning and tilting. The Insect was lying awkwardly on the ground, but they quickly rose again.

The wall dematerialized and the Insect rushed out into a featureless corridor. Before Edge could follow, the wall became solid again.

She wasn't alone for very long this time. A few minutes later, a new Insect with extremely long, neatly folded arms hopped into the room. They had bulbous green eyes and a wedge-shaped head, protruding from a chitinous neck plate. Their forearms were covered in sharp looking spikes.

The Insect hopped around Edge, their head jerking and tilting this way and that. One moment, they were leaning in to examine her silky tail, the next they hopped onto the ceiling, hanging upside down to scrutinize her terrified face. Edge stood as still as possible to avoid getting skewered by one of the Insect's sharp spikes.

Although they jumped here and there, and often leaned in very close, the Insect didn't touch her. When they were finished inspecting her, the Insect crouched in front of Edge and rubbed their wings together, producing a sound that made Edge jump away with a yelp.

"Fffooorrraaaxxx..."

"Did you just say *Forax*?" Edge yelped again in surprise. "You know how to *talk*?"

The Insect stared at her with huge, unblinking eyes.

"Wwwhhhyyy aaarrreee yyyooouuu hhheeerrreee?"

"*Wow*," whispered Edge.

In her wildest dreams, she had never imagined that Insects could speak her language. As a scientist, she was elated. As a prisoner, she was horrified. There was no way to predict what the Insects might do. After years of studying them, she realized she didn't know very much about them at all.

Maybe we should have tried talking to them, Edge thought regretfully.

The Insect stared at Edge and waited.

"Okay, well... I hope you can understand this..." Edge collected her thoughts with difficulty.

"The rover who brought us here made a mistake. We're not supposed to be here. Can you let us go please?"

The Insect did not acknowledge any of her words. Edge had no way of knowing whether they understood, but they seemed to be listening.

"I just want to find my mother and leave," Edge continued, wishing she had paid closer attention when Mana explained her ideas about Insect communication. "We really *like* Insects. We don't want any trouble."

The Insect did not respond.

"Do you... do you understand me?" Edge whimpered.

The Insect moved closer.

"Wwwhhhyyy sssaaapppiiieeennnsss fffiiiggghhhttt?"

"I'm not fighting!" Edge cried desperately, "I just want to leave!"

The Insect's antennae brushed her temples. Edge closed her eyes.

"Ssshooowww yyyooouuuu..." rasped the Insect.

This time, the connection felt similar to what she'd experienced with Sole. Time raced past, and Edge's awareness of her own mind dwindled. She was insignificant. She witnessed the diversification of the Insects from an uncountable number of perspectives, feeling them evolve and specialize over hundreds of thousands of years. What started as a diverse multitude of individuals competing for food and territory became a delicately balanced, collective society. Edge was witnessing Hive Mind's collective memory, passed along from one generation of Insects to the next.

"Wwwooorrrkkk tttoooggggeeettthhheeerrr. Nnnooottt fffiiiggghhhttt," the Insect droned.

Hive Mind shared memories of sapiens who looked like Sole leaving the ocean. The Insects welcomed them. For generations, the sapiens remained near the water, but over time, they travelled inland and built more permanent homes. They turned wild forests into fields, and harnessed energy from the earth and sun.

Edge watched the sapiens diverge into Forax, Amphs, and Avians. They formed a cooperative system surrounded by stone shells and supported by iron veins, and they called it Marrow. Edge watched as Marrow expanded. She felt anger, but it wasn't her own anger.

The memories faded, but the anger remained. Hive Mind was angry.

The Insect stepped away abruptly and Edge was entirely back in her own mind.

"Sssaaapppiiieeennnsss dddeeessstttrrroooyyy Gggrrrooottooo," the Insect droned accusingly.

"I'd never do anything to The Grotto," Edge insisted. "My friend Xalma lives there!"

The Insect twitched thoughtfully for a few moments.

"Cccooommmeee," they buzzed and clicked. A wall dissolved, and the Insect stepped through, gesturing for Edge to follow.

Chapter Sixteen

Unintended Consequences

S ole followed the Insects to the great chamber where they had delivered their report a few weeks earlier. The fountains continued to dance, but the steam was gone. Fewer Insects were present this time, and they seemed distracted.

Sole begged the Insects to release Edge and Mana, backflipping awkwardly and rolling on the floor. The Insects didn't understand why the rover was asking them to return the sapiens without resetting them first. Nothing of the sort had ever happened before. The Insects worried that something might be wrong with Sole. They assured the rover that everything was proceeding normally, but Sole continued dancing eccentrically, trying to explain that Edge and Mana didn't need to be reset. Hive Mind was always in agreement, so the Insects didn't have movements to express the words 'mistake' or 'regret'. Sole was improvising.

A group of Insects replied by balancing on top of one another. The Insects on the top stood on their heads and clapped their wings together in a complex rhythm, while those on the bottom moved gracefully around the room, carrying their friends.

This meant, "Your bad dancing is making us uncomfortable, and we have a lot going on right now. Please wait."

Finally, a long-limbed Insect delivered Edge to Sole with a dance that meant, 'she could not be reset.'

"Are you okay?" Sole asked Edge.

"Where's Mana?" Edge demanded as another Insect returned her pack.

A moment later, Mana was carried out and placed gently on the ground beside her belongings. The Insects disappeared, leaving them alone in the great chamber. Edge noticed that the music of Hive had become discordant. The air vibrated to a buzzing drone as every Insect worked to keep Hive warm.

"Mana!" cried Edge. She shook her mother until Mana looked up. Her eyes were bleary. She gazed at her daughter and Sole in confusion.

"Where am I? Who are *you*?" yelled Mana, backing away.

Edge tried to hug her mother. "It's me, Mana. You're going to be okay," she said.

"Don't *touch* me!" yelled Mana, hitting Edge hard enough to knock her off balance.

"Mana! It's *me*!" Edge looked at Sole desperately. "What did they do to her?"

Mana tried to run away. Sole grabbed her. She shrieked and thrashed in the rover's arms.

"We have to get out of here!" Sole yelled over Mana's frenzied cries.

"*No*! They have to *fix* her!" cried Edge.

Sole held Mana in one arm and grabbed Edge in the other, lifting them away from Hive while they struggled uselessly. Sole finally landed on a pile of debris where the ocean entrance to The Grotto had once been and examined the destruction.

Mana was no longer screaming, but she refused to interact with Edge or Sole.

"Now we know what that huge boom was," Sole observed. "The Grotto was destroyed. It looks like it was a pretty big explosion. No wonder Hive is in an uproar."

As Edge took in the sight of the ruined mountainside, Harbeshi's shawl caught her eye. It was dusty and torn, and trapped under a sizable boulder. Burned logs and what looked like the remains of a camp were strewn across the nearby rocks.

Then she saw Harbeshi's pack. It was full of food. Edge tied it to her own pack with a heavy heart.

"We should go back to Limbic," Sole said quietly.

"I'm not going *anywhere* with you!" Edge answered angrily. "Look what you did to Mana! Just stay away from us!"

"This is my fault," Sole admitted. "I'm still learning how to think for myself, and I did a poor job of explaining what I was doing. Tsoci told me to bring you to the Insects so you'd be prepared for Cowrie. Mana said she wanted to go there. I didn't realize the Insects would reset her until it was too late."

"What does that mean?" Edge cried.

"They locked her memory," Sole replied. "I expect it makes the transition to Cowrie easier for sapiens from Marrow. Tsoci must have known this would happen."

"But *you* didn't?" Edge demanded.

"No. I didn't. I'm so sorry," Sole replied. "I think we have to go back to Limbic and find out what Tsoci wants you to do. It must be something they knew you wouldn't do without a pretty big incentive."

"Why would I help Tsoci after they tricked us?" Edge growled.

"To get Mana's memory back," Sole answered.

Edge glared at the rover. She didn't have a word for the corrosive, gnawing hatred she felt. She never wanted to see Sole again.

"What exactly *is* Limbic?" Edge asked angrily.

"Limbic is where chemical signals from Tsoci's body are received and analyzed," Sole explained, "and where responses are initiated. You could say Limbic is the place where Tsoci's feelings happen."

Edge was intrigued despite her anger. "Tsoci has feelings? What makes Tsoci feel happy? Being a jerk?" she asked.

"Truth," Sole answered. "That's why Limbic created me. It's why all rovers are created. Whatever Tsoci's task for you is, it will ultimately be part of their search for truth."

"What *is* Tsoci?" Edge wondered. "Are they just plants and stuff?"

"Tsoci is the vast web of life that connects us all."

"Are sapiens part of Tsoci, too?"

"Your bodies are part of Tsoci," Sole answered carefully. "You produce chemicals and influence the environment in ways that affect Tsoci. But your mind - your individual consciousness - is particular to you. Tsoci isn't capable of experiencing reality the same way that you are. That's why Tsoci needs your help."

"Why didn't they just *ask* for my help?" Edge asked.

"Why don't you ask your lungs to help you breathe? Or your heart to help you pump blood?" Sole replied reasonably. "Tsoci doesn't think the way we do. They use chemicals and feelings."

Sole's right. I don't want to help Tsoci, thought Edge. *But what choice do I have?*

"Fine," she said. "Take me to Limbic."

When they arrived, the wormhole appeared in front of the thicket, but Sole refused to enter.

"Go ahead," they said. "I'll stay here with Mana. I don't want to find out what'll happen if Tsoci examines me and discovers I've been questioning my task."

"*Are* you questioning it?" Edge asked in surprise.

"Well, yeah," Sole replied. "I didn't mean to hurt anyone. I *do* want to help Tsoci," they added quickly. "But I should have considered whether visiting the Insects was necessary. I didn't know they'd lock up Mana's memory."

Mana sat near the bushes in silence, anxiously rocking back and forth. Edge tore her gaze from her mother and willed herself to be brave as she stepped through the wormhole.

Maybe the secret to bravery is accepting that things are scary and terrible, and trying to make them better anyway, thought Edge.

Patterns of light rippled over the walls and floor. Tsoci was waiting for her, their crackling, distorted voice shifting invisibly around the room.

"*Edge Anomaly.*" The voice fluttered and crunched. "*Why have you come?*"

"I'm here to find out what you want from me," answered Edge defiantly. "The Insects locked my mother's memory. I want you to give it back."

"*Your mother violated her purpose,*" answered Tsoci.

"Please! I'll do whatever you want," Edge begged. "Sole said you have a task for me!"

A sound like gravel sliding down a hill filled the room. The patterns of color and light on the walls morphed and twisted. Limbic was laughing.

"*The rover is mistaken. You can do nothing for us, little deviation.*"

"There must be *something* I can do," Edge insisted.

Tsoci was silent for a while. The patterns of light across the walls grew increasingly complex. Finally, they answered.

"*You will go to Cowrie,*" rasped the ancient voice.

"To do what?" Edge asked hopefully. "Tell me what to do. I'll do anything."

The room around Edge crackled and roots shot from the walls and roof, wrapping around her body and holding her motionless. She had no time to react. The transition from being Edge to becoming everything was immediate. Edge lost herself completely and became the entire island. Somewhere at the fringes of her awareness, Edge's body writhed in pain as Limbic connected her directly to Tsoci.

Tsoci's attention rippled from microscopic to the size of a continent and back, their sleepy awareness encompassing everything. They saw and felt and smelled and tasted and heard things at every size and time scale at once. Rain poured from the sky in a single instant; a single sunlit day lasted a lifetime; water and wind caressed and shaped the land over eons. Each year was a breath, each season a heartbeat.

Life evolved. Their body grew in diversity and complexity and perspectives, until their component parts began to develop an awareness of their own. For a long time, these pinprick awarenesses popped in and out of existence, lasting just long enough to learn and carry out Tsoci's wishes.

Trees and fungi and uncountable microbes covered every surface, anchoring themselves deep in the soil and rocks of the island, and stretching far out to sea.

They expanded until a thought from Tsoci took a season or more to trigger a reaction from the furthest connections.

They expanded until they touched Something Else, and then they contracted, because it hurt.

The pain was unlike anything Tsoci had ever felt, and infinitely worse than the simple pain of death. It was like rotting and being born and rotting again, endlessly, without a purpose.

Tsoci's immune system kicked in. Earthquakes shivered through the bones of the land. Floods washed toxins from the soil. A massive volcanic eruption violently severed the connection to the most damaged part of themselves.

The pain eventually subsided, but so much had changed. Tsoci didn't know themselves anymore. They started probing the damaged place. Conscious life continued to multiply, descendants of the original immune response, but unchecked. Malignant.

The vines retreated and Edge returned to her own mind. She felt sick and weak.

"Help the rover discover why you exist." Tsoci's voice was inside her head and all around her. *"If you succeed, we will unlock your mother's memory."*

The lights in the room grew dim and the wormhole opened. Edge stumbled outside, disoriented and nauseous. Her muscles convulsed and flashes of light erupted painfully across her field of vision.

"I'm supposed to help you finish your task," she informed Sole through teeth clenched in agony.

"I'm not surprised at all," Sole said.

Edge grimaced. It felt like needles were being pulled from her brain, one after another.

"I can't do this," she whimpered. "I'm not strong enough. Everything hurts."

"I'll help you," Sole assured her gently. "We can do it if we work together."

Edge wasn't sure she wanted Sole's help, but the rover knew more about the world than she did.

"Can you take us home?" Edge groaned. "Fly slowly, or I might throw up."

Sole complied, carrying Edge and Mana, who no longer resisted. Long before they arrived at the treehouse, they could see that it was gone. The trees had been burned to the ground and the buildings were in ruins.

"Who could have done this?" Edge cried in horror.

"I suspect it was whoever blew up The Grotto. Do you still want to go there?" Sole asked.

"No. Take us to the canyon," Edge replied with a heavy sigh. "That's where Jessop is."

The last thing Xalma remembered was seeing a patch of light through the ice over the lake. She used the last of her strength to swim towards it. A door opened in the sky, and Xalma went through it.

Maybe I'm dead, she thought.

Fearing the judgement she was going to face if there was an afterlife, she pointed out that she'd recently made the ultimate sacrifice, hoping to prove that she was a good sapien.

"Jessop and Ashmara are safe," she announced.

I hope death isn't going to be boring, she thought before passing out.

Regaining consciousness was the most painful thing Xalma had ever experienced. Blood pounded in her veins. Her skin was on fire. Her empty stomach heaved. Xalma tried to open her eyes, but the world around her was blurry and unstable.

Harbeshi carried Xalma as he flew low over the forest, looking for a safe place to guard The Child Queen while she transformed. He briefly visited the treehouse and picked through the wreckage, terrified that he was going to find Edge and Mana. Thankfully, there were no bodies, but he didn't find anything useful, either.

My nest is not safe anymore, he thought sadly. *I will have to find my supplies and camp in the forest.*

On the way, they flew over what remained of the lake entrance to The Grotto. A huge swath of forest was burned away. Where the swamp had been, nothing was left but a wasteland of dust and ashes. The stone entrance and the statues were reduced to rubble.

Harbeshi found his shawl first. He tore it out from under a boulder before recovering his blanket, his shelter, a canteen, and a stove. His pack was gone.

I will have to hunt today, he thought wearily, *but first I must find a place for us to hide.*

Xalma moaned as he lifted her into the air, but she remained unconscious. Harbeshi had never felt so alone.

Chapter Seventeen

Three Spirits

Jessop and Ashmara heard Mana's screams as Sole searched the channels and gullies around the canyon. They were hiding behind the tree when Sole landed. Jessop ran out and hit the rover with an empty pot until he noticed Edge.

"Hey!" exclaimed Sole. "Quit it!"

Mana was still screaming, so Sole clamped a hand firmly over her mouth, lifting her off her feet. Mana kicked the air uselessly.

"Okay, this is easier," Sole said.

"Put her down!" hollered Edge.

"Tell them what's going on first," Sole replied.

"Mana and I went into Hive," Edge explained quickly, watching her mother struggle in the rover's arms with concern. "The Insects took Mana's memory, and now she doesn't remember me. I have to find out why I exist so I can get her memory back."

"...and I'm Sole," added Sole.

Ashmara and Jessop stared at Edge speechlessly.

"They used to be Rover," Edge explained.

A strained silence followed this news.

"Xalma's gone," Jessop said finally.

"Where did she go?" asked Edge in surprise.

"She jumped into the river while we slept," Ashmara replied dejectedly. "I do not think she survived."

Things can't get worse, thought Edge. Then she remembered Harbeshi's shawl.

"I'm really sorry," she said, untying Harbeshi's pack from her own and passing it to Ashmara.

"*Where did you find this?*" Ashmara asked.

"By the ocean," answered Edge. "The Grotto is destroyed. Harbeshi's shawl was under a big rock. I'm so sorry."

Ashmara wailed and fell to the ground. Mana wrestled free of Sole's grip.

"Are you hurt?" she asked curiously, approaching Ashmara. Her voice was pitched strangely.

"I think someone I care about is gone forever." Ashmara's grief threatened to overcome her.

Mana put her arms around Ashmara. "You'll be okay," she said. "Everything is okay."

"Mana?" Edge asked hopefully. Mana didn't respond.

"What now?" Jessop asked.

"Tsoci said I have to go to Cowrie and find out why I exist," Edge replied.

"Tsoci? Do you mean Fangowl? The moon spirit?" Jessop asked in disbelief. Ashmara stirred.

"Moon spirit?" Sole asked.

"Amphs, Avians, and Forax all tell a slightly different version of the Tsoci story, but everyone knows it," Ashmara replied. "Tsoci lived alone on the moon. The only thing to look at was our planet, and it was covered in water and ice. One day Tsoci dipped their hand into the water and pulled up a great island."

"Tsoci *did* come from the sky," Sole replied with a smile. "Their soulseed landed in the ocean and catalyzed the molecules that became the first life."

"What does catalyzed mean?" Jessop asked.

"It's when something makes a chemical reaction happen faster by getting molecules to move around more," Edge explained. "The catalyst itself stays the same, but the things around it change."

Sole smiled encouragingly. "The first living things to evolve were microbes, and they were inextricably bound to Tsoci from the very beginning. Plants evolved from partnerships between microbes and fungi. They're Tsoci's nervous system."

"What does that make you?" Ashmara demanded.

"I'm part of Tsoci's short term memory," Sole replied proudly. "Tsoci's mind is so big, they can't perceive time in small increments, but a lot of things can happen in short amounts of time. That's what rovers are for."

"For Amphs, the moon spirit is a great, ancient froggle named Horndrum who wants to spread life to other planets," Ashmara said. "Avians believe Fangowl wants ecological balance and stability."

"What do Forax believe?" Jessop asked.

"Mana told me that Sewlich wants sapiens to obey the laws of nature," Edge replied. "She said it was just a story, though."

"Which of them is correct?" Ashmara asked Sole, her eyes narrowed.

"None of them," replied Sole. "Tsoci is a superorganism, and we are all tiny parts of their whole, but only Tsoci can ever completely understand what Tsoci wants."

"I don't feel like I'm part of a superorganism," said Jessop.

"You're too small to connect to Tsoci's greater awareness," Sole explained. "Your individual pattern would be torn apart. The Insects have to form a Hive Mind just to understand a few of Tsoci's messages. That's why Edge's ability is such a big deal."

"I don't care if they *are* a superorganism, or a moon god, or whatever," Edge said bitterly. "Tsoci and the Insects had no right to take Mana's memory."

"I'm not saying it was the best way, but they did it so you would help them," Sole replied. "You're basically a miracle."

"I don't want to be a miracle," Edge objected.

"No one ever does," Sole assured her.

"What if I refuse to help?"

"I don't think Mana's memory will come back unless you do," Sole answered sympathetically, "but you don't *have* to do anything. It's your choice. Whatever you decide to do, I'll help you."

"Can't you go to Cowrie without me?" Edge asked.

"Yes," Sole answered, "but if Tsoci told you to go with me, it means the odds of finding the information we're looking for are better if you come."

"I do not understand all of this, Edge," Ashmara admitted, "but I believe you are meant to do something important. Mana told me she raised you here for a reason, though she did not tell me why. I will care for her while you are gone."

"I don't even know what I'm supposed to do, though!" Edge cried. "This is so unfair!"

"I think we need to find The Resistance," Sole replied. "They sent Mana to Far Crescent. They might know where your abilities came from."

"I'm coming with you," Jessop declared.

Ashmara opened her mouth to argue. *I said I would support him when the time came,* she reminded herself.

"Are you sure?" Ashmara asked. "It will be very dangerous."

"Dad would have wanted me to protect my friends," Jessop said, his voice cracking.

"I still don't know if *I* want to go," Edge reminded them.

"Your abilities are really special," Sole said quietly. "If they evolved because of environmental pressure, they might even be essential."

"This is *wrong*," Edge objected. "Tsoci is holding Mana's *memory* hostage!"

"Right and wrong are concepts invented by sapiens, not by Tsoci," Sole said gently.

"Fine, I'll go," growled Edge. "But this isn't fair."

As the last light of day slipped from the depths of the channel, they watched the fire die in silence. Sole flew to the top of the tree and stared at the infinite sky long after the others were asleep, wondering why the stars looked so lonely.

The next morning, Ashmara helped them pack. She gave them the blankets Xalma had taken from the treehouse, and insisted they take the food and supplies from Harbeshi's pack. Edge tried to speak with Mana, but her mother still didn't recognize her.

"We'll get Mana's memory back before you know it," Sole said optimistically.

Edge didn't know how far they had to travel, but the thought of being carried by Sole the entire way made her even less happy about the task.

"I *hate* flying that fast. My eyes sting, and my ears roar," she said.

"Oh! I have an idea!" Jessop retrieved their swimming goggles and some rope from his pack.

"Remember these?" His face clouded for a moment as he thought of Xalma. Jessop turned to Sole.

"If we use the packs as harnesses, can you pull us? That way we can still kind of fly on our own. The goggles will help us see. It should be more comfortable."

"That sounds fun!" Sole carefully examined Jessop's goggles. "It'll create some drag if I drag you. Haha! Get it?"

Jessop and Edge looked at Sole blankly, and Ashmara rolled her eyes. Sole looked momentarily disappointed, but they continued cheerfully.

"Uh, so anyway, we won't be able to go *quite* as fast. But it won't hurt to have three pairs of eyes instead of just one. Let's try it!"

Jessop fashioned a harness out of his pack and tethered himself to the rover.

"You start flying first," Sole suggested. "It'll be easier."

Jessop launched himself into the air, and Sole followed him.

Edge and Ashmara watched nervously as the rope between Sole and Jessop became taut. They disappeared over the edge of the surrounding cliffs.

Long moments passed. Edge held her breath until Jessop reappeared, twirling down gleefully.

"Wooo!" he yelled. "That was AMAZING! You've *got* to try that, Edge!"

He and Sole were smiling broadly as they returned to the ground, but Jessop's cheerful optimism soon faded under the weight of losing Xalma and Harbeshi. He was subdued as he fastened Edge's harness.

Ashmara gave Jessop a long hug. Edge approached Mana and tried to say goodbye, but Mana pushed her away. Devastated, Edge watched Jessop and Ashmara finish their farewells.

Moments later, Sole was towing them across the lake and out of the valley. Within minutes, Edge was further from her home than she'd ever been before.

Chapter Eighteen

The Artists

Harbeshi followed Xalma's directions to the tree in the canyon, but when he arrived, he found only the empty tub and the remains of a long-extinguished campfire. After a fruitless search of the adjoining gullies and channels, he returned to the shelter in the forest.

On the way, he noticed tracks in the snow at the edge of the lake. He examined the traces carefully, but he didn't recognize them. Before he could leave, he heard shouts.

"This way!" yelled a deep, sibilant voice. Harbeshi ducked behind a tree.

They're the sapiens who destroyed The Grotto, Harbeshi realized with horror as two Amphs ran past.

"No sign of the Forax. Call the Avians. Tell them to search the sky," ordered one of the sapiens.

Harbeshi waited until they were gone before returning to Xalma. He stayed below the cover of the treetops, dodging the branches and melting snow. When he arrived, he circled the camp, brushing away their tracks. Xalma was awake and shivering next to the cold stove. She was no longer crying. Her skin looked angry and red, as though she'd been burned.

"Where's Jessop?" Xalma whimpered, her face full of pain.

"I did not find him," Harbeshi replied gruffly.

Xalma continued to shiver miserably as Harbeshi built up the fire in the stove.

"What's happening to me?" she asked weakly.

"You are becoming an adult," Harbeshi answered. "Ashmara and I were supposed to prevent this from happening. We failed you."

"Jessop is becoming an adult, but it doesn't hurt *him*," Xalma whimpered. "Why does this *hurt* so much?"

"Jessop is aging at a steady pace," Harbeshi explained. "When Amphs reach a certain age, they transform into adults more quickly. It is not normally painful."

"Why does it hurt for *me*, then?" Xalma wept.

"No Amph has ever delayed adulthood for as long as you have," Harbeshi replied. "I do not know what is going to happen, but I am not surprised that it hurts."

"Am I going to die?" Xalma asked pitifully.

"I do not know," Harbeshi answered honestly.

"Will you stay with me?" Xalma pleaded.

"Yes," Harbeshi assured her.

They sat together in silence. Xalma felt too miserable to speak, and Harbeshi was worried about Jessop, and angry with Ashmara. Finally, Xalma broke the silence.

"What will happen when I transform?" she asked.

Harbeshi looked at Xalma for a long time. He had never cared much for The Child Queen. He thought she was selfish and silly, and he did not believe that keeping Xalma in The Grotto was unkind. Harbeshi thought Xalma was unprepared for the world, and undeserving of the power that was her inheritance.

"You will dream," he replied dispassionately. "Your skin will grow thick and hard. If you wake up, you will break out of your old skin, and you will be in a new body."

"What kind of body?" asked Xalma, horrified.

"That depends on the dream you have."

Harbeshi's anger and fear still dominated his mind, but thinking about the traditions of Amph transformation reminded him of a more peaceful time.

"Young Amphs normally spend many years preparing to transform," he told Xalma. "They study and explore so they can discover who and what they want to be as adults, and they choose physical traits that will help with their intellectual pursuits. I was once a painter, and I have helped Amphs imagine what they want to become. Maybe I can help you."

As Harbeshi spoke, he picked up a small branch and cleared some pine needles from the ground. He traced the shape of an Amph in the dirt.

"Some Amphs become strong protectors," Harbeshi explained, adding spikes to the figure. "Some wish for nimble hands." He added long fingers. "Some desire speed or stealth." Harbeshi lengthened the legs and made the figure leaner.

He looked at Xalma.

"What do you like to do?" he asked.

"I like to make things," Xalma answered weakly. "I make pictures and sculptures and stuff. At least, I used to."

"I also like to make things," Harbeshi admitted. "I cannot promise that you will survive your transformation, Xalma, but I may be able to help you prepare for it."

"How?" Xalma whispered.

"We will make a picture together," Harbeshi answered. "We will draw the dream you want to have."

As Xalma watched, Harbeshi spread a sheet of bark in front of the fire, covered it with snow, and scraped it with a sharp stone until it was smooth and pliable. Then he placed a large, flat rock in front of him, and crushed a handful of fragrant leaves with a few small stones. He mixed the resulting pulp with ash, tree sap, snow, and other things from the forest, producing several colors of paint.

Harbeshi plucked a few of his feathers, pulling them evenly from both sides. He twisted some of them into brushes, and fashioned quills with the rest. When he was finished, he addressed Xalma.

"What is the first thing you want to do as an adult?" Harbeshi asked.

"I want to find Jessop," Xalma answered without hesitation.

"What will you do when you find him?"

"I'll keep him safe," Xalma replied immediately. "I'll protect him."

"How will you protect him?" Harbeshi asked, a quill poised over the sheet of bark. "There are many ways to protect someone."

Xalma thought for a while. Harbeshi was right. She could protect Jessop by fighting, or she could hide him. She could even protect him by attracting danger to herself.

"I want to be strong and dangerous," Xalma decided. "I want anyone who threatens Jessop to be afraid of me."

Harbeshi considered what might frighten the sapiens who threatened Jessop and sketched the rough shape of a soldier Amph, not unlike the statues at The Grotto's entrance. As he drew, Xalma made suggestions.

"Put some spikes on my head... there." She pointed. "Can I be poisonous?"

Xalma found it easier to tolerate her pain if she focused on the drawing. Many hours passed, and she was struggling to stay awake. The picture was not finished.

"Will I transform if I fall asleep?" she asked.

"I do not think so," Harbeshi replied. "But I cannot know for certain."

Xalma yawned and yelped as the skin on her face cracked. Blood trickled down her cheeks.

"Go to sleep," Harbeshi said. "I will keep watch."

Xalma fell asleep almost immediately, but Harbeshi stayed awake for a long time. He was thinking about The Child Queen. Now that she was focusing on helping Jessop, she was no longer feeling sorry for herself.

Ashmara was right, he thought. *She cares about Jessop enough to face becoming an adult. Maybe she will help us. If she survives.*

When she woke, Xalma started painting. Harbeshi watched as she added details and adjusted proportions.

"You are very talented," he said approvingly.

"Thanks," Xalma croaked. Her voice was raw. Tears streamed from her eyes and the skin all over her body cracked and bled.

Harbeshi gave Xalma his blanket and took her soiled bedding. He filled the shawl and Xalma's blanket with snow and hung them over the fire, so the melting snow could soak into the fabric. As Xalma continued drawing and painting, Harbeshi scrubbed the soaked fabrics with fresh pine needles to remove the blood and pus. He repeated the process a few times throughout the morning, taking a break to make breakfast. When he was satisfied that Xalma's blanket was as clean as he could get it, he hung it near the fire to dry, and sat next to Xalma.

"I think I'm done," she said, looking at the picture critically. Harbeshi was impressed with the level of detail. Each scale and claw was distinct. The Amph in the picture was black and muscular, with vivid red stripes and huge, pale green eyes.

"Why did you choose these colors?" asked Harbeshi quietly.

Xalma shrugged reflexively and winced.

"That's just how I feel," she answered. "Inside. Do you know what I mean?"

Harbeshi had studied art with the Amphs for many years. It was the first form of expression through which he felt he could truly communicate. He understood exactly what Xalma meant.

"Would you like to know about the colors you have chosen?" Harbeshi asked. "I do not think you should change them," he added quickly, "you have made good choices."

"Yes," sighed Xalma, closing her eyes. "Tell me about the colors."

"The color red is reserved for The Child Queen," Harbeshi told her. "It is not genetically possible for any other Amph to be red." He spoke softly. Xalma's eyes closed as she listened.

Harbeshi gently removed the soiled blanket from Xalma's shuddering body. She was covered in a slimy film that was rapidly forming a crust. Harbeshi wrapped her gently in the clean, dry bedding.

"It is rare for an Amph to be black," he continued, "it is the rarest and most sought-after color. It is a color of strength."

Xalma half opened her eyes. Harbeshi could see that they were filmy and unfocused.

"Will I be able to protect Jessop?" Xalma murmured.

"I believe you will be able to do much more," Harbeshi told her. "There is great injustice in the world. Resources in Marrow are not equally distributed."

"What are resources?" Xalma whispered.

"Food. Water. Education." Harbeshi could not keep the bitterness from his voice.

"Everyone should have those things," sighed Xalma as she slipped into the deepest sleep of her life.

"If you survive, you will have the power to give those things to the sapiens of Marrow, Queen Xalma." Harbeshi moved Xalma closer to the fire. He didn't know if she would wake up.

Chapter Nineteen

Two Journeys

F lying with Sole was exhausting and exhilarating. The first flight was punctuated by frequent stops to adjust the harnesses, look for food, and explore the mountains. None of the travelers had ever ventured this far from the valley.

Edge watched the world race past through the distorted lenses of her goggles. It took all her concentration to keep a safe distance from Jessop, who was tethered beside her performing aerial acrobatics. He was as excited as Edge had ever seen him, so she didn't have the heart to ask him to stop careening through loops and spins, even though she was worried about a collision.

They landed in the mountains and camped near a cold, clear stream. Jessop lit a small fire and prepared some of the food he was carrying. They ate in silence, lost in their own thoughts. After dinner, Jessop offered Sole a blanket and settled near Edge, who was already curled up next to the fire.

"What's this for?" Sole asked.

"It will keep you warm while you sleep," Jessop answered.

"What *is* sleeping?" Sole asked.

"It's when your brain rests and you have dreams," Edge replied. "Mana told me that dreams are how you remember your story."

"My parents said it's your brain cleaning itself out," Jessop added.

"If sapiens don't sleep, do they forget their stories?" asked Sole.

"It's harder to remember things if you don't sleep," Edge answered. "We can even die if we don't get enough sleep. I think Insects die without sleep, too, but Mana and I never saw that happen, and there's no ethical way to test it."

The three travelers were silent for a long time. The fire slowly died down, and soon the only light came from the dim embers and the bright, colorful stars and galaxies scattered across the night sky.

"When I was very little, I used to wonder if my life was just someone else's dream," Jessop whispered into the darkness.

"We're all part of someone else's dream," Sole answered, closing their eyes, "but I guess we can have our own dreams, too. I'm looking forward to it."

Edge didn't reply. She was fast asleep.

Harbeshi kept Xalma's chrysalis warm. The forest was as quiet as a grave. Shortly after midnight, he decided to risk a quick flight to look for Ashmara and Jessop again. Moments after he left the shelter, two sapiens appeared from the darkness. They had been waiting silently in the trees since the previous day. A thin wisp of smoke had given the shelter away.

They knew The Child Queen's chrysalis was inside. They also knew that moving her at this point would be a delicate matter. Fighting with the Avian inside might damage her chrysalis. When Harbeshi finally left the shelter, they moved very quickly. They had a net, originally intended to capture the outcasts in the woods. Together, they loaded the chrysalis into the net and carried it back to their submarine.

Harbeshi was careful to remain concealed as he flew through the forest. He stayed beneath the trees, and didn't set foot on the forest floor for fear of leaving tracks. When he reached the tree in the channel, he perched on a branch and spent a long time thinking about where Ashmara and Jessop might have gone. He decided to search the canyon again.

She is probably moving around to avoid being caught, he thought.

Harbeshi spotted light from a fire coming from a small cave at the edge of the raging river. Ashmara didn't hear Harbeshi's arrival over the roar of the water. He spoke very quietly, hoping not to startle her.

"Ashmara?" he whispered.

"Who is there?" exclaimed Ashmara, jerking upright and wielding a blade.

She was sleeping with a knife, thought Harbeshi sadly. *What have we come to?*

His heart ached at the thought that his actions were responsible for so much fear and pain, but then he felt a wave of anger.

Ashmara broke her promise, he reminded himself. *She helped The Child Queen grow up. This is her fault, too.*

"I found you," answered Harbeshi in a harsh whisper. His next words were interrupted as Ashmara caught him in a fierce embrace.

"Ashmara, too tight!" he gasped, and she let him go. "Where is Jessop?"

Ashmara glanced at Mana, who was fast asleep.

"You had better sit down," she said. She lit a small lamp and set it between them. Her face was full of despair.

"Where is our son?" Harbeshi demanded.

"He and Edge left with an emissary of Tsoci."

"What?" Harbeshi cried, leaping to his feet. Ashmara shushed him and pointed at Mana, who groaned in her sleep.

"Sit down," she ordered in a whisper.

Harbeshi obeyed, but he was glaring at Ashmara. She did her best to sum up the past few days as succinctly as she could.

"You let our son go with the Forax?" Harbeshi was shaking with rage by the time Ashmara had finished. "What were you *thinking?*"

"Keep your voice down," Ashmara hissed.

"Ashmara!" Harbeshi snapped, but she interrupted him.

"We raised Jessop to be strong and clever, and to care about other sapiens," Ashmara said fiercely. Tears streamed down her face. "Leaving was his choice. I would have discussed it with you first, but I thought you were dead."

Harbeshi's anger subsided a little.

"Xalma is alive, at least for now," he grunted. "She is transforming. She wants to protect Jessop. If she survives, she may be able to rescue him from the consequences of your poor choices."

"She is *alive?*" Ashmara looked at Harbeshi, her expression a mixture of wonder and shame. "How?"

"I found her in the lake," Harbeshi answered shortly. "What is this nonsense about Tsoci?"

"Edge has some kind of mutation," Ashmara answered. "She can merge with Tsoci without dying."

"These mysteries can wait," Harbeshi declared after staring at Ashmara in silent disbelief for a few long moments. "Xalma's chrysalis is in the forest. I think it may be safer if I move her here, but I will need help – there are unfriendly sapiens searching the forest."

"I have to take care of Mana," Ashmara replied. "She has forgotten who she is."

"Then I will help you watch her." Harbeshi said. "We should stay together. Can you carry her to my shelter?"

Ashmara looked at Harbeshi gratefully.

"I am afraid to feel hopeful," Harbeshi admitted.

"As am I," Ashmara agreed. "I used the last of my hope to raise a child. Jessop is stronger than we are, Harbeshi. He was raised to be free."

"What is freedom without safety?" Harbeshi growled angrily. "One is nothing without the other."

Ashmara took Harbeshi's hand.

"Jessop has had freedom without safety, and Xalma has had safety without freedom. Perhaps between them, they can find a balance."

Harbeshi carried Mana back to his shelter, but when they arrived, it was immediately clear that the chrysalis had been stolen. Harbeshi roared and Mana cowered behind Ashmara, whimpering quietly.

"Hush!" Ashmara whispered urgently. "We must leave. Quickly."

Harbeshi retrieved his stove and tarp, and they returned to the cave next to the river.

Mana seemed relieved to return to a familiar place. Ashmara was soon occupied with feeding and entertaining her. Harbeshi stared at Xalma's picture, and wrestled with the thought of searching for Xalma and Jessop on his own.

"We have to *do* something," he yelled in frustration.

"We *will*," Ashmara answered. "But right now, we must wait."

"Wait for what?" Harbeshi paced anxiously.

"A few hours ago, I believed you and Xalma were dead." She took Harbeshi's hand and held it to her heart. "I think we should wait for another miracle."

Chapter Twenty

Holy Father

Thanks to Sole, Jessop and Edge passed through the enormous mountain range much more quickly than they could have managed on their own.

We'll be in a lot of trouble if we lose Sole, Jessop realized with concern. *I'm not sure we can make it back on our own.* He didn't share this thought with Edge.

Every evening, they camped near a river or a lake, and Edge fished while Jessop went foraging and set traps. Although both friends were devastated by their losses, they were able to find moments of happiness in the simple routines of a traveler's life.

A few days into their journey, Edge returned from foraging with a nest full of eggs.

"Ew, you eat *eggs?*" Jessop grimaced with disgust.

"Sure. Why not?" asked Edge curiously.

"Because it's *gross,*" Jessop answered. "Eggs are baby birds! You know that, right?"

"Not yet," Edge disagreed. "They're just embryos, and that's only if the egg is fertilized. Anyway, they're delicious!"

"Erg," Jessop said. "*I* was an egg once. That's like eating a baby."

"It's not," Edge argued. "Eating a *baby* is like eating a baby. This is an egg. You weren't *you* when you were an egg."

Jessop looked away. "It's still gross," he insisted.

"I came out of an egg," Sole added. "At least, I think I did…"

"Oh yeah!" Edge had forgotten the egg in the middle of Limbic. "You and Jessop have something in common!" Her brow furrowed as she remembered the terrifying room.

"Why was the egg room full of body parts, Sole?" she asked.

"Those were parts of old rovers. When a rover is done collecting information, Limbic reabsorbs them, dismantles the parts, and recycles whatever can be reused." Sole shrugged. "What's left just sort of piles up."

"That's not so bad," observed Jessop. "Better than actual bodies, right?"

"How is it any different, though?" Edge asked. "Do rovers get to choose whether they get reabsorbed?"

"No," Sole replied. "Rovers don't normally make choices. I copied some of your neural patterns the first time we merged so I could communicate with you more efficiently, and it changed me."

"How did it change you?" Jessop asked curiously.

"I started to *want* things," Sole explained. "I started to feel more feelings."

"Like what?" Jessop tried to imagine what it would be like to go through life without any personal desires. It didn't seem like much of a life.

"I want to be me, and I want to help Edge," Sole replied simply.

"How do you know you're not just following Tsoci's programming?" Edge asked skeptically.

"I'm aware that I have a choice," Sole explained. "I can choose to find a quiet place to live my life out. I would be safer, but I would be alone. I wouldn't feel happy. I feel happy when I'm helping you."

The next day, they flew higher into the mountains. Edge was getting better at controlling her flight as Sole towed them. Bizarre plants and colorful crystals burst from the rocks below, and Edge watched them speed by with regret. She wanted to stop and study them, but Sole insisted on travelling as quickly as possible.

"We're getting closer to the center," Sole explained when Edge asked about the changes in the environment. "Cowrie is near the impact point of the soulseed. It'll start to get warmer the closer we get to the rainforest."

"Is that where The Resistance is?" Edge asked.

"Yes," Sole confirmed. "In their last report, the Insects said The Resistance has built up a base in Cowrie."

"What *is* Cowrie?" asked Jessop "Is it like Marrow?"

"It's much older than Marrow. Long before sapiens came ashore, Cowrie was a great forest Hive. It's supposed to be a place of healing and restoration for sapien anomalies after they're reset. It's where Insects and rovers first taught sapiens how to tell stories."

"What are we supposed to do when we get there?" Edge asked. "Are we just going to ask The Resistance why I exist?"

"That depends on all the variables," Sole answered dismissively. "We have to figure it out as we go."

"That's not much of a plan." Edge saw the hurt look on Sole's face. "I'm sorry... I didn't mean..."

"It's fine," Sole replied. "I'm probably not explaining this very well. Tsoci thinks really big, amazing, thoughts. But their mind is huge, right?" Sole stretched their arms out to the side. "Their mind is bigger than the whole island. So, their thoughts are slooow."

"Time feels different when I merge with them," Edge remembered.

"They experience time more quickly," Sole confirmed. "Just as you experience time more quickly than a very small animal does."

"But we're all part of Tsoci, right?" Jessop asked. "You said you were their short term memory or something. So what does that make me and Edge? What are sapiens for?"

"Sapiens are an immune response," Sole explained. "When an organism gets big enough, their immune cells have to be self-aware."

"Does that mean Tsoci's sick?" Edge asked.

"One way or another, yes," Sole confirmed. "Either you're the result of an autoimmune response, or your mutation was triggered by a pathogen that Tsoci doesn't know about yet. That's why it's so important to understand why you exist."

"You want to find out if I'm a disease or a cure," Edge said quietly.

"Neither one of those sounds good," Jessop observed.
"No," Sole admitted. "They're both bad. That's why I
want to help. Now that I know what it's like to be an
individual, I understand that this is a lot for an individual to
deal with."

Xalma knew she was not in Harbeshi's shelter anymore.
She was confined by the hard shell of her chrysalis. Voices
were talking about her, and they didn't sound friendly.
I guess I didn't die, she thought.
"She must be allowed to emerge," said a high, wavering
voice.
"Of course. If she won't cooperate, we can easily contain
her," a second voice declared. "We can't risk anything
interfering with our plans, especially now."
"Her authority is absolute among the Amphs," the
wavering voice continued. "She might lead the revolution."
"Perhaps. When she emerges, bring her to the helm,
Cato."
Xalma waited until the departing footsteps faded. Very
quietly, she scratched a hole in the chrysalis.
"Hey!" she whispered as loudly as she could, "Look, I
don't want to cause trouble. Can you tell me what's going
on? Where am I?"
"So, you *are* alive." Cato's shadow fell across the
chrysalis. He was smaller than Xalma expected.
"Yeah, I'm alive, but I'm squished up pretty bad. Is it safe
for me to come out?" Xalma shifted uncomfortably and her
shell started to crack.
"It depends on your choices," Cato replied calmly. "You
are on a submarine. When the camera screen in The Grotto
made contact, The Resistance was already on their way to
fetch a Forax I was observing."

"*You* sent the screen? Wait a second... *you were spying on Edge!*"

"She commands a great power. The Resistance wants to direct this power towards saving the lives of millions of sapiens. Tell us where the Forax is, and no harm will come to you."

"An Insect took her, but they brought her back. She's in her treehouse."

"By the time we searched the treehouse, the Forax was gone." Cato tapped the chrysalis. "If the Insects have her, they may yet deliver her to us, but for now, you are our backup plan."

"That's... uh, I have no idea what that means," groaned Xalma. The shell of the chrysalis was crushing her. "Look, I *really* need to get out of here."

"Before you come out, you should know that I ordered our soldiers to destroy The Grotto. It was time for you to grow up," Cato replied. "Despite the lies you've chosen to tell yourself; you would not have transformed if you could have returned to The Grotto."

Xalma felt a wave of anger and hatred roll over her, but she didn't argue. She knew Cato was right, and she still felt guilty about the things she'd learned from Ashmara.

"You must choose to fulfill your purpose," he said, "or we will throw you off the ship."

"You're going to tell me what my purpose is, right?" Xalma squeaked. She was running out of room to breathe.

He said I was his backup plan, Xalma thought. *He wants Edge, not me. I just have to find Edge.*

"We are deep under the ocean," Cato continued. "You are an adult now. You will not survive this deep under the water."

Shows what you know, jerk, thought Xalma.

She wasn't sure if all her anatomical choices had materialized, but she could feel gills hidden under her bony neck plate. Harbeshi had insisted that adult Amphs were never truly aquatic again, but Xalma was not ready to give up living underwater. Not if she could help it.

The chrysalis burst apart.

"Tell me what my destiny is!" Xalma stretched luxuriantly as pieces of glittering shell rained down around them. She looked at Cato, a beautiful, sinuous creature made of spikes and claws and needle sharp, venomous fangs.

"I'm starving," Xalma announced. "I hope you have some food, because otherwise I'm probably going to eat you."

Edge, Jessop, and Sole left the mountain range as the morning sun peeked over the horizon. A dark canopy of trees stretched from the base of the mountains to the distant shore.

They flew above a wide ribbon of clouds that billowed and swirled over and through the treetops.

"It's a river in the sky!" Jessop called in wonder as they raced through the air above a lively, turbulent torrent of vapors. Above them, the sky was equally changeable. The sun beamed through the clouds, and rainbows danced around shafts of light. When they first descended below the canopy to rest, the noises, smells, and colors were far more vibrant and varied than Edge had ever experienced. Her senses felt overwhelmed. The air was heavier and gloomier than it was above the trees.

"This place is getting inside me," Edge whispered to Jessop. "Do you feel it too?"

"I can feel *something*," Jessop replied after a moment. "It's dangerous here."

Edge nodded.

No one suggested exploring. As soon as they were rested, they returned to the open sky. The oppressive feeling lifted as they broke through the canopy into the light.

They had been flying for several hours when a twinkling streak appeared on the horizon. It grew bigger and brighter as they approached. When they were closer, they identified the source of the glare. The leaves here were different from the surrounding forests, each one a flashing, green-tinted mirror. Instead of each leaf blowing independently, these leaves moved together like slow, golden waves.

"Welcome to Cowrie," said Sole.

They removed their tethers and descended together into Cowrie, flying slowly so that they could talk. The oppressive sense of danger they'd felt the first time they descended into the trees was not as strong.

With his sharp eyes, Jessop noticed that wires wound down the branches from the glittering leaves. He pointed it out to Sole and Edge.

"I think they're sun collectors!" Edge gasped. "There are so many! How many sapiens live here?"

"I'm not sure," Sole answered, "but the Insects reported that a lot more have come in the past decade or so."

As they descended, the trunks of the trees widened. The branches below were shaped into buildings and machines, as though these things had grown directly from the trees.

"What kind of tree is this?" Edge wondered.

"The trees here are modified," Sole answered. "The Insects trained them originally. Some of these trees were already here before sapiens left the ocean. The buildings you see in their highest branches were once near the forest floor."

The trees were full of sapiens. Cowrie's vertical density stirred Jessop's dim memories of Marrow, but it was strikingly different in many ways. Instead of being divided into different areas, every race lived together. Forax treehouses, Avian nests, and Amph terrariums clustered together in the branches of the towering trees, connected by countless platforms, ladders and bridges. As they approached the ground, dens and caves appeared.

The lower they descended, the darker it became. They flew past ponds, fountains, and bramble-covered buildings. Curtains of vines and colonies of giant fungus bordered winding paths. Lights twinkled everywhere, keeping the gloom of the rainforest at bay. Occasionally, between the clusters of buildings and paths, ancient looking structures jutted from the ground. Spiral cones poked through heavy blankets of leaves and flowers, reminding Edge of half buried shells at the bottom of The Grotto.

Jessop noticed them too. "I wish Xalma were here," he said.

The sapiens in Cowrie went about their business. Most did not even glance up as the three visitors passed. Sole led them to a paved square near the bank of a wide river. A small crowd gathered below to watch them land.

Edge glimpsed two large, round eyes flashing from the shadows next to a vine-covered building, but when she looked more closely, they were gone.

"Greetings, new recruits! Welcome to Cowrie," said tall, slender Forax.

His wedge-shaped face tapered into a small mouth full of sharp white teeth. His ruddy fur darkened at his hands, feet, and the tip of his bushy tail. He was the first Forax Edge had ever seen besides Mana, and he was not a scout.

Imposing, serious Amphs stood on either side of him. They reminded Edge of Xalma's statues.

"Welcome to Cowrie!" said the Forax pleasantly. "What an unusual rover! Can it speak?"

"I *can* speak," Sole answered blithely, "and I'm not an *'it'*."

"Of course not! My sincere apologies!" The Forax bowed to Sole.

"My associates will show you where you can rest so you may get on with whatever business you have left to do. These two will be safe with me."

One of the guards gestured for Sole to follow them. Sole smiled at Edge reassuringly.

"Remember Edge," Sole advised as the guard led them away, "follow your feelings."

"*Curious*," observed the Forax. "Rovers don't *usually* speak."

He caught the incredulous look on Edge and Jessop's faces.

"I see you are surprised that I know what a rover is," he continued. "The Resistance discovered the truth about Tsoci and the rovers a few years ago."

"Who are you?" asked Jessop.

"My name is Hiro." The Forax bowed deeply. "I am the Holy Father of The Resistance. We will bring you to a place where you can rest until the ceremony tonight. Then, we will welcome you properly."

Chapter Twenty One

The Warning

"I don't know if I like being split up like this," Jessop admitted when he and Edge were alone in a guesthouse. "Maybe we should find Sole."

"We can cover more ground this way," Edge pointed out. "I want to learn more about this place. I'm pretty sure that's what Sole wants us to do."

"I'm glad *you* understand them," Jessop snorted. "I don't know what they're saying half the time."

The door was locked, so Edge slid open a window and she and Jessop slipped outside. A silent, shadowy figure left the overhanging branches and followed them as they glided away. The thick, dark forest made it difficult to tell how many sapiens lived in Cowrie, but there were far more than Edge had ever dreamed of.

To think, a few weeks ago I didn't even know any of this existed, Edge thought.

"Is this what Marrow is like?" she asked.

"Kind of, but everything's alive here," Jessop answered thoughtfully. "Even the buildings are alive. I wonder if it's actually as nice as it looks."

"What do you mean? Why wouldn't it be?" Edge asked curiously.

"When lots of sapiens live together, they need rules," Jessop replied. "My parents said that bad things happen when the rules aren't fair."

"You think that's happening here?" Edge recalled her outrage when she'd learned that Forax were forced to grow food for other sapiens.

"I don't think that Hiro fellow follows the same rules as everyone else," Jessop replied wisely.

No one stopped them as they flew through Marrow, passing thick trees laden with buildings and connected by a network of bridges and ladders. As they approached the outskirts of the forest-city, the buildings became simpler and the lights were more widely spaced, leaving swathes of dark forest between motes of electric light. The buildings here looked newer - constructed rather than grown from the trees.

When they reached the first farm, Edge assumed it was a meadow, like those in Far Crescent. Then she noticed that the shrubs in the fields had too many straight lines and right angles. They were all identical. She and Jessop landed next to one of the shrubs. Bunches of tiny bodies dangled from leafy tails like ripe fruit. Bright yellow eyes with vertical pupils stared at them from feline faces.

"Are these vinecats? They look like adults! Why are they still attached to the shrub like this?" Edge asked. "Are they in pain?"

"This is a farm," answered Jessop. "They're not like the wild vinecats at home. They've been domesticated."

Edge reached for one of the vinecats and a voice behind her yelled "Stop!"

Turning around, Edge saw an Avian peeking around a hedge behind them. They had been followed.

Edge and Jessop examined the newcomer carefully. He didn't seem very threatening. His face was flat and wide. Huge round eyes warily followed their movements.

He looks terrified. Is he afraid of us? Edge wondered.

"Do not go to the ceremony," said the stranger, staring at them even more intently. Edge couldn't tell if he was outraged, afraid, or just deeply concerned.

"Who are you?" she asked.

"My name is Mahali," answered the Avian, taking a step closer.

"Tell us about the ceremony, and we'll decide for ourselves whether we want to go," Jessop suggested. "Will Sole be there?"

Mahali looked confused. "Who is Sole?"

"Our friend," Jessop explained. "The rover we arrived with."

"You are *friends* with the rover?" gasped Mahali in surprise.

"Don't worry, we think it's weird, too," Edge assured him. "But yeah, Sole is our friend, sort of. It's a long story."

"No," Mahali replied, his eyes bulging. "The rover will not be there."

"What's the ceremony?" asked Edge.

"It is a ritual for newcomers. Hiro will brainwash you."

"I *knew* this place was too good to be true!" Jessop huffed.

The vinecats whimpered in distress.

"Can't we do anything for the vinecats?" Edge asked with concern.

Jessop shook his head. "I know what it looks like, but if we pull them off their host plant, they'll die. That's how they've been bred."

"That's awful!" Edge exclaimed.

"The hybrid farms are new, and they are cruel," Mahali agreed. "Domesticated vinecats were brought here by The Resistance."

"The brainwashing guy and his friends did this?" Edge asked. "Well, I *definitely* don't want to be brainwashed. Now what?"

"We need Sole," Jessop replied. "If Hiro's planning to brainwash us, I doubt he'll help us find the answer you're looking for."

"Come with me," Mahali offered. "I will help you find the rover."

Jessop and Edge exchanged a glance.

"Can you give us a moment alone?" Jessop asked.

"Certainly," answered Mahali politely, flying a fair distance away.

"What do you think about this?" Jessop asked when Mahali was out of earshot. "Sole told you to follow your feelings."

"I feel like not being brainwashed," Edge said firmly.

"What if Mahali is lying?"

"Oh! I didn't think of that." Edge looked uncertain. "Why would he do that?"

"Maybe he's friends with a bunch of outlaws and he's luring us to them? Maybe Hiro had him follow us to test us? Or he really might want to help us. There's no way of knowing for sure."

Edge's eyes grew wider. "For real?"

"Yes," Jessop answered. "Avians want to kill my family. Some sapiens are bad. We can't trust everyone we meet."

"I don't know what to do then," Edge admitted. "What do *your* feelings tell you?"

"Well, I think we could beat Mahali in a fight if we had to, so let's not get brainwashed, for starters," Jessop decided after a moment's thought. "But if I say we should run, let's fly away from here as fast as we can go, okay? With or without Sole."

Edge nodded solemnly.

"I have been living secretly on the outskirts of Cowrie for a long time," Mahali explained as he led Edge and Jessop through the dark forest. "I know how to get around without being seen."

Shortly after nightfall, they arrived at a simple shelter suspended from a tree and mostly hidden by curtains of vines. Inside was a bed of soft grass, a hammock, and a shelf full of books and boxes.

"Get some sleep," Mahali told them. "I will keep watch. Tomorrow we can retrieve your friend and move somewhere more comfortable."

Edge didn't entirely trust Mahali, but she couldn't keep her eyes open. The two friends slept soundly until a cacophony of animal and bird cries filled the morning air.

"It sure is loud here," Jessop observed irritably as he left the shelter with Edge.

Mahali was perched on a branch far above them. His amber eyes appeared through the gloom as he glided down to them.

"Good morning," he said. "I hope you slept well. It is very loud in the rainforest in the morning. This is where Tsoci is the most alive," Mahali gestured to the forest around them. "It gives me great joy to hear the free animals, but I wonder if they are crying for the release of their kin," he said.

"The vinecats we were looking at when you found us... they were being..." Edge struggled to find the words to describe it.

"Being juiced," finished Mahali. "A terrible practice."

"It's awful. Has that always happened?"

"No," Mahali answered, offering them some food. "Because of The Resistance, there are many more sapiens here than there once were. Modified crops are the easiest way to feed everyone." Edge and Jessop gratefully accepted the berries Mahali offered them.

"How do you know all this? Were you born here?" Jessop stared at Mahali with open fascination.

"No," answered Mahali. "I was brought here from Marrow after the Great Pact."

"I'm from Marrow, too!" Jessop exclaimed.

"What's the Great Pact?" asked Edge before Jessop could ask Mahali what part of Marrow he came from.

Mahali considered Edge carefully.

"Are you *really* from Far Crescent?"

Edge hesitated. She looked at Jessop, who gave a small nod.

"Yes," Edge answered. "How did you know?"

"While you slept, I visited your rover friend," Mahali said quietly. "They told me that you are from Far Crescent. They said Tsoci gave you a task, and that you are doing this task to get your mother's memory back. Is this the truth?"

"Yes," Edge confirmed. "It's true. Where's Sole? Did you bring them here?"

"They were not ready to leave yet. Your mother's name is Mana?" Mahali's eyes bulged.

Edge didn't know whether to laugh or scream. She glanced at Jessop again. He was examining Mahali with obvious interest, but he did not seem afraid.

"Mana is my mother," Edge said.

Mahali nodded, as though Edge had confirmed something important. He vanished into the shelter and returned with a photograph.

"Is *this* your mother?" he asked, passing the photograph to Edge.

The image was old and faded, but Edge could still make out Mana's face. She was standing in front of someone who looked vaguely familiar.

"Yes!" Edge exclaimed. Her eyes filled with tears as she gazed at her mother's face. Mana looked so happy.

"Where did you get this?" Edge whispered.

"I stole it from a Forax named Cato."

"Who's Cato?" Jessop asked.

"Cato and a few other sapiens discovered Cowrie many years before I was brought here," Mahali replied. "They were the first sapiens to come here without losing their memories of Marrow. This is where rovers used to bring the sapiens who did not fit into Marrow."

"Used to? What happens now?" Edge asked.

"Now they bring sapiens here to join The Resistance."

"How do you know?" Jessop asked.

"Because the Insects told us," Mahali said. "Cato arrived here with a sapien named Sopa. She could speak to the Insects." Mahali's expression softened. "When I arrived, she protected me."

"From what?" Edge asked.

"From Hiro," Mahali answered, looking at Edge carefully.

"The jerk who wants to brainwash us?" Jessop scoffed. "He sounds like a bad guy."

"He is a deeply misguided sapien," Mahali agreed. "He is also the spiritual leader of The Resistance. Cato commands the army, Vera runs the lab, and Hiro gives the soldiers a sense of purpose."

"Are they here now?" Edge asked, wondering if one of these sapiens might be her father.

"Only Hiro is here," Mahali answered. "Cato travelled to Far Crescent several years ago. He only returns for short visits. Vera is leading a resupply mission to Marrow. Hiro is supposed to be a prophet, but he does terrible things. He punishes sapiens who do not want to join The Resistance, and he abuses the Insects."

"There are *Insects* here?" Edge said, surprised.

"Not as many as there once were," Mahali replied regretfully. "Cato and the Insects formed the Great Pact about twelve years ago. Since then, Insects have delivered sapiens to Cowrie without erasing their memories. That way, Hiro can question them before he brainwashes them. All the Insects who have delivered sapiens since the Great Pact was made have stayed in Cowrie."

"Where are they?" Jessop asked.

"They are in the lab, along with your friend Sole," Mahali answered. "The Resistance is trying to turn them into weapons."

"Weapons?" Jessop looked alarmed. "Why?"

"They are preparing for war. I am trying to stop them." Mahali looked at them defiantly.

"All by yourself?" Jessop asked in disbelief.

"Yes," Mahali confirmed.

Edge was perplexed. "Who are they planning to fight?"

"The Resistance wants to overthrow Tsoci," Mahali answered, his voice low.

"Why are *you* here?" Jessop asked. "It doesn't sound like you wanted to join an army."

"I was taken with about a hundred other sapiens," Mahali continued. "None of us wanted to leave Marrow. We tried to escape, so Hiro punished us."

"Punished you how?" Jessop asked.

Mahali was silent for a long time. "He ordered the other sapiens to hurt us. We ran into the rainforest to escape. That is where Sopa found me. I was the only survivor. The rainforest is a dangerous place."

"Hiro sounds like a *jerk!*" Edge was outraged.

"Hiro claims that Tsoci has gone mad," Mahali told her. "The sapiens in The Resistance believe him."

"What do *you* believe?" Jessop asked.

Mahali blinked slowly.

"Before he left, Cato said that he would return with Hiro's daughter, and that she would have greater power than her father. He said that Hiro's daughter would lead The Resistance to victory."

Slowly, Edge realized what Mahali was saying. "Hiro is *not* my dad," she spat vehemently.

"Look at the photograph again," Mahali urged.

Now that she knew what to look for, the resemblance was undeniable.

There was her mother, smiling broadly. Standing behind Mana, his arms wrapped lovingly around her waist, was Hiro.

"But he didn't even *know* me! He *can't* be my dad. He's *awful!*"

"Many fathers are," Mahali said sympathetically.

"Why didn't Mana *tell* me my father was a monster!" Edge exclaimed. "Why didn't she tell me The Resistance was bad? Why didn't she tell me *anything?*"

"Hiro may have been different when your mother knew him," Mahali suggested wisely. "The ceremony changes sapiens, and he has partaken many times."

Edge was still furious.

"*Are* you here to lead The Resistance?" Mahali asked Edge pointedly.

"No!" she replied emphatically. "I came here to find out why I exist."

"Why you *exist?*" Mahali look perplexed. "What do you mean?"

"The Insects took my mother's memory away. Tsoci said they'll only give it back if I help Sole find out why I exist," Edge added, her eyes filling with tears. "I just want my mother back."

Mahali looked at her thoughtfully. "You have spoken with Tsoci?"

"Yeah," Edge glanced at Jessop, who shrugged. "I can merge with them. I can remember Tsoci's memories and feel their feelings for a little while. It hurts."

Mahali was silent for a long time.

"Sopa did not like how The Resistance was using the Insects, or the way they changed Cowrie so quickly," he concluded. "She said she could feel Tsoci's pain. Maybe you exist to put an end to what The Resistance is doing."

"What exactly *are* they doing?" Jessop asked. "Why do they need the Insects?"

"They are taking the Insects apart," Mahali replied. "They are learning how to change them the way they changed the vinecats you saw."

Jessop and Edge were horrified.

"We have to stop them!" Edge declared.

"The Insects *did* take Mana's memory," Jessop pointed out.

"It's still not right," Edge said firmly.

"I will consider how we can help the Insects," Mahali answered, "but first we must retrieve your rover friend. Follow me, and stay silent. The lab is near the very center of Cowrie."

Mahali flew into the trees.

"Are you sure we should follow him?" Jessop asked.

"Yes," Edge replied. "I definitely feel like we need Sole right now."

Chapter Twenty Two

Strange Friend

"I'm totally ready to fulfill my purpose," Xalma assured the leaders of The Resistance when Cato brought her to the helm of the submarine.

She bared her sharp teeth in what she hoped was a winning smile. Many of the sapiens in the room took a step back.

"I'm sure we're all grateful that you have finally decided to do your job, Your Highness," Vera replied scornfully.

"Uh, yeah," Xalma said, her smile turning into a grimace. "Sorry I'm late. I'm not sure what happened... but you guys destroyed my home and everything. I kind of think we're even, don't you?"

"That will depend on whether you repair the damage done in your absence." Vera turned away from Xalma dismissively. "Keep us updated, Cato."

Cato led Xalma to her quarters. A simple room had been prepared for her, with a cot and a small table. To get there, Xalma and Cato walked through a long room full of crates and barrels. Rows of beds lined the wall.

"Is this where everyone sleeps?"

"Most of us, yes," Cato replied. "There are just over a hundred sapiens on board. The containers are for supplies. Let's get some food," he suggested, noticing the ravenous look on Xalma's face.

Xalma couldn't remember hearing a more beautiful sentence.

She could not stop eating. For the first few days after transforming, eating was Xalma's main activity. She grew at an impressive rate. Her bones and muscles became stronger. Her body lengthened. Before long, the top of her spiked head scraped the roof of the submarine, and she had to duck everywhere she went. She felt stronger and more powerful with each passing day.

While Xalma ate, Cato explained the history of Marrow. It was long and complicated, and it involved a lot of sapiens Xalma didn't know. She ate and pretended to listen.

"We will go ashore today," Cato announced when Xalma had reached her full height. "It's time for you to learn to use your new body."

"Oh cool!" Xalma exclaimed when Cato shared the news. "Who's going to teach me?"

"*I* am," answered Cato. Xalma tried not to look disappointed. Now that she was grown, Cato's head barely reached her waist.

"Sure thing, *Master Cato*," snickered Xalma. Cato smiled, and Xalma assumed he hadn't noticed her sarcasm. But he had, and he was going to make her pay for it.

Mahali led Edge and Jessop to the lab to find Sole. They travelled most of the way on foot, squeezing through narrow gaps, climbing into buildings full of pipes and wires, and sneaking down the hidden corridors connecting the power and water systems of Cowrie. Like everything else, the pipes and wires were surrounded by living vines and moss, and seemed to have grown alongside the trees and shrubs.

"These are service tunnels," Mahali explained. "We must stay hidden. I am surprised Hiro did not assign a guard to keep you from wandering away. He must not have thought you were very important, but by now he will know you have escaped. His soldiers will be looking for you."

"Why did you follow us?" Jessop whispered.

"When you arrived, I knew you were different," Mahali replied. "The rover looks unusual."

He led them to a looming stone building next to a wide, deep river. The building was new. Most of the structures in Cowrie were overgrown with vegetation, but the windowless stone walls of the lab were free of vines and moss.

"This is a research lab?" Jessop asked. "It looks like a prison."

"It is both," Mahali answered darkly.

Two huge sapiens guarded the only entrance.

Edge and Jessop hid around the corner while Mahali approached the door. A few moments later, both guards walked away, guffawing as they passed the shadow where Edge and Jessop were hidden.

"I gave them some berry loaf," Mahali explained. "Sopa taught me how to make it." He motioned for Edge and Jessop to follow him inside.

"We only have a few minutes," Mahali whispered. He led them to a steep, stone staircase.

The torchlit halls were empty and bare. Heavy wooden doors lined the walls. They descended several flights of stairs. Edge was about to ask how much further they had to go when she heard Sole's cries. It sounded as though the rover was screaming in pain.

"Sole's in trouble!" whispered Edge urgently.

"They are faking it," Mahali responded calmly. "Stay here."

Edge and Jessop waited nervously next to a doorway while Mahali entered and spoke to someone inside. There was a loud thump. A few moments later, he poked his head out of the doorway.

"Enter," he said. The cries had stopped.

"Hey Edge!" Sole called cheerfully. The rover was strapped to a table. Pins were embedded across their brow, and patches of fur and feathers were ripped or burned from places all over their body.

"Oh *Sole!*" Edge exclaimed, "Are you okay? What have they done to you?"

"What, *this?*" Sole glanced at their injuries. "It's nothing, I'm fine! I'm a *rover*. I can *choose* whether or not to feel pain."

Edge ran towards Sole and tripped over a figure lying prone on the floor.

"Don't worry about him," Mahali said, removing a huge thorn from the prone scientist's neck. "He's just sleeping." Mahali dropped the thorn and crushed it into the stone floor. "Sticklethorn," Mahali explained, seeing the look on Jessop's face. "It will put you to sleep if it stings you."

"You're not hurt?" Edge examined Sole anxiously.

"No, just bored. It's fun to yell," Sole grinned. "The scientists here didn't think rovers *could* feel pain, so when I did, they were surprised. I turned it off pretty quickly, but you should see how much it messes with them when I yell." Sole was giggling. "Sometimes I laugh, too. That *really* messes with them."

"But they were *trying* to hurt you!" Edge cried angrily, turning to Mahali. "Did you know about this?"

"Yes," Mahali answered. "When you told me Sole was your friend, I found them and offered to release them, but they said they were not ready yet."

"I was still learning things!" Sole remarked. "I don't want to *stay* here," they added quickly, noticing Edge's appalled expression.

"Can we get out of here?" Jessop asked. "This place gives me the creeps."

"I did what I came here to do," Sole said. "Mahali, can you go get Mary? She's in the next room."

"Who's Mary?" Jessop asked.

"She's my new friend," Sole smiled, as Mahali rushed into the hall.

Edge and Jessop helped Sole remove the pins and wires attached to their body. When Mahali returned, Sole was free of the machines.

An unfamiliar voice said, "Sssooollleee?"

"Who is *that*?" exclaimed Edge.

"Cool, right?" Sole said. "I taught her to speak!"

The Insect stood as tall as Jessop. She had a segmented body and huge mandibles.

"How do you know Mary is a she?" Jessop whispered, eyeing the mandibles with concern.

"She told me," Sole replied. Then, to Jessop's surprise, Sole and Mary started dancing.

"What's going on?" Jessop asked.

"They're talking," Edge gasped. "Sole knows how to talk to the Insects."

Mary clicked in a way that reminded Edge of laughter. Together, Mary and Sole started digging through the stone wall of the room. Once they'd tunneled through the wall, Sole collected the tumbled stones and mortar and expertly stacked them back in place. The only light that remained in their escape tunnel was the soft red glow of Sole's eyes.

"Hiro's going to be *so confused*!" Sole giggled. Mary clicked affirmatively.

"Hiro's my dad," Edge informed Sole.

"Oh wow, that's some great information! Good work!"

"I don't know what to do next," Edge said.

"We'll figure it out," Sole assured her.

Digging their way out took less time than Edge expected. Mary tunneled through the ground with expert efficiency. Edge was horrified by the state of Mary's body. Her wings had been violently torn from her back. She was covered in fresh injuries and scars, and she walked with a noticeable limp.

"If they can dig themselves out, why don't the Insects escape?" she whispered.

"They believe they're supposed to be here," Sole explained.

"Shhh," hissed Mahali.

They slipped out of the tunnel, and Mahali led them down hidden paths until it was safe to fly. Sole lifted Mary into the air and the small group flew the rest of the way to Mahali's shelter. When they arrived, Sole gently lifted Mary into the shelter and tended to her wounds until she fell asleep.

Sunrise barely reached the murky forest depths, but the morning cacophony of sound woke them early. Wisps of fog drifted across the eternally damp ground. In the dim light, Mahali led them over rocky hummocks and around the trunks of enormous, unmodified trees. Now and then, an eager shaft of sunlight snuck through a crack in the dense foliage, throwing a fleeting spotlight on a random patch of ground and highlighting the strange and fascinating denizens of the rainforest floor.

"Everything here is so *alive*," Jessop whispered in wonder. "Even the *stones* are alive."

"This place is amazing," Edge agreed. "I could spend my whole life trying to understand this place."

"Isn't that what the scientists in that lab are doing to the Insects?" Jessop asked.

"Experiments are shaped by the questions you ask," Edge replied. "The scientists in Cowrie are asking awful questions, so their experiments are awful."

"Awful or not, these sapiens have learned quite a bit about Insects," Sole remarked.

"They must know that what they're doing is wrong, though," Edge insisted.

"I'm not sure they do," Sole replied. "They really believe that Insects and Rovers can't feel pain, and that what they're doing is going to save the world from Tsoci's madness."

"But Tsoci isn't mad, are they?" Edge asked.

"I'm not sure I'd know if they were," Sole admitted, "but I don't think so."

Mahali opened a moss-covered door behind a curtain of thick vines. Once inside, they climbed down a ladder to a winding underground tunnel that branched off into many passages. Mushrooms of every shape and color lined the walls.

"We know who Edge's dad is now, but we still don't know why she exists," Jessop said as they followed Mahali through the dimly lit passages. "What should we do next?"

"I think we should get the Insects away from here," Sole replied.

"I feel the same way," Edge agreed.

"The Insects are really strong." Jessop glanced at Mary's mandibles. "Why don't they just leave on their own?"

"They won't leave unless Hive Mind tells them to," said Sole. "The Resistance has some kind of agreement with Hive."

"The Great Pact," confirmed Mahali.

"Can't they make their own choices?" Edge asked. "I'm pretty sure Hive Mind didn't intend for them to be tortured and killed." She looked at Mahali. "What exactly *is* the Great Pact?" she asked.

Mahali shrugged. "Nobody knows what Cato and the Insects agreed to."

The tunnel walls were made of a smooth iridescent material that reminded Edge of the inside of a shell.

"Where are we?" Edge asked.

"This is part of the very first Hive, where the first Insects lived," said Mahali. "It has been abandoned for a long time. In Cowrie, they call it the Ruins. Sopa said it once had another name."

"Where *is* Sopa?" Edge asked. "Maybe we should talk to her ourselves."

"She was banished for trying to rescue the Insects," Mahali replied. "No one knows where she is now. I miss her."

They continued in silence until Mahali stopped in front of an elaborate carving of an Insect standing on a hill in front of an expansive tree. He motioned the others to step back.

"Oh!" exclaimed Sole. "It's a *dancing* door!"

"A *what* kind of door?" asked Jessop.

"Watch," answered Mahali.

He bowed low and spread his arms to the side. When his hands touched the floor, he extended his wings before tucking in both arms and wings and gracefully flipping backwards. He landed lightly, spread his wings and touched the door. The carved section of the wall slid silently into the ceiling. He turned to Sole and Mary. "Did I perform well? I am afraid I do not know what it means."

Sole giggled and Mary clicked. They both seemed amused.

"Why are you laughing?" Mahali had hoped to impress his new friends.

"It means *Open up, door.*" Sole laughed. "It's kind of obvious, right?"

Mahali performed another series of graceful movements when they were inside, and the door closed again.

"I bet you know what *that* dance means." Sole teased.

Mary clicked in amusement again.

"Your dancing is beautiful." Jessop said earnestly, ignoring the rover. "Can you teach me?"

Mahali looked slightly mollified, even though Sole continued to snicker.

"We should get some rest first," Mahali replied. "There are bedrooms along the left hall. We will be safe."

"Oh *yeah!*" Sole exclaimed, skipping eagerly down the hallway. "I forgot all about sleep! Maybe I'll even dream this time!"

Mary followed Sole, her huge head turning from side to side as she looked around.

Sopa's hideout reminded Jessop of the treehouse, except that it didn't have any windows. Instead, light shafted down from skylights in the ceiling. When he stood underneath one of these lights and looked up, Jessop realized that the light was travelling down tall, hollow trunks. The inside of each trunk was riddled with holes and lined with angled mirrors and crystals, which directed countless tiny beams of light down from the very top of the canopy and into Sopa's home. The beams danced and changed as the day advanced. Mahali lit a fire in the hearth and the hideout became warmer.

"This is where I lived when Sopa was still here," Mahali explained. "I spend most of my time in the forest now, so I can keep an eye on The Resistance."

The walls were lined with bookshelves. As Jessop examined the books, Edge wandered into the adjacent room and discovered that Sopa, like Mana, had a lab. It did not seem to be home to any active experiments.

"Is Sopa a scientist?" Edge asked curiously. "Is she a Forax, like me?"

Mahali's huge eyes gleamed as he looked up from the fire he was tending.

"Sopa is a mycologist. She always said she preferred fungus to folks. She was a Forax exterminator before The Resistance took her. She was working for Vera when she found me."

"What's an exterminator?" asked Jessop.

"Pest control for the farms," Mahali explained. "Sopa was designed to destroy anything that might damage the crops grown for Marrow."

"Designed?" Jessop asked.

Mahali seemed surprised by the question. "Avians design every Forax," he replied. He looked at Edge. "Were you not designed in Marrow, Edge?"

"I don't know what you mean." Edge was perplexed. "I was born in Far Crescent."

"Surely you were implanted in Marrow, though. No Forax has reproduced naturally for at least five generations. Are you *sure* you were not designed, and given to Mana and Hiro to raise?"

"My mother said I was born in the treehouse." Edge looked uncertain. "Mana had a lot of secrets, though."

"I *lived* in Marrow and I never heard anything about Forax being *designed*," Jessop said. "What does that even mean?"

"Your mother's name is Mana and she is a scout, correct?" Mahali asked Edge.

"Mana is a scientist," Edge answered firmly.

"But she has the body of a scout, like you," Mahali insisted.

Edge nodded reluctantly.

"Before the Mana you know now, there was another Mana. Before that Mana, there was another one. That is how Forax are made. When one dies, they are replaced by an exact clone, unless their job is no longer needed, or another kind of Forax is engineered to do the job better. In fact, there are not many scouts left since Marrow built the network."

"Do you mean all the Forax are just copies of someone else?" Edge asked.

Mahali nodded.

"Did *you* know this?" she asked, turning to Jessop.

"No!" Jessop exclaimed, clearly just as shocked as Edge.

"I knew you were Hiro's child, but I assumed you were assigned to Hiro and Mana, to be raised in Marrow." Mahali walked to the hearth and stoked the fire. "I thought Mana stole you. You see, Forax cannot reproduce."

"You think I'm a *clone*?" Edge looked at Mahali in shock.

"I do not think you can be Hiro's literal child," Mahali replied softly. "You have seen him for yourself. He looks nothing like you."

"We knew you were different," Jessop reminded her. "I wonder if Sole knows about this."

"Your friend Sole is very strange," Mahali said in a low voice. "Are you sure you can trust them?"

"We don't have a choice," Edge replied before Jessop could answer.

"If you *are* the natural offspring of two Forax, you are very unique, Edge. Such a thing has not happened for a very long time." Mahali looked at Edge with renewed interest.

"We could ask Hiro," Jessop suggested. "Maybe he can explain why you exist."

"I think we should avoid Hiro," said Edge. "But there's got to be someone here who knows."

"If anyone knows, it will be Vera. She is a geneticist," Mahali said. "Maybe when she returns to Cowrie, we can find a way to speak with her."

"When will that be?" Edge asked, yawning.

"Not for a few days," Mahali replied. "There is time to rest and make a plan."

After several nights of falling asleep watching the stars together, Edge and Jessop felt safer staying in the same room. Jessop wrapped himself in a hammock. Edge curled up inside a bed of dry, sweet smelling moss that had recently been piled into the corner. Neither of them could fall asleep.

"I've been thinking," Jessop said quietly, "what if you have to decide for *yourself* why you exist?"

"What do you mean?" Edge asked.

"Well, it seems like a lot of your power has to do with choice. Your brain made it possible for Sole to make choices. You can even choose to stay an individual when you merge with Tsoci. What if the reason Tsoci doesn't know why you exist is because you haven't decided yet?"

Edge stared into the darkness.

"I don't want to be *for* anything. I just want to go back to how things were," she whispered.

Chapter Twenty Three

Disappointment

"Where are we going?" Xalma asked Cato.

"We are picking up supplies in Marrow and travelling on to Cowrie," he answered. "There is an army waiting for you there."

Xalma had grown tired of pointing out that she didn't want to lead an army. Arguing wasn't much fun, so she started playing along instead.

"Oh goody," she said. "I can't wait to meet them."

Once a day, Xalma and Cato rode to the shore in a small boat and trained together for an hour before returning to the submarine. Two Amphs remained behind to guard the boat. They bowed as Xalma and Cato passed. Xalma assumed they were bowing to Cato, and thought it was very silly.

An Avian circled above, watching for danger until they returned to the submarine.

On her first day of training, Xalma learned that they were travelling with a whole fleet of submarines. Dozens of them bobbed in the distant water like fat, metal ducks. She was trying to count them when Cato interrupted her thoughts.

"Knock me down," he ordered.

"No offense, but you're a tiny old Forax," Xalma objected. "That doesn't seem right." Xalma wobbled a little, still adjusting to being on land again.

"You are a coward," sneered Cato.

"No I'm not!" Xalma objected. "I just feel weird about beating up an old guy."

"You will not succeed," Cato assured her. "You are weak and slow, and I am strong, and possibly the smartest sapien you have ever met."

Xalma argued for a while, but Cato did not relent. He criticized and belittled her. Xalma grew frustrated.

"*I'm* weak?" Xalma snarled as she half-heartedly lunged at Cato. "What about *you*? What kind of jerk makes someone feel bad for being nice?"

Cato stepped aside easily and pushed Xalma into the sand.

"You're not trying," he snapped. "Don't insult me with your low expectations. *Knock me down*!"

"You *want* to be attacked?" hissed Xalma. "Fine!"

Xalma ran towards Cato at top speed. Once again, he easily sidestepped her. She blinked and he was behind her. As she tumbled past, Cato brushed her lightly with his hand. Xalma flew sideways and rolled across the beach.

"*Again*," Cato commanded.

All day, Xalma tried to knock Cato over. She never improved, but she became more determined with each failure. Her respect for Cato grew. At nightfall they returned to the submarine. Xalma was exhausted.

"Thank you for teaching me, Master Cato," she said breathlessly.

"I am not teaching you," he replied harshly, "because you are not *learning*, Your Highness."

Before Xalma could reply, Cato stormed out of the room.

At nightfall, Mahali woke the others. He'd prepared a feast. Bowls and plates of berries, fish, seeds, and roots were set for Jessop and Edge. Moss and pleasant-smelling fungus were artistically arranged on a platter for Sole and Mary. Jessop eagerly grabbed some of the mushrooms after verifying that they weren't poisonous.

"This is delicious!" raved Jessop. "I've never tasted mushrooms like these before!"

"Thank you!" Mahali beamed.

"Will you teach me how to find them and cook them?" Jessop asked eagerly.

Edge snorted. "Maybe mushroom hunting can wait?"

"Oh yeah. Of course," Jessop replied briskly. "So what are we doing next?"

"I understand that you want to release the Insects from the lab," Mahali said. "I will help you, but I have already tried many times to set the Insects free, and they will not leave."

"*Mary* left," Jessop pointed out. "Maybe she knows how we can convince the others."

Sole performed a series of graceful movements. Before long, Mary was dancing too. The two of them moved silently and gracefully for a few moments before sitting down again.

"The Insects won't leave unless Hive Mind tells them to. They think they're supposed to be here, because of the Great Pact," Sole explained.

"Even if they're being hurt?" Jessop asked in disbelief.

"They'll endure great sacrifice if they believe it's for the good of their Hive," Sole answered. "Even if we convince them to escape, they won't be able to fly home. They're really badly hurt. We need to find a way for them to get home."

"This just keeps getting harder," Edge complained. "Is there some way to convince them to fight for themselves?"

"They won't fight willingly," Sole replied. "Mary and I merged when the scientists experimenting on us tried to make us fight. I merged with her to ask her why she was attacking me. She was being forced to. When we merged, Mary changed the same way I changed when I merged with you, Edge. She started thinking of herself as *I* instead of *we*."

Mary clicked affirmatively.

"Why can't you merge with the rest of the Insects and change them, too?" Jessop asked Sole.

"Even if Edge helps me, that will take a long time," Sole replied. "If we're caught, we might not be able to save them all."

"Is there some way to communicate with all the Insects at once?" Edge asked.

"Maybe you can ask Tsoci for help," Sole suggested.

"Unless Edge can ask Tsoci to heal all the Insects so they can fly home, that doesn't really help them escape," Jessop pointed out.

"I think if Tsoci could have freed the Insects, they would have," Edge remarked.

"Not if they don't know what's happening," explained Sole. "This has only been going on for a few seasons. Tsoci probably doesn't even know about it yet."

"Okay, but even if I wanted to tell Tsoci that a bunch of Insects are being tortured here; I don't know how. Don't I need to be in Limbic? Do I have to find a magic hole in a bush somewhere and talk to a creepy invisible thing in a room full of crazy light?"

"I can take you to a place where you can try merging," Mahali offered. "There is a special dome in Ruins. No one goes there. It is a sacred place."

"Now?" Jessop asked. The light filtering down from the skylights above had grown dimmer. Although they had slept all afternoon, Jessop was reluctant to leave the hideout when night was falling.

"It is not far," Mahali assured him. "We will not leave the tunnels. Edge can try merging and we can return before it gets late."

"Yeah, okay," Edge agreed, standing up. "I'd rather do *something*. I still don't understand how I'm supposed to figure out why I exist. Am I just supposed to ask someone?" She looked at Sole, who shrugged.

"Follow me," Mahali said. He danced open the door.

They passed through ancient tunnels and elaborately carved chambers. Lofty ceilings rose high above the travelers in colorful spirals. The chambers were often cracked and crumbled, leaving large sections of the walls and ceiling open to the darkness outside.

"This place kind of looks like Hive," Edge whispered, carefully examining the chambers. "The rooms are the same shape, but Hive isn't covered with carvings, and the walls are made of something different. Who carved all this?"

"The Insects," Mahali replied.

Jessop stopped the party so he could examine the walls more closely. "A lot of the carvings look like Insects dancing. Maybe these are lessons."

Mahali motioned for the group to be quiet as they paused outside the entrance to a massive, dusty chamber. The vaulted space was as large as the biggest dome in Hive. After waiting in complete silence for what felt to Edge like a very long time, Mahali slowly led them into the chamber.

The floor, tiled in the opalescent scales of some ancient creature, flashed dully through a layer of dust. Walls, the color of bone, spiraled up towards the peak of the chamber in sweeping bridges and coils.

It's like a huge, twisted flower, Edge thought, *but it's inside-out.*

"We're inside a fractal cone!" Sole exclaimed in wonder. "This is incredible!"

The pointed top of the ceiling was so elevated, it broke through the canopy of the trees. The last light of dusk highlighted ornately shaped windows high above their heads.

"I do not know the name of this place," Mahali whispered, "but it is full of strength and beauty." He pointed at the arched doorways bordering the room. "There are many entrances. If The Resistance discovers us, they could surround us. I do not believe they will look for you here, but I am sure there are soldiers nearby, and the forest is full of dangerous creatures. We should not draw attention to ourselves."

"Mary and I will keep a lookout!" offered Sole.

"I'll watch, too," said Jessop.

"Circle the perimeter of the chamber," Mahali advised them. "Listen for sounds in the passages. If you hear anything, call us. We will escape by a different exit."

Jessop, Sole, and Mary circled the room, watching and listening for signs of danger. Mahali and Edge continued towards the center of the chamber, where clusters of moss and mushrooms were draped over the spiraling hill of an enormous shell bursting through the middle of the floor. They climbed a winding staircase to a platform carved into the top.

"Would you like me to leave you so that you can concentrate?" Mahali asked Edge.

"Please stay. It'll be good to have company," Edge answered nervously. "The last time I merged with Tsoci, it was really painful. If this works, I might need your help."

Mahali nodded and sat nearby. He closed his eyes and waited patiently.

Edge sat on the flat surface of the platform. Following Mahali's example, she closed her eyes. She recalled everything she knew about merging. Something was always touching her when she merged; Sole's antennae; the roots in Limbic. Edge placed her hands firmly on the iridescent surface beneath her. The shell felt warm and alive.

Edge breathed slowly and deliberately. Nothing happened. She forced herself to focus on the idea of Tsoci. She imagined the life all around her, picturing individual cells in her mind's eye. She imagined microscopic life all around her.

I'm already part of Tsoci, she told herself. *We're already connected. I just need to let myself expand.*

A tiny whisper of another awareness brushed her thoughts. She felt little sparks, like the pins and needles of blood returning to a limb, but they were not inside her.

Mahali gasped as tendrils of light erupted from Edge's hands and crept across the shell in streaks and ripples.

"Whoa!" Jessop yelled as he soared overhead. He flew closer to Edge. "Are you okay?"

Edge heard Jessop, but she could also hear and see and feel everything around her as her senses joined the web of life around her and pulled her attention in a million different directions. She was incapable of filtering the new input or reconnecting her own thoughts.

The shell under Edge pulsed with light. Complicated patterns, like those on the walls of Limbic, radiated from her hands and spread across the vast, ancient room. Delicate webs of glowing mycelia emerged from the floor, weaving their way over every surface. Jessop and Mary watched in silent wonder. Sole grabbed Mary and lifted her into the air.

Mahali left the platform and circled the room, patrolling the entrances for signs of danger.

"I think it's working!" Jessop called in excitement.

Mahali was growing increasingly concerned. "Will the light stop spreading when it reaches the walls? It is very noticeable."

Jessop immediately understood why Mahali was worried.

"I don't know how this works at all. We have to ask Sole," he replied, heading towards the rover without waiting for Mahali to reply.

Before they could reach Sole, air started to rush in through the entrances around the chamber. It started as a pleasant breeze, but quickly rose to a roaring, howling, bitter wind that tossed Jessop and Mahali through the air like leaves. Something large was crashing through the tunnels and passages towards them.

"What is that?" yelled Jessop in alarm. "Something big is coming!"

"We must leave now!" Mahali cried back. "Get Sole and Mary."

When Edge's consciousness reached the boundary of the chamber and made contact with the forest outside, her mind expanded exponentially. Her perspective fluctuated wildly, from the transient, binary perception of a particle, to the massive, slow sea of information circulating over eons across an ancient, dreaming awareness too vast for Edge's stretched mind to understand.

Somewhere, the atoms and molecules of her transient body remained intact, but they were meaningless points in an endless sea of life. Edge lost herself completely.

"Sole, what should we do?" Mahali called as he unsuccessfully tried to wake Edge.

"Leave her!" Sole commanded hovering overhead holding Mary. "If you move her, she might be scattered inside Tsoci forever."

"But something's coming!" Jessop cried. "We have to go!"

Branches and roots and fungus crashed through all the doorways of the chamber, climbing up the walls in an explosion of greens and browns. Flowers of every color bloomed from every plant, and moss and mushrooms glowed from every crevice. Luminescent spores filled the air.

Creeping vines and roots snaked quickly up the shell and converged on Edge. They wove and wrapped and bound her body in a tangled and impenetrable matt of branches and leaves, obscuring the light. Mahali and Jessop took flight to avoid being buried by the crush of vegetation.

Mary struggled out of Sole's grasp and climbed to the top of the platform, shredding Edge's living cocoon with her mandibles. She tore through the plants, but they grew back as quickly as she could pull them apart. Jessop and Mahali landed beside her, ripping moss and vines and branches away as fast as they could.

"Sole, *help us!*" Jessop yelled desperately. The rover still hovered a few feet above them and didn't respond.

"Sole!" Jessop yelled again.

As soon as Sole touched the fibrous cocoon, they were engulfed. Jessop and Mahali watched in helpless horror as vines and moss wrapped around the rover and pulled Sole inside. Sole focused on how much they cared about Edge, and how much they wanted to help her.

I hope this works again, they thought as their consciousness scattered through Tsoci's ancient mind.

Who are we? What am I?

You're Edge. You're my friend. Sole thought, clinging desperately to their sense of individuality.

As soon as she perceived Sole, Edge's sense of herself grew stronger. The distances between the patterns that made Edge an individual started to contract. She floated inside the dream of something ancient and vast, but she was herself again. She was aware of her body shivering in pain, but the sensations couldn't reach her.

Edge felt something else, something new and small and terrified, reaching for her mind across the vast consciousness of Tsoci. It was Sole. They were being reabsorbed.

Don't go, she thought. *Don't take them! Sole!*

I'm here. The thought was just a whisper.

An unfathomable, unending, torrent of agony washed over Edge. She tried to pull away, but she was spread too thin. She became the pain. Tormented images raced and tumbled before her eyes.

Small groups of sapiens worshipping and fearing Tsoci as the literal and unknowable creator of the entire universe. Communities growing. Sapiens living their whole lives in the same place and never meeting all their neighbors. Different groups of sapiens reimagining Tsoci in ways that favored their groups and turned anyone outside their group into an enemy. Sapiens stopped getting to know their neighbors. They stopped trusting each other.

Edge watched as the Insects diligently taught the sapiens to write. They were in the very same chamber that she was in now. The Insects danced, explaining that the purpose of writing was to share ideas and work towards a common goal, and to keep mistakes from being repeated. Once again, Edge felt her individual thoughts drifting further and further away. She was no longer able to follow the thread of Tsoci's memory, but she felt their excruciating pain.

Let us go! We can't help you if you absorb us! she thought desperately.

Mary, Mahali and Jessop continued ripping through the vegetation, tearing at the branches and vines until their hands were scraped and bleeding. Finally, they stopped. Mary bowed her head, whether out of sadness or exhaustion, Jessop and Mahali couldn't tell. Mahali put his hand gently on Jessop's shoulder.

"We cannot force Tsoci to release them," he said. "We must wait. I am sorry, Jessop."

Jessop groaned. He pulled away from Mahali, his eyes wide with terror and loss. Without another word, he flew to the highest window of the chamber and out into the night, looking for a way to free his friends.

"Jessop!" Mahali yelled. "Stop! You will be caught!"

But Jessop was gone. Mahali looked at Mary's tattered wings. If he followed Jessop, he would be leaving three helpless individuals on their own. Clouds of spores glittered in the air and settled silently to the floor.

Chapter Twenty Four

Hypothesis

"It seems my trust was misplaced." Hiro looked tired. "I should have been more prudent."

Jessop struggled to focus, blinking blearily through the bars of a metal cage in the center of a dark cell. There were no windows. Jessop didn't know what time it was, or how long he'd been trapped.

Why is the world tilting? Jessop thought uncomfortably. *Why can't I move?* Heavy shackles around his ankles secured him to a perch. His wrists were tied behind his back with thick rope, pinning down his wings.

"I'm very busy," Hiro continued, "so I won't waste my time convincing you to be reasonable. As Holy Father, I am responsible for the spiritual well-being of The Resistance. I can't have outcasts barging into Cowrie and running around Ruins with a defective rover."

He knows the others are in Ruins. Fear crossed Jessop's face, confirming Hiro's suspicion.

"I don't know what you're talking about," answered Jessop sullenly. "Let me go."

"I know you're from Far Crescent. I know you arrived with a Forax scout. She looked to be about twelve. Is she Mana's daughter?"

"I'm not telling you *anything*," Jessop replied stubbornly. "Let me go!"

"*Where is the rover?*" Hiro demanded.

Jessop said nothing.

Hiro sighed heavily. "This would have been much easier if you had participated in the ceremony."

"So you could brainwash us? No thanks," Jessop snapped defiantly. He and Hiro stared at each other, one angry and afraid, the other cold and calculating.

"As I've already mentioned, I'm very busy," Hiro said finally, breaking the silence. "You have one day to reconsider. If you tell me where the scout and the rover are, I'll let you go. If not, I'll force you to tell me, and I assure you that it will not be pleasant."

"I'll never help you," Jessop snarled. "I know what you're doing to the Insects. I know you hurt sapiens who don't want to fight for you."

To Jessop's surprise, Hiro looked remorseful.

"I have hurt many sapiens," he admitted. "So have Marrow and Tsoci. Sometimes righteous rebellion is the only way to end a greater violence."

"That's stupid," Jessop muttered.

"You are innocent." Hiro's eyes were full of compassion. "You don't understand the burden of a leader during a time of great change. I have many sapiens to protect, and they are all as deserving of freedom and safety as you are."

Jessop did not respond, but Hiro's words made him uncomfortable.

He's right. I don't understand any of this, Jessop realized.

"Perhaps I will have time to explain the urgency of my need when we meet again," Hiro said. "Until then, I'll ask the guards to release you from your shackles and provide you with food and water."

The door slammed shut behind him.

A few moments after Hiro departed, a guard opened Jessop's cage, and roughly unfastened his cuffs.

"Thanks," Jessop said gratefully. The guard grunted and locked the cage again, leaving Jessop alone to wait for Hiro to return.

Mahali and Mary watched over the impenetrable thicket surrounding Edge and Sole. The sun rose and the chamber filled with the fresh light of morning. Eventually, they both drifted into an uneasy sleep.

They woke up many hours later when the vegetation retreated, leaving Edge and Sole unconscious on the surface of the enormous shell. Mary and Mahali carried their companions back to Sopa's hideout.

As soon as Edge and Sole were safely in their beds,
Mahali left the hideout to search for Jessop. His search led
him to the prison. He waited quietly in the shadows, hoping
the guards would mention something that might give him a
clue about Jessop's whereabouts. He wasn't disappointed.

"I heard they captured the Far Crescent Avian," said one
of the guards.

"Hiro's planning to perform the ceremony today," replied
the other.

"Shame, I would've liked to ask what it's like in Far
Crescent," said the first.

"You can still ask." The guard chuckled. "Maybe Hiro
will leave some of his memories intact. I doubt it, though.
Our Holy Father is pretty angry about the whole escape."

Sole was awake when Mahali returned to the hideout.

"Is Edge okay?" Mahali asked. "Are *you* okay?"

Sole shook their head.

"We were almost absorbed by Tsoci, but they let us go.
Edge is asleep. I think she'll be fine, but I know she was hurt.
Tsoci released us because we still have a task, but I don't
think Edge asked for help. I don't think she could. Did you
find Jessop?"

"Jessop is in prison," Mahali frowned. "The Ruins is
crawling with soldiers. Hiro is planning to perform the
ceremony. He will ask Jessop where we are. We have to
leave."

"We can't leave until Edge wakes up," Sole replied. "Tell
me how to find Jessop. Maybe I can rescue him. I can move
faster than you."

"The prison is a fortress, surrounded by guards and
protected by weapons that you cannot defeat," Mahali
explained. "Even if you move quickly enough to reach Jessop
undetected, you will not get him out of there without being
caught. Hiro *expects* us to try to rescue Jessop. It is a trap."

"I just want to look," Sole insisted. "Maybe I'll notice something you didn't see."

"The prison is the windowless stone building next to the square where you landed when you arrived." Mahali replied with a heavy sigh. "The entire surface is electrified. You will not be able to tunnel in. Stay hidden."

Sole returned several hours later.

"You're right, that place *is* a fortress," Sole confirmed. "Are you *sure* Jessop is there?"

"I overheard the guards." Mahali said.

"What should we do?"

"Leave. As soon as possible. Hiro could question Jessop at any time. There is no way we can stop it."

"If they find us, can they open the door?" Sole asked.

"Yes," Mahali answered. "They are good at blowing things up. The dancing door will not help us if they find out where we are."

"You're sure Hiro can make Jessop talk?"

"Yes," Mahali answered grimly. "Our only hope is that Jessop cannot remember how to find this place."

"Will he lose his memory?" Sole asked quietly, thinking of how Edge would feel if Jessop also had his memory stolen.

"It is likely," Mahali confirmed. "The ceremony is a way for Hiro to learn everything a sapien knows before erasing what he does not want them to remember."

"When she wakes up, I'll help Mary dig another way out of the hideout, in case we need to escape," Sole suggested.

"Good idea." Mahali agreed. "We can pile furniture against the door. If they find us, we may be able to escape before they can reach us. I will help you find a hidden location for the exit before you start to dig."

Xalma was frustrated and confused. She tried to follow Cato's instructions, but day after day he responded with disappointment.

The more she disappointed him, the more Xalma wanted Cato to like her.

"Master Cato, I'm *really* trying."

Cato didn't respond immediately. He was lost in thought.

"I should not have expected so much," he said finally. "You are not to blame."

"Why?" Xalma asked. "It's not your fault if I'm stupid."

Cato sighed heavily. "Walk with me," he said. One of the guards started to follow them, but Cato waved him back.

"I must speak with my student alone," he said.

He and Xalma walked along the shore in silence.

"I have made many mistakes," Cato said, "as have those who came before me."

Xalma looked at Cato in surprise. "What do you mean?"

"I spent my life planning to destroy Marrow. You've never been there, but it *is* a terrible place."

"It sounds pretty bad," Xalma said, relieved that Cato seemed willing to talk. "Like, there's a war or something? And the Amphs are being jerks to the other sapiens."

Cato frowned and shook his head.

"Those in power are unfair to those with less power," he said dismissively. "That has always been the way. That's not why Marrow is a bad place."

"Why is it bad, then?" asked Xalma.

"Marrow is a big machine," Cato explained, "and sapiens are part of the machine. The machine itself is not evil, but it keeps growing bigger. Marrow is running out of resources."

Xalma remembered her conversation with Harbeshi.

"Do you mean resources like food, water, and education?" she asked.

"No," Cato answered. "I mean chemicals. Marrow uses chemicals just like you do. Like all living things do."

"By 'uses', do you mean 'eats'? Because that's pretty weird," Xalma chuckled. "Isn't Marrow just a lot of sapiens living together in a city? How can a city eat anything?"

"Marrow is made of sapiens, factories, farms, livestock, buildings, power lines, sewers, ships, schools... it has many parts. It is the place sapiens created for themselves when they were cast out of Cowrie."

"What *is* Cowrie? That's where we're going, right? If we were cast out of it, how can we be going there?" Xalma asked, eager to learn as much as possible while Cato was in the mood to answer questions.

"Cowrie is a hidden place in the rainforest, far from Marrow," Cato explained. "For many generations, Tsoci sent rovers into Marrow to retrieve special sapiens."

"What the heck is So-See?" Xalma asked.

"Tsoci is everywhere," Cato replied. "They are part of you and you are part of them. *You* especially, Xalma. Tsoci has kept you young far beyond your years."

"If you're doing what Tho-Sea is telling you to do, you're a good guy, right?" Xalma asked innocently. "Marrow is bad, and See-saw or whatever is good? That's what it *means* to be good, right? Doing the right thing? Beating the bad guys?"

"Tsoci is not like you and me," Cato sighed. "Tsoci doesn't care if sapiens get hurt."

"What does Tsoci want?" Xalma asked.

"Tsoci wants to grow and learn," Cato replied. "They want all their parts to work together to help them get bigger and stronger and smarter."

"That doesn't sound so bad."

"It's bad because Sapiens grow and learn a lot faster than Tsoci does. We're a threat, and Tsoci is doing whatever they can to keep us from thriving. You can help us overthrow Tsoci, Your Highness, but you will have to work a lot harder."

"I'm honestly not that interested in fighting Soo-see or whatever you call it," Xalma admitted. "I just didn't want you to chuck me off the submarine. I have my own mission." Cato looked at her with interest. "What is your mission?" he asked.

"I want to make sure my friend Jessop is safe," Xalma said. "I really like him, and I think he's in trouble because of me."

Cato laughed. "You are talking about the Far Crescent outcast? He is meaningless, Xalma. You don't understand the power you have, do you?"

"I don't have *any* power," muttered Xalma. "I can't even knock you down."

"Your mission is too small," Cato informed her irritably. "If your mission was to defeat Tsoci, you would be able to knock me down."

"Yeah well, I don't really want to *do* that mission," Xalma answered. "Why should I? You admitted it yourself - *you* made mistakes. Why should *I* fix them?"

The Avian guard circling above landed in front of Cato and Xalma.

"I have a message from Cowrie, Master Cato," said the Avian.

"What is it?" snapped Cato. The Avian whispered something in Cato's ear.

Cato burst out laughing.

"Well then! This changes things!" He smiled at Xalma. "I think your mission just got a lot bigger," he announced.

"What's *that* supposed to mean?" Xalma asked.

"Your friend Jessop is in Cowrie. He is going to join The Resistance."

"Why would he do that?" Xalma realized that although Harbeshi had implied that Jessop was in danger, she didn't actually know what the danger was.

Is this what Harbeshi meant? she wondered. *Did he know Jessop was going to join a rebel army? That doesn't seem like something Jessop would do.*

"Take me to him!" Xalma demanded.

"I intend to," Cato replied. He walked back towards the boat. "The submarines must continue to Marrow to resupply. You and I will travel over the mountains to Cowrie. Pack your things. I will train you on the way."

Everything hurt. Thinking hurt. Moving hurt. Lying still hurt. Breathing hurt.

Being alive hurt.

Edge felt as though she was made of pure pain. Every cell in her body was struggling to process the effects of merging with a superorganism.

Is this what Mana was protecting me from? Edge wondered. *Did she know this was going to happen?* She considered whether it was better to be prepared for the horrors of the world or sheltered by a false sense of security that she might never experience again.

There's no way for me to know whether I'd be better at this if I'd known about The Resistance and Tsoci when I was younger, she decided finally. *I wouldn't be me if I grew up knowing different things.*

As soon as she was able to sit up, Edge asked Mahali to bring her some ink, a quill, and paper. As the worst of the pain subsided, she wrote down everything she could remember about her experience, just as Mana had taught her to do. She recorded her memories carefully and honestly.

"Don't start asking questions until the details of your observations are recorded," Mana told Edge. "Otherwise, the answers you *expect* to get can change the way you remember things."

When Edge was finished recording everything she could remember, she started asking questions, narrowing the possible answers down to those that seemed the most probable, based on what she knew about the world. *Why can't I communicate with Tsoci when we merge?* she asked herself. *I'm too small. I'm nothing compared to Tsoci,* she answered herself. *If a single one of my cells tried to tell me something, I'd never notice.*

Edge absentmindedly doodled diagrams of different types of cells. *My cells* do *deliver messages I can understand, though,* she realized. *That's how I feel hungry, or tired, or cold. My cells have to work together to tell me things. Maybe communicating with Tsoci is the same.*

Throughout the day, Hiro's patrols searched the rainforest and the extensive, maze-like tunnels of Ruins, but the hideout remained undiscovered. A rotation of guards checked on Jessop from time to time. Eventually, a group of sapiens entered the room carrying a cot, a chamber pot, a bowl of over-ripe fruit, and a pitcher of water. They opened Jessop's cage before leaving and locking the door behind them.

Relieved to be out of the cage, but feeling utterly helpless, Jessop lay down on the cot and waited for Hiro to return.

Chapter Twenty Five

Research

Xalma had never walked so much in her life. By the middle of the first day, her feet were blistered and sore.

"Can I just swim upstream and meet you there?" she begged Cato, wincing with each step.

"You will walk, and you will learn to walk properly," Cato answered sternly.

Throughout the day, Cato commented on Xalma's gait and posture. Time after time, he knocked her over as they trudged uphill, often with just a small nudge. Xalma was exasperated, bruised, and filthy when they finally stopped for the night.

"You made progress today," Cato acknowledged gruffly, "but you will need to work harder tomorrow. You must improve more quickly."

"Improve at *what*?" Xalma demanded. "Falling in the dirt?"

"You need to be faster and stronger to overthrow Tsoci," Cato answered sternly.

"Is Toe Cheese *also* going to shove me around for no reason and tell me I walk funny?" Xalma snarled. "You know what? It doesn't matter! I'm not fighting Toe Cheese! I'm just getting Jessop and going home."

"Fine," Cato growled. "Even if you find your friend, it will be a long, dangerous journey back to Far Crescent. You're weak. Your balance is poor. You do not pay attention to what's happening around you. How will you keep him safe?"

Xalma realized that Cato was right. The next morning, she was ready to try again. Calluses had formed on her blisters, and her wounds had healed.

"You will not always heal so quickly," Cato warned her. "*Now* is the time to perfect your skills and finish becoming who you want to be. Focus on becoming a strong, smart warrior so you can protect your friend."

By midday, Cato could no longer knock her over. By evening, she had learned to strike back fast enough to push him away.

"Very good work today," said Cato approvingly when they stopped for the night. "You're learning quickly. You have earned a reward."

"What's the reward?" asked Xalma eagerly.

"Tomorrow, you will be allowed to swim upstream," answered Cato.

The next morning, Cato led Xalma to the bottom of a cliff covered in waterfalls. Silver streams roared down from unknown, cloud covered heights. Hundreds of ledges jutted from the steep rock wall like fungus on the side of an old tree. Atop the ledges, the water carved shallow, overflowing pools before streaming down the cliff again.

Xalma eyed the turbulent lake at the bottom of the cliff with distaste.

"You're *kidding*, right?" Xalma shook her head.

"I will meet you at the top," said Cato. He leapt into the air and spread his wings. Xalma realized it was the first time she'd seen him fly. As she watched him slowly ascend, she wondered how someone so tiny and old could have so much energy and spite.

Xalma made a valiant effort to swim up the vertical maze of the waterfall, but she quickly grew tired. She was resting in one of the pools, about a third of the way up the cliff, when Cato glided down from above and landed next to her.

"This is no place to stop," he berated her. "Get moving."

"I'm *exhausted*," Xalma snapped. "You can just flap straight up to the top. You have no idea how *hard* this is."

"You said you wanted to swim," Cato reminded her coolly.

"I didn't say I wanted to swim straight up a *mountain*," Xalma complained. "Besides, I don't have as much energy as you."

"I have no more energy than you do," Cato growled. "I just *care* more. I know that many sapiens will die if I do not succeed."

"I can't *care* about sapiens I don't *know*," insisted Xalma.

Cato considered her for a moment.

"Many of those sapiens care about *you*," he said.

"How *can* they care about me?" Xalma asked. "They don't even *know* me."

"All Amphs revere The Child Queen, Your Highness," Cato told Xalma, watching her face carefully. "You give them hope."

As Xalma ascended the rest of the waterfall, she thought about how, when she arrived in Cowrie, she would meet sapiens who cared about her.

Every day, Xalma grew faster, stealthier, and smarter. As they passed through the mountains and started the descent into the rainforest, Cato asked her if she wanted to learn how to fight.

"I thought I *was* learning to fight, Master Cato," she said.

"You have learned to control yourself," Cato answered. "Fighting is about controlling someone else."

"I *definitely* want to learn how to fight," Xalma said enthusiastically.

Cato showed Xalma how to fashion a spear and a bow, and how to wield them. He showed her how to throw a punch, and how to disable opponents by using their weight and momentum against them. Xalma loved sparring. The strength, balance, and speed she developed came together as a kind of dance, and took all her concentration.

She chose traits that make her a great fighter, Cato thought privately. *Yet she would waste them on one outcast Avian traitor. I must guide her mind.*

When Xalma successfully defeated Cato for the third time in a sparring match, he showed her how to use a gun.

"Why didn't we *start* with this?" asked Xalma after shooting a sizable hole in the side of a tree. The power of the gun was exhilarating. Holding it made Xalma feel like she controlled everything she could see.

"This is one of the city's weapons," Cato answered. "Marrow's defenses can kill millions of organisms in less time than it takes for you to blink, without sending a single living soldier to the fight."

"Wow!" Xalma exclaimed. "*We* have guns too, right?"

"Guns are no use against Tsoci," he replied, smiling. "That's why Mana was training your Forax friend. The war against Tsoci will take place inside the minds of sapiens, and Edge was created to have the ability to connect minds."

Xalma felt a twinge of jealousy. "I can do whatever Edge was supposed to do," she said, trying to sound casual.

Cato didn't reply, but he noted her envy.

Xalma didn't want to lead The Resistance, but she wasn't sure what she *did* want. Some of the things Cato told her sounded nice. Xalma thought she would enjoy having a lot of new sapiens who cared about her. She liked the idea of being someone important, but she missed being free to do whatever she wanted. She missed Jessop. She wanted things to go back to the way they used to be, but she also wanted to be famous and admired.

If I control an army, Jessop and his family might be able to go back to Marrow, Xalma thought. *We can all live there together, and I'll never be lonely again. But The Resistance destroyed my home, and Cato is a jerk.*

Cato marched a short distance ahead. Watching him, Xalma felt anger rising inside her. The spines along her back and tail stood on end, and her scales smoldered.

I'll rescue Jessop and take over The Resistance, she decided. *Then I can hang out with Jessop forever, and we can lead Marrow together.*

After several days of rest, Edge finally stumbled from her room.

"I think I know how to get the Insects to go back to their Hive," she announced.

"How?" asked Sole.

"I have to make a Hive Mind," answered Edge.

"If you can start a Hive Mind outside of a Hive, you will have done something that even the Insects have never done," Sole informed her.

"Mahali said Cowrie used to be a Hive. Maybe we can start a Hive here. It's the only way to convince all the Insects to escape at once."

"How will you do this?" Mahali asked in wonder.

Edge looked at Mary, who was sitting quietly nearby.

"If she'll let me, I'd like to merge with Mary," she replied. "Maybe her memories will teach me how a Hive Mind works."

"Will that hurt you?" Mahali asked with concern.

"I don't think so," Edge answered. "I've merged with individual Insects before. It wasn't comfortable, but it didn't hurt."

Sole danced. Even though she knew what Sole was asking, Edge couldn't connect the movements to the question.

Mary dipped her head and twirled, stretching her arms towards Edge.

"She says yes," Sole reported.

Edge finally realized someone was missing. "Where's Jessop?" she asked.

As soon as she understood what had happened, Edge wanted to rescue her friend.

"I can't break him out," Sole told her. "I checked."

"We will have to ask the Insects for help," Mahali said. "While you learn how to make a Hive Mind, I will search for a way to help everyone escape the rainforest." He left without another word.

Edge turned to Mary. "Are you ready?" she asked.

Sole translated the question. Mary approached Edge. Her antennae started to glow.

"Okay," said Edge, squaring her shoulders. "Let's do this."

Mahali had many sources of information. Most of them were sapiens who had been taken from Marrow against their will and forced to join The Resistance. He visited one trusted contact after another, asking for the latest news and hoping to learn something that might inspire an escape plan.

When he learned that a submarine fleet would soon dock in the wide river near the lab, he smiled.

If we can hijack a submarine and make it to the ocean, we can all escape, he thought.

Many of his contacts also mentioned that The Child Queen was returning. At first, Mahali thought it was a joke, but after speaking to almost every one of his connections, he had to admit that they believed what they were saying. He couldn't go back to the hideout yet. Not without finding out whether The Child Queen was really coming to Cowrie. Mahali perched above a pool on the outskirts of Cowrie until nightfall. From the darkness, he heard a group of young Amphs approaching.

If anyone is skeptical about news concerning The Child Queen, it will be the neo Amphs, he thought.

"Hoi! Anchor! Is it true that The Child Queen is coming?" Mahali asked from the shadows of the tree above.

Two of the Amphs jumped in fright, but the third smiled and yelled back into the trees.

"Come down, Mahali. It's rude to lurk in the shadows."

"I am comfortable where I am," Mahali replied calmly.

"The Child Queen is a myth," Anchor replied, walking to the base of the tree and peering up at Mahali.

"Are you certain? I hear she is coming to Cowrie with Cato."

"I wouldn't put it past Cato to show up with some crusty old lizard painted up and trained to be a mythical leader," Anchor sneered. "When he left, he said he was fetching Hiro's magical kid. He's full of lies."

Mahali chuckled.

"Thanks," he said. "I knew you would be honest with me. Hiro's guards believe he is telling the truth."

"Well, that's *Hiro's guards*, right?" Anchor leaned nonchalantly on the trunk of the tree. "They all had their minds wiped. No one I know actually *believes* in The Child Queen."

Without warning, Anchor raced up the tree, her wide, flat fingers and toes sticking effortlessly to the trunk. She climbed quickly, but she was not quick enough to catch Mahali.

"Don't be a stranger, Mahali!" Anchor yelled as Mahali disappeared. "Come back any time!"

"Can you show me how you learned to join the Hive Mind?" Edge asked Mary. Sole translated her words into dance. Edge still couldn't interpret the movements, but Mary seemed to understand.

Edge closed her eyes as Mary's glowing antennae brushed her temples. Mary's memories were difficult to decipher at first. She could see very little, and the sounds were muffled. She slowly realized that she was inside a translucent egg. Occasionally, an Insect passed nearby, casting long, delicate shadows on her shell. Edge recognized the pulsing rhythm of Hive.

This is Mary's childhood! Fascinated, Edge took in every detail.

Outside the shell, mandibles clicked, wings and legs droned, and insectile instruments bellowed and chimed, but Edge could see none of these things. Instead, she heard and felt them. As she listened to the melody, Edge found herself relaxing.

What an amazing lullaby, she thought. She felt Mary's perspective shift. Edge was suddenly perceiving the world from the inside of hundreds of different eggs. The memory shifted again, and Edge saw the world through the segmented eyes of a group of larvae cleaning decaying matter from the forest floor. They moved in unison, tapping a rhythm with their many feet.

With a little concentration, Edge found that she could shift her perspective from all of the larvae at once to Mary's individual awareness. The music was louder and more present when she was perceiving the world as an individual. She was aware of the rich scents of loamy peat, pine needles, and the dusty spores of ferns and moss.

Edge was familiar with all of the smells, but as the Hive Mind, she understood their full message for the first time.

We appreciate you, Tsoci proclaimed joyfully. *You are a good part of us. You will be welcomed back when your tasks are done.*

"It's been an hour," Sole said, gently removing Mary's antennae from Edge's temples. "Are you both okay?"

Mary bowed her head and looked at Edge. An inquisitive smell wafted through the air, and Edge understood that the Insect was wondering whether the memories she'd shared had been useful.

"That was so helpful, Mary! Does every Insect learn the egg dance?" Edge asked hopefully.

Mary clicked affirmatively.

Edge turned to Sole. "I have a theory. I need to write."
Sole nodded. "I'll get your papers."

Chapter Twenty Six

Manipulation

A burly Forax with long incisors and a wide, flat tail appeared in Jessop's cell and ushered him back into the cage.

Bewildered, Jessop watched as a group of sapiens entered the room and installed wainscotting and finely carved wooden trim. The harsh electric lights were replaced with simple, warm oil lamps. Abstract paintings were arranged on the walls. Jessop's hard prison cot was swapped for a comfortable hammock. Finally, a proper dining table was carried in, surrounded by perches and topped with bowls full of berries and nuts.

Jessop's attempts to convince any of the sapiens to talk to him failed. They didn't acknowledge him at all, except to shift his cage so they could lay down a plush, colorful rug.

When they were done, the burly Forax returned and opened the cage door, motioning for Jessop to come out.

"What's going on?" Jessop asked as he left the cage.

The Forax silently dismantled the cage and carried it out of the room, leaving Jessop to wonder what his upgraded prison conditions could possibly mean.

Definitely something bad, he concluded.

A hundred sapien soldiers met Cato and Xalma at the edge of the rainforest. Xalma was surprised that they were so young. None of them were Amphs.

"They're just kids," Xalma said, "like Jessop and Edge! What are they doing here?"

"They are here to protect you," Cato said. "Hiro sent them to meet us. The rainforest is full of jackbears and thornwolves, and other, even more dangerous creatures, and they are closely connected to Tsoci. Sapiens are not safe in the rainforest unless they are in Cowrie."

Why is Cowrie safe?" Xalma asked curiously.

"Tsoci doesn't know we're there yet, and the animals rarely enter the city," Cato replied. "We must be silent now."

Avians flew ahead of them, patrolling the canopy. Groups of Forax walked in formation around Cato and Xalma, alert for signs of danger. The first attack came only an hour into the journey. Although Xalma had never seen a thornwolf, Jessop had described them. The animals that appeared out of the shadows and dragged several soldiers away were bigger, faster, and more terrifying than Xalma could have imagined.

Cato and a group of soldiers pulled Xalma away from the blood curdling screams as a group of young soldiers pursued the thornwolf pack. Xalma heard the snap of gunshots, and the rainforest grew silent again.

"What happened to the soldiers?" Xalma asked anxiously. "Are they okay?"

"We always lose a few sapiens when we walk through the rainforest," Cato said. "The thornwolves should never have been allowed so close."

"Couldn't someone carry us over the trees?"

"The animals in the upper canopy will attack anything that doesn't move very quickly. Hunting above the trees is easier than hunting below. But you make a good point. Your friend may be able to fly, but surely he cannot lift you anymore. Who's going to carry you back out?" Cato asked. "Pay attention to the forest, Xalma. I want you to be prepared when you venture back."

Xalma noticed eyes peering from the shadows and her heart raced. Half-seen creatures skittered and skulked in the darkness. Xalma glimpsed them out of the corner of her eye, but they were always gone by the time she turned her head.

There were several attacks throughout the day, but Xalma didn't see another animal, and the sounds of the attacks were distant. The soldiers guarding the perimeter kept anything dangerous from getting within Xalma's line of sight.

"Your friend Jessop is the son of Ashmara and Harbeshi, is he not?" Cato inquired, noticing Xalma's nervousness.

The question caught Xalma off guard. "How do you know that?" she asked.

"The Avian outcasts are quite famous," Cato smiled. "You see, Harbeshi and Ashmara started the most recent war in Marrow."

"That's stupid," Xalma declared confidently. Although she'd never been particularly interested in their past, Jessop and Ashmara talked about it a great deal. "Jessop's family was *escaping* the war. They didn't *cause* it. They were just trying to save their friends."

"Harbeshi and Ashmara were Ambassadors, but they turned on their own race," Cato informed her. "Perhaps they *were* trying to save their Amph friends, but that does not change the fact that they betrayed the Avians and started a war."

Xalma snorted in disbelief, but she felt a twinge of doubt.

"Haven't you ever wondered why *Avians* were sent to guard you, rather than Amphs?"

"The *Deejii* are my guardians," Xalma argued.

"The Deejii are supposed to be your *friends*, but you don't *have* any friends, do you, Xalma?" Cato fixed her with a knowing look. "Jessop isn't a real friend. You know that, right?"

"Shut up," snapped Xalma.

Cato continued, still speaking calmly and reasonably, as though explaining something obvious to a stubborn child.

"Harbeshi and Ashmara betrayed the Avians and helped the Amphs gain control of Marrow."

A chill shot down Xalma's spine despite the damp heat of the rainforest.

"Many Avians died because of them," Cato added.

"Jessop cares about me. He's my best friend," Xalma growled. "You don't even *know* him."

"Perhaps," Cato agreed smoothly. "Though I wonder why Jessop and his family did not encourage you to leave The Grotto, or tell you who you were. Instead, they kept you ignorant. That does not sound like something a friend would do."

Xalma stalked ahead of Cato and refused to talk to him for the rest of the day. When they stopped for the night, Xalma camped as far from Cato as she could, while soldiers stood guard around her.

The attacks became less frequent over the course of the next day, but Xalma still caught glimpses of bright eyes and bristling shadows lurking in the darkness. She was relieved when they reached the border of Cowrie.

Every sapien in Cowrie seemed to know Xalma was coming. Young Amphs watched her from the ponds, their sparking scales and bright eyes twinkling through the mist. Flocks of Avians swooped through the air and perched on the overhead branches. Sapiens scurried out of buildings and climbed down from trees to watch as Xalma slowly made her way down a well-trodden path towards the middle of Cowrie.

There are so many of them, Xalma thought in wonder.

She enjoyed the attention. Their soldier-escort formed a barrier around Xalma and Cato, preventing the other sapiens from coming too close.

"Hi!" Xalma called cheerfully, waving to her new followers.

They smiled and whispered to one another. By the time they reached the center of Cowrie, Xalma's following had grown. The soldiers raised a barrier, keeping the onlookers at the edge of the square.

Hiro met them, flanked by his guards.

"Cato!" Hiro exclaimed. "Welcome back!" He turned to Xalma and bowed low.

"It is an honor, Your Highness."

The guards on either side of Hiro bowed and did not rise. Xalma realized they were bowing to her. She squirmed uncomfortably.

"I look forward to updating you, Hiro," Cato said. "Has the fleet arrived?"

"They will dock tomorrow," Hiro replied. "A comfortable home has been prepared for you. You have time to rest."

Hiro turned to Xalma and indicated the prostrate guards. "Your Highness, my soldiers are at your command."

"Um, thanks," said Xalma. "Can I see Jessop now?"

"Have you prepared Her Highness' friend according to my instructions?" Cato asked.

"Every detail was followed exactly," Hiro confirmed.

Cato nodded and the guards rose to their feet.

"Follow us, Your Highness," they said.

"I will return shortly," Cato told Hiro as he departed with Xalma. The onlookers continued to follow them. Xalma could hear laughter and shouts of surprise. The soldiers continued to form a living wall between Xalma and her admirers.

Cato was right, these sapiens do *care about me,* Xalma thought. *Wait until Jessop sees this!*

Mahali was on his way back to the hideout when the soldiers appeared.

Why are they marching through Cowrie? he wondered. When he saw Cato and Xalma in the middle of the crowd, Mahali's heart skipped a beat.

Cato did *find The Child Queen.*

Mahali followed the crowd as Cato and Xalma were escorted to the prison. He overheard snippets of gossip as he made his way closer to Cato and the Amph.

"Did you *see* her? Her stripes are red!"

"I thought for sure that this was just some trick of Hiro's, but she looks real."

"That's the scariest Amph I ever saw."

Mahali slipped through the crowd until he was close enough to overhear the conversation between Cato and The Child Queen.

"I haven't changed my mind," Xalma said. "These sapiens seem cool and this place is nice, but I still don't want to lead The Resistance. I just want to rescue Jessop."

"You may find that there is nothing to rescue him from," Cato replied pleasantly, "but if you wish to leave Cowrie with the son of traitors, we will not keep you here. You may go."

"Really?" Xalma asked doubtfully.

"I had hoped to change your mind," Cato answered, looking disappointed, "but it's clear to me that you do not have the qualities of a leader. We will find someone more suitable."

"Oh," said Xalma. "Okay. Good."

"I will say goodbye to you here," Cato said as they reached the heavily guarded door into the prison. "Is everything ready?" he asked.

"Her Highness is cleared to proceed," barked one of the guards.

The door opened and Xalma was ushered inside. "Thank you for everything, Master Cato," she said, pausing in the doorway.

"I'm sorry I expected too much of you," Cato replied, "I hope you are able to return to The Grotto. Perhaps you can continue as you were before, and forget this ever happened. You may never be a child again, but I'm sure you've learned a great deal about forgetting things that you'd prefer not to remember."

The door closed before Xalma could reply.

Mahali perched in a tree nearby. He was the only one who noticed the satisfied smile on Cato's face as he walked away from the prison.

"The Child Queen needs time to decide whether she wants to lead The Resistance," Cato announced to the crowd. "We must all do our best to make her feel welcome here. Hiro will make an announcement about our future the evening after tomorrow."

After the crowd dispersed, Cato turned to the soldiers guarding the prison door.

"When she leaves, follow her. Do not let her out of your sight. She will lead you to Hiro's daughter."

Mahali waited and watched from the shadows of the trees.

Mary remembered a huge, dead fish, washed up on the shore. Hive Mind asked Tsoci what to do, communicating their question with a frenzied burst of chemicals. Tsoci's answer was complicated and subtle. The Insects followed Tsoci's instructions, carrying moss and mushrooms to the carcass and placing them gently in the sand next to the body. Mycelium penetrated the dead creature. It swelled and burst, releasing a cloud of smells that communicated the story of the creature's death and its composition. Hive Mind used this information to transform the carcass, returning the components to the body of Tsoci.

Edge explored the memory, taking note of every detail. It was a difficult task. Edge's language relied mainly on sounds, symbols, and patterns. Tsoci's language was made of chemicals and interactions, interpreted by senses that Edge could only experience through Mary's memory.

Mary's Hive was not the Hive Edge knew. The flowers and plants were unfamiliar. The air was warmer, the sun higher in the sky. When she was done merging, Edge wrote down everything she could remember. She asked questions. Sole translated the questions, and Mary answered them. Edge wrote everything down.

"Where was Mary born?" Edge asked.

Sole squatted down and traced the shape of a circle. Mary faced the southern wall of the room and Edge could smell dust and salt and rain.

"Mary says there's a new Hive at the end of the southern desert," Sole explained. "That's where she's from. It's strange though..."

"What is?" Edge asked.

"When I collected the report from the Insects, they didn't tell me there was a new Hive," Sole replied thoughtfully.

"Maybe they didn't know?"

"Maybe. Or maybe they thought Tsoci already knew," Sole mused.

"Can Insects tell lies?" Edge asked.

Sole covered both eyes with one hand, and their mouth with the other. The rover swayed like a reed in a strong wind, breaking and crumpling to the floor.

"Are you okay?" Edge asked with concern.

"Of course," Sole answered, standing up. "I was translating your question."

Mary spread her arms and opened her mouthparts wide.

"She says no. Insects can't deceive each other because a Hive Mind requires honesty."

"Can a Hive Mind be deceived, though?"

Sole looked puzzled. "What do you mean?"

"Does Mary know what The Great Pact is?"

Sole's interpretation of the question was clumsier than usual, but Mary understood.

"Tsoci told Hive Mind to... help The Resistance destroy Marrow." Sole translated as Mary danced around the room. "Hive formed a pact with the sapiens... in Cowrie? What?" Sole looked confused. "That can't be right, can it?"

"That means Tsoci is *helping* Hiro." Edge frowned. "Why would Tsoci do that? Why would they send Insects here to die?"

"I don't know," Sole replied. "It doesn't seem right. Maybe The Resistance *did* deceive Hive. But how?"

"Maybe Mary knows?" Edge suggested.

"She won't," Sole replied without asking Mary. "She wasn't there. It happened before she was born."

"Mary's still a child?" Edge was shocked.

"Most of the Insects here are children. So are most of the sapiens."

"Can you show me your family?" Edge asked Mary gently. "I'd like to learn more about where you come from."

"She says she'd like to learn about your family, too," Sole replied when he'd relayed Edge's question.

When they merged again, Mary remembered making music with her friends, and Edge remembered studying the Insects with Mana. Mary shared the feeling of being connected to a big family. Edge shared the freedom of a childhood spent alone. Mary and Edge enjoyed exchanging their unique perspectives. They found places where their experiences overlapped, but they became friends because of their differences.

When she and Mary were finished, Edge spent many hours reviewing her notes and thinking about how to help the rest of the Insects.

"Music is the secret to making a Hive Mind. It helps the Insects align their thoughts and feelings," Edge explained. "If we're going to convince the Insects to leave, we're going to need a way to make music with all of them."

"Your plan sounds surprisingly simple and incredibly hard at the same time," Sole observed. "Where do we start." "I have no idea," Edge replied wearily. "We'll figure something out," Sole assured her optimistically. "You should get some sleep. I'll keep watch." Edge could barely keep her eyes open long enough to trudge back to bed, but she felt a glimmer of hope.

Mary curled up next to Edge, her cool, smooth body pressed against Edge's side. Edge leaned against Mary's sturdy back and gently stroked her antennae.

"Isn't it lonely without a Hive?" Edge asked quietly.

Mary clicked her mandibles sadly. For a few moments, Edge thought she could smell the ocean.

Chapter Twenty Seven

Reunion

Saving Jessop was Xalma's sole purpose. Her smoldering scales, her poisonous spines, and her towering, muscular body were all traits she'd chosen so she could rescue Jessop and keep him safe. Until now, she had not considered how Jessop would react to her new appearance.

What if he doesn't like me anymore? Xalma worried.

She followed the guards down a dark, damp hallway lined with heavy doors. Xalma had lived her entire life inside a windowless cave, so she didn't think windows were important. She had no idea she was inside a prison. The door opened into a comfortable, tastefully decorated room. Jessop was perched next to a table eating grapes. Their eyes met. Xalma stooped under the doorframe and entered the room.

"What do you want?" Jessop snapped angrily. "When are you going to let me go?"

"Hey Jessop. It's me..." Before Xalma could finish, Jessop hopped across the entire length of the room and crushed her in a fierce embrace, tears streaming from his eyes. The top of his head barely reached her chin.

"You're *alive!*" he managed to squeak between sobs. "Oh Xalma, you're *alive!*" The two friends shared a brief moment of absolute happiness.

Jessop looked closely at his friend. Spikes crowned Xalma's head, and dangerous looking spines cascaded down her back like a mane. Her body was armored with obsidian scales. Red stripes framed her face, slashing across her broad shoulders and limbs. Xalma looked strong and deadly, from her clawed hands to the spiny fin on the tip of her tail. She reminded Jessop of the beautiful, poisonous fish in The Grotto.

"You look *incredible!*" Jessop gasped. "How did this happen? Did it hurt? How did you find me?"

"I transformed!" Xalma answered. "Just like Ashmara said I would! When I was done, I woke up on a submarine with a bunch of sapiens!" Xalma fixed Jessop with a stern gaze. "One of them was named Cato and he said you were going to join The Resistance. I'm here to rescue you."

"You *know* Cato?" Jessop asked in surprise.

"Yeah, he brought me here to find you," Xalma answered. "He said I could take you home."

Something about Xalma's story didn't feel right. Mahali had described Cato as an enemy. Why would he just let Jessop and Xalma walk away?

"I'm not here to join The Resistance," Jessop said firmly. "Cato lied to you. The Resistance caught me and locked me up. You can't trust Cato."

"Oh, I *totally don't* trust him," Xalma answered, rolling her eyes. "He *sucks*. That's why we should get out of here *right now*. I don't know how hard it's going to be to get away from him, but I'm ready to fight if we have to."

Xalma's scales smoldered.

"Me too," Jessop agreed boldly. "Let's go."

Xalma knocked on the door. To Jessop's surprise, the guards opened it and allowed them both to pass into the hall. Jessop followed Xalma down the passage, up the stairs, and out of the door. A growing crowd of curious sapiens followed them as they walked through Cowrie, but no one stopped them.

Mahali followed Xalma and Jessop away from the prison, hiding among the following crowd. As soon as he was sure of their direction, he left the crowd and flew ahead.

"Where are we going?" Jessop asked, eyeing the crowds apprehensively.

"Anywhere but here," Xalma answered. "I just want some privacy. We have to get away from all these sapiens."

"Why are they following you?" Jessop asked. "Do you know?"

"They want me to be their *leader*," Xalma snorted.

"Whoa," Jessop gasped.

"If I'm in charge of The Resistance, I can make sure nothing happens to you and your family." Xalma looked at Jessop. "I'll do it if you want me to."

"I… well, that's *really* nice of you, Xalma," Jessop said, "but the sapiens here, Cato and Hiro and The Resistance, they do really bad things. I don't think you should get involved with them."

"Oh. Okay," Xalma replied. Her new face was better at hiding her feelings, so Jessop couldn't see Xalma's disappointment.

The trees around them were heavy with buildings full of machines and wires. Thick bundles of pipes connected the buildings, running from tree to tree. Sapiens continued to follow Xalma and Jessop, but it was difficult to see anything but flashing eyes and teeth through the growing darkness.

Jessop was about to suggest that they go back when screams erupted from the crowd. Sapiens around them started panicking and running away. Jessop and Xalma looked around fearfully, but they couldn't see any reason for the screaming.

"Let's get out of here," suggested Jessop, his eyes wide with fear.

They raced through the murky twilight, dodging around the complicated shapes of what Jessop now thought of as machine-trees. A scream just ahead stopped them in their tracks. A moment later, the air was full of shrieks and wails. Jessop and Xalma ducked into a narrow alley and crouched in the shadows between two buildings.

The screams grew louder. Someone landed in the alley with them.

"Follow me," said a voice.

Xalma pounced on the newcomer, pinning him to the ground.

"Mahali, is that you?" Jessop asked.

"Yes," Mahali coughed, struggling to breathe under Xalma's weight.

"He's a friend, Xalma!" Jessop said, pulling Xalma off Mahali.

"Sorry to frighten you," Mahali said when Xalma released him. "I used screamers to drive the crowd away. The sound of screaming usually means someone is being attacked by the creatures of the rainforest. We have to escape before they realize no one was attacked. They will try to find you again." Mahali didn't wait for a reply. He ducked into the shadows, leading them from shadow to shadow until they reached the base of a wide tree.

"Jessop cannot carry you on his own, Your Highness," he explained, "so they will not expect you to be in the air. With your permission, we will carry you through the trees together. We can fly safely under the canopy as long as we remain quiet."

"Whatever gets us out of here is fine with me," Xalma agreed.

Mahali perched on Xalma's shoulders and, with extreme difficulty, lifted her a few inches off the ground. Jessop put his arms around Xalma's waist and wrapped his taloned feet around each of her legs, pulling her body horizontally into the air. Together, they rose through the branches.

"This is *fun!*" Xalma squealed with delight.

"Please remain silent, Your Highness," Mahali whispered.

Xalma watched the forest floor fall away. As they ascended, the light increased. Soon they were soaring, almost silently, just under the leafy ceiling of the rainforest.

Xalma managed to remain quiet for the rest of the trip. Mahali lowered her onto a branch and explained that they were going into a tunnel as soon as they reached the ground. Xalma grinned and nodded, but she didn't make a sound. When they reached the end of the tunnel, Mahali pushed a pile of furniture aside and they crawled into the hideout.

"Edge! Sole!" Jessop called at once. "Xalma's here! She's alive!"

"Welcome back!" Sole answered cheerfully. The rover was keeping watch alone. "Edge and Mary are sleeping. You look *great*, Xalma! Now that you're here, we'll be able to finish the task in no time!"

"*What* task?" Xalma asked.

"We have to help Edge," Jessop replied, "Tsoci sent her here to find out why she exists."

"I'm not here to help *her*," Xalma objected. "I'm here to help *you*."

"I know." Jessop smiled at Xalma reassuringly. "I'm really grateful. Let's talk about it in the morning, okay? I was in that prison for a really long time. I need some sleep."

Xalma thought about the newly renovated room where she'd found Jessop. "*I've* been walking and sleeping on the ground for *days*, and *I* don't need sleep," she grumbled.

Mahali broke the awkward silence. "I am sure your stamina is much greater than ours, Your Highness," he said with a polite bow. "You are The Child Queen, after all. Still, I think you will enjoy a warm bed after your long travels."

I guess it would *be nice to rest somewhere comfortable,* Xalma realized.

"Fine," agreed Xalma.

Jessop hugged her and said goodnight, and Mahali led her away, returning briefly.

"You did not tell me you knew The Child Queen," Mahali said, looking at Jessop and Sole intently.

"I thought she was dead," Jessop replied honestly.

"Are you certain she is truly who she claims to be?" asked Mahali.

"She's definitely The Child Queen," Sole confirmed. "It's a really good sign that she's here, too. Tomorrow will be interesting."

"What are you talking about?" Jessop asked, but Sole only winked and disappeared into their room.

"I am very glad you are safe," Mahali said quietly. "I would still like to teach you to dance."

Before Jessop could reply, Mahali followed Sole's example.

Jessop tiptoed quietly into the room he shared with Edge. She was fast asleep. The joy and confusion of rediscovering Xalma kept him awake for a long time. Jessop still cared about Xalma, but he didn't feel like he knew her anymore.

"It's *amazing* to see you, Xalma!" Edge exclaimed.

Sole was resting, and Mary was still asleep. Mahali, Jessop, Edge and Xalma gathered in the main area of the hideout.

Seeing Jessop and Edge together made Xalma uncomfortable. "I came here to get Jessop," she declared. "He's basically my only friend."

"Well, we're all really glad to see you!" Edge replied, ignoring Jessop's awkward cough. "We had no idea how to get Jessop out of that prison. Even Sole couldn't do it. Mahali said you just walked right out with him!"

"Cato let them go. He was hoping to have them followed," Mahali said.

"Followed?" Jessop asked. "Here?"

"Oh yeah, that makes sense," Xalma said. "Cato wants to find Edge. Ha! I bet he thought we'd lead him right to her! I wish I could see his face right now."

"Why does he want to find Edge?" Jessop asked.

"Cato wants *you* to lead The Resistance, Edge." Xalma chuckled. "He wants you to defeat Tsoci. That's his big plan."

"Well, that's not going to happen," Edge replied. "The Resistance is terrible. Did Jessop tell you what they're doing to the Insects?"

"Speaking of Insects, this is Mary," Jessop said as Mary and Sole joined them.

"Uh, nice to meet you," Xalma said insincerely. The rescue she'd been planning was unravelling.

"Have you figured out a way to convince the Insects to leave Cowrie?" Mahali asked Edge.

"I think I know what we have to do," Edge replied, "but I'm not sure how to do it. The Insects use music to form a Hive Mind. We have to help them make music together."

"What *exactly* is this task you're doing?" Xalma asked.

"This isn't the task. The Resistance is hurting Insects," Jessop explained. "Sole convinced Mary to escape, but the rest of the Insects think they're supposed to be in the lab, even if they're being hurt. We want to help them escape."

"So what?" Xalma asked callously. "No offense, but that's none of our business, is it?"

Edge frowned.

"Xalma!" Jessop scolded. "Mary is our friend! Friends help each other. Don't be a jerk."

"I just don't understand why it's *your* problem," Xalma insisted. "Why can't Mary rescue her *own* friends? *I* don't expect *her* to help me rescue *you*."

Jessop looked like he was about to lose his temper, something Mahali very wisely understood would not be a good idea. He quickly changed the subject.

"I may have found a way for the Insects to get home safely," he said. "A fleet of submarines is arriving today."

"What's a submarine?" asked Edge.

"It's a big boat that travels underwater, I came most of the way here on one," Xalma answered, her tone suggesting that Edge ought to have known.

"Do you know how many submarines are in the fleet, Your Highness?" Mahali asked politely.

Xalma shrugged. "A lot. Way more than fifty."

"How many Insects can fit on a submarine?" Edge asked.

"How should *I* know?" Xalma answered. "Just because I got *abducted* by one doesn't mean I'm an *expert*." *Cato was right,* she thought bitterly. *Jessop has new friends now. He doesn't need me to rescue him.*

"Do you know how many *sapiens* can fit on a submarine?" Jessop pressed.

"It's not like I was counting them," Xalma answered sullenly. "I was too busy trying to keep them from *killing* me."

"Look, Xalma," Jessop said firmly, "I'm *really* glad you're here. I thought I'd lost you forever. I'm so grateful that you came to find me, but I'm not the only one in danger here. We have to save the Insects. Will you help us?"

"Maybe a hundred," she sulked.

"What?"

"I think a hundred Insects could fit on a submarine," Xalma answered tonelessly. "If they're all the same size as this one." She glanced at Mary.

"We only need one submarine," Edge concluded. "That's good, right?"

"I can probably just order The Resistance to let the Insects go, and *give* you a submarine," Xalma offered. "I'm in charge here, if I want to be."

"We can't trust Hiro and Cato," said Edge firmly. "We'll find another way to get a submarine."

"Well, since you obviously don't need *my* help, I guess I'll just *leave*," Xalma snarled. She stomped to her room and slammed the door.

"She is not what I expected," Mahali said quietly.

Jessop sighed and stood up. "She's been through a lot. I'll talk to her."

Chapter Twenty Eight

Jealousy

When Xalma didn't answer Jessop's soft knock, he opened the door very slightly and whispered.
"Can I come in?"
Jessop could hear Xalma crying in the darkness. He slipped into the room and put a hand on her shoulder, waiting for her tears to subside.

"I… don't know… what to do," Xalma gasped. "I thought... when I found you… you'd *want* to be with me. You don't *like* me anymore, do you?"

"Of *course* I like you, Xalma," Jessop replied quietly.

"Why are you helping Edge and an Insect and sapiens you barely *know*, then?" Xalma asked. "Why won't you *leave* with me? We could go right now."

"It wouldn't be right," Jessop explained gently. "I can't leave if I know I can help someone who's in trouble."

"I was going to lead The Resistance to Marrow and make it safe for you and your family," Xalma said sadly.

"I *do* want to go to Marrow with you," Jessop assured her, "but there are right ways and wrong ways to get there. Leading an army into a battle you don't understand is the wrong way."

They sat in silence for a long time.

"I don't like sharing you with other friends," Xalma confessed.

"You never had to before," Jessop replied sympathetically. "They're also *your* friends. I'll be sharing you, too."

"I don't trust them." Xalma's eyes flashed in the darkness and her smoldering scales filled the room with a soft orange glow. "They don't care about you as much as I do. I've known you the longest."

"Friendship isn't a contest, Xalma."

"I want things to go back to the way they were," said Xalma, looking confused. "Well, no. I don't. I'm *glad* I can learn things now. I'm *strong* now. The Amphs all love me. Maybe I *should* lead The Resistance. At least they *want* me."

"Cato just wants to use you." Jessop held Xalma's gaze. "He doesn't care about you, Xalma. He's a jerk; you said it yourself."

"Cato cares about me enough to tell me the *truth*," Xalma
insisted, sitting up and staring back at Jessop with an
intensity he'd never seen before. "You and your family just
wanted to keep me trapped and helpless forever."

"You know that's not true!" Jessop met Xalma's burning
gaze. "My parents wanted to keep us safe. They kept secrets
from me, too!"

"Your parents lied to both of us. Cato told me *they* started
the war. Don't you think they should have *told* us that? I *hate*
them!" Xalma's scales flared like embers in a high wind, and
her eyes flashed.

Jessop fell back in surprise.

"Cato lied to you, Xalma," he argued. "He lied about me
joining The Resistance, and he lied about my parents. He's
just messing with you, manipulating you."

"I don't think he was lying about this." Xalma sounded
uncertain.

"My mother cares about you. My father did, too. He... he
died keeping watch over you when The Grotto was
destroyed."

"Harbeshi's not dead!" Xalma replied in surprise. Her
rage subsided a little when she remembered Harbeshi's
kindness. "He helped me transform."

"My dad is *alive*?" Jessop stood up. "Why didn't you *tell*
me?"

"I didn't know you thought he was dead," Xalma
answered honestly. "Who else do you think is dead?"

Jessop wrapped his arms around Xalma joyfully.

"This is amazing!" Jessop cried. "I thought I'd lost both of
you forever!"

"I thought I'd lost you, too," Xalma said, the last of her
anger subsiding.

"I care about you *so* much," Jessop whispered. "I'm *really* glad you're here. I know a lot has changed, but we'll get through it together, okay? I'll go to Marrow with you when we're done helping Edge. Just promise me you won't go back to Cato."

"I promise," Xalma agreed. "Thanks Jessop. You're my best friend."

"The Child Queen seems a bit insecure," Mahali observed. "Have you known her for a long time?"

"No," Edge answered. "I met her about a month ago. Before Jessop and I left, her home was completely destroyed. We thought she was dead."

"I am worried about what Cato has told her," Mahali admitted. "Insecure sapiens are easy for him to manipulate."

"I don't think Xalma will do anything bad." Edge spoke with confidence, despite her nagging doubt. "She gets jealous sometimes, but she cares about Jessop. She just wants him to be safe."

Mahali looked uncertain, but before he could voice his concerns, Jessop and Xalma returned.

"I still don't really know what happened to you Edge. After I left, I mean." Jessop said. "I'm sorry about that, by the way, I shouldn't have panicked."

"You followed your feelings and did what you thought was the right thing to do at the time," Sole interjected. "If you hadn't been caught, Xalma might not be with us."

"I guess that's true," Jessop admitted.

"I wrote down what happened when I merged," Edge said quickly. "You can catch up when we have more time. It was confusing and it hurt a lot."

"Won't merging with a Hive Mind hurt?" Jessop asked.

"Merging with a Hive Mind is different from merging with Tsoci," Edge replied. "When I merge with Tsoci, I become a very tiny, very spread out part of something really big. I'm too scattered to think. Hive Minds spread their thoughts across a lot of different individuals, but the individuals don't lose themselves. No two Insects understand everything the Hive Mind is thinking, but when Hive Mind decides something, all the Insects know why they're all agreeing."

"What if an Insect doesn't like one of Hive Mind's decisions?" Jessop asked.

"Insects think of themselves as 'we' most of the time," Edge said after concentrating on her memories. "They don't think the way we do. The opinion of the group means more than the opinion of a single Insect."

Mahali looked impressed. "You have an astonishing gift, Edge."

"There's a song every Insect hears when they first learn to join the Hive Mind," Edge continued. "If the Insects in the lab hear that song and join in, I think it will make a Hive Mind. Mary knows the song, but I have no idea how to get the music into the lab."

"What about my screamers?" Mahali said. "They amplify sound."

"That's how you distracted the sapiens who were following us, isn't it?" Jessop realized.

Mahali opened his sack and removed a handful of tiny disks.

"Yes," he said. "I placed screamers around the buildings ahead of you. There are only a few left, though. We would have to place them very carefully."

Edge was confused. "I don't understand how screaming will help with this."

"We can use the screamers to make *any* sound louder," Mahali explained. "They were called 'talkers' until sapiens started using them to scare other sapiens. If we put screamers around the lab, the Insects will be able to hear Mary's song. There is still a problem, though."

"What's that?" Jessop asked. He examined one of the screamers with interest.

"These disks can receive sound, and they can transmit sound, but they cannot do both at once," Mahali explained. "Either the Insects will be able to hear us, or they will be able to share their song with others. They will not be able to hear us and make music at the same time."

"What if we place two of them together, and set one for only listening and one for singing?" Jessop pointing at a button underneath a tiny display. "This has a lot of settings for something so tiny."

"If we double them up, we have just enough of them to place two screamers at the end of every hallway," Mahali said, "but we will have to do it without being seen."

"I can do it!" Sole exclaimed. "I'll use the escape tunnel Mary and I made to get back into the lab. Once I'm inside, I can move so quickly no one will see me."

Mahali passed the screamers to Sole. "I will keep two of them. We will need them to start the song."

"Okay, that's half a plan," said Jessop when Sole had departed. "How are we going to get a submarine?"

"The submarines dock in the river near the lab," Mahali replied. "They will be guarded, but I do not believe the guards will be prepared to fend off all the Insects at once. If we move quickly, we may be able to capture one before it can submerge."

"Cato has a gun," Xalma said. "A lot of the soldiers have guns. They'll just shoot everyone who tries to escape."

"Good point, Your Highness," said Mahali. "Outside the prison, I heard Cato announce that Hiro and the other leaders are addressing The Resistance in the square tomorrow evening. We should try to get to the submarines while everyone is distracted."

"That doesn't give us very much time," Edge said. "What if the Insects won't leave? We don't even know for sure if my idea will work."

"If it doesn't work, we'll hide and think of something else," Jessop said. "It's the only plan we've got."

"Great, your plan is done," Xalma said. "Do you have anything to eat around here?"

"Of course. You must be hungry," Mahali said. "I will prepare some food, Your Highness."

"Just call me Xalma," she replied, eagerly following him to the kitchen.

"She's changed a lot, hasn't she?" Edge asked quietly.

"She's growing up," Jessop replied. "She said my dad is alive!"

"Oh Jessop, that's great!" exclaimed Edge.

"Xalma thinks she can make Marrow safe for my family again," Jessop continued. "I'd like to help her once we rescue the Insects. She needs to fix things in Marrow. That's her job."

"Are you sure?" Edge asked. "That sounds pretty dangerous."

"Yes. Will you be okay? Do you think you can figure out why you exist?"

"I'll be fine," Edge said, turning away. "Sole will help me. We'll figure it out after we save the Insects."

"I'm sure you'll be okay," Jessop grinned. "You're the smartest sapien I've ever met. Xalma needs me. If I don't help her, she might get into serious trouble."

"Yeah, you're right," Edge agreed. "She listens to you."

"All the screamers are in place," Sole reported when they returned from the lab. "Also, the submarines are here. There sure are a lot of them."

Mary was trying to teach Edge, Jessop, and Mahali the egg dance. Since it was a dance used to teach unhatched Insects to join Hive Mind, it wasn't very difficult, but it didn't come naturally to the sapiens.

"You all look *ridiculous*," laughed Xalma.

"It's *really* fun, Xalma. You should try it!" Jessop exclaimed as Mahali twirled around him. "If this works, it's going to be the coolest rescue party ever!"

Mahali caught the look on Xalma's face. He offered to pack supplies for the rescue so that she could dance with Jessop, but she still refused to dance. In the end, all three of them headed to the kitchen to pack food and supplies, leaving Edge, Sole, and Mary to practice.

"What was it like to transform?" Jessop asked Xalma.

"I thought I was going to die," Xalma answered matter-of-factly. "Then I fell asleep and my cells all rearranged themselves. I woke up on a boat full of sapiens who wanted to kill me for no reason, and I did everything I could to stay alive so I could rescue you."

"Thank you," Jessop said gratefully.

Xalma smiled.

No one knew how difficult it was going to be to rescue the Insects, or how long it might take. They decided to go to sleep early, and Mahali slipped out to collect as much food as possible. Even though he knew how important it was to be well rested for the rescue, Jessop couldn't sleep. He slipped out of his room. A few candles were burning, and a low fire glowed in the hearth.

He was leafing through Edge's notes when Mahali returned.

"Have you looked at these?" Jessop asked without looking up from the papers he held.

"Yes," Mahali nodded. "Edge has an impressive mind."

"She's just a kid, though." Jessop looked up at Mahali, his eyes full of tears. "The way she describes the pain... no one should feel like that! She said it felt like nothing mattered. She stopped caring about being herself. What if that happens to her tomorrow?"

"She said merging with a Hive Mind was different," Mahali replied slowly.

"She's twelve years old and all this stuff just happened to her. If this happened to me, I'd have no idea how to deal with it." Jessop stood up and started pacing. "Maybe we shouldn't be letting her do this."

"If you think it will hurt her, we can find another way," Mahali said consolingly. "Maybe Mary can tell the Insects, and Edge will not have to merge. We can talk about it in the morning."

"I'd feel a lot better things if Edge didn't have to risk herself again." Jessop started walking back to his room, but Mahali stopped him.

"Would you..." Mahali hesitated.

"What?" asked Jessop.

"Would you like to dance with me?" Mahali's eyes glowed like moons in the candlelight.

"Um, okay," Jessop answered shyly. "But I don't know if I can do it without Mary guiding us."

Mahali looked excited and nervous.

"Avians have dances, too," he said.

"Really?" Jessop was intrigued. "I don't know much about Avians. I was raised with the Amphs."

"It shows," Mahali smiled. "You are different from other Avians."

"I'm sorry," Jessop apologized. "You must really miss your friends."

"I do not think it is bad that you are different," Mahali hastened to explain. "You are more open. Kinder."

"Oh," said Jessop. He wasn't sure what else to say, so he returned to the subject of dancing. "What are you going to show me?"

"We will need music," Mahali said. He held out a screamer.

Jessop looked alarmed. "Won't that thing wake everyone up?"

"I have adjusted the volume," Mahali explained. "I put some songs on this one to remind me of home." He set the small disk on a table nearby and a deep, pulsing beat filled the room.

Mahali approached Jessop slowly. He was only a little taller, but quite a bit wider. He stood opposite Jessop and placed one arm across Jessop's shoulder.

"Just do what I do," he directed.

Jessop mirrored Mahali's movements. The beat of the song pulsed between them like a shared heartbeat. Mahali demonstrated a set of movements and poses, moving slowly at first, transitioning through the movements every four beats. And then every two.

Soon, they were flowing effortlessly through the steps of the dance, bowing and twirling; taking one another's hands; lifting one another from the ground.

"The full dance includes flying," Mahali explained as they circled the room, "but we would need more space."

As they danced, Jessop grew more confident. Laughing quietly, they took turns leading each other through the steps. Neither of them noticed Xalma in the shadows.

A nightmare had shaken her from sleep. Xalma didn't want to be alone, so she decided to look for Jessop. When she saw Jessop and Mahali dancing, every terrible thought she'd had since leaving The Grotto flooded through her mind.

He doesn't want me here. He has new friends now. Friends who can fly with him. Friends who are like *him.* Silent tears ran down her face. *He doesn't like me anymore.* She felt the spines all over her body rising as anger and pain coursed through her. Her scales smoldered and her muscles tensed. She felt an overwhelming urge to destroy; to lash out at everything around her. *He's still my friend!* Xalma struggled to control her rage. *He's not doing this to hurt me. It's* good *that he found someone who understands him.*

No matter what she told herself, Xalma couldn't hold back the waves of fury threatening to drown her. Her body was preparing to attack, whether she wanted to or not.

I've got to get out of here before I hurt someone, Xalma realized desperately. She rushed into the main room, pushing the shelves aside and vanishing into the tunnel before Jessop or Mahali could stop her.

They chased her through the forest until she reached a pond. Xalma disappeared into the water. For a long time, Jessop and Mahali waited at the pond's edge, but Xalma did not return.

Chapter Twenty Nine

Dwarka

Throughout the day, Cato, Vera and Hiro exchanged updates with their generals and discussed the announcement that they were going to make the following evening.

The Resistance was ready to mobilize, but they couldn't march all the way to Marrow together, nor could they all fit in the submarines. Cato was preparing to move waves of the ground troops across extremely dangerous terrain. He expected the full mobilization to take several months. His goal was to capture Marrow and build a better, stronger army for the real war.

"Are you certain it was Tsoci's will to let The Child Queen go?" Cato asked Hiro.

"That is what I felt," Hiro replied. "I told you not to follow her. She needs to prove her character, free of our influence."

"We discussed this, Hiro. Her *character* is irrelevant." Vera glowered. "We just need someone that sapiens will take risks for. She's legendary."

"Tsoci believes that Edge and Xalma are both potential leaders," Hiro explained. "This is how they operate. The fittest survive. That's why I told you to destroy The Grotto. This fight was set into motion by Tsoci."

"How much longer must we keep following Tsoci's orders?" Vera asked. "Who knows how many plants and animals were destroyed in that explosion! It's clear that our host can no longer maintain equilibrium. When are we going to take control?"

Cato was carefully watching Hiro's reaction, looking for the slightest sign of doubt. "You want to let Tsoci pick a champion," he concluded.

"It will happen tomorrow," declared Hiro.

"Did Tsoci tell you that?" Vera asked. Hiro shook his head.

"I think it's inevitable," Cato answered. "Xalma is due for a massive temper tantrum. She wants her Avian friend to leave with her, and the Forax is in the way."

"This will be an interesting battle," smiled Vera. "Have you seen any evidence that our modification of Mana and Hiro's genes yielded the results we wanted? Can the child interface with Tsoci?"

"There was no sign while I was watching her," Cato admitted. "She's a precocious child, though. Much more intelligent than the average sapien, but feral."

"They may both become tools of Tsoci," Hiro suggested. "Have you considered that?"

"The Child Queen is jealous of the Forax," Cato replied. "They will never join forces."

"Well then, let's hope my daughter wins," Hiro remarked as he prepared to leave. "She's the savior *we* created, which makes her story easier to tell. As your spiritual leader, I'd rather not retrofit the story of another culture's savior."

The warm water reminded Xalma of home, but there were no bioluminescent plants or animals to guide her through the dark depths of the pool. The soft red glow of her own fiery scales revealed a path on the bottom of the pond.

Someone made this place, she thought, following the path. It led to a tunnel, which led to more tunnels. If Xalma had entered the hideout through the dancing door and seen the passages of Ruin, she would have noticed that the tunnels underwater looked just like the passages on the land.

Even though nothing around her was familiar, Xalma found the solitude comforting. She was grateful that her gills still worked. She swam slowly through a confusing network of ponds and tunnels.

I guess I could live alone down here, she thought sadly. Just as she was accepting a lifetime of solitude, Xalma passed through a tunnel and found herself looking down at an underwater city.

"Hey, you're The Child Queen!" yelled a voice behind her. Xalma turned to see a neotenous Amph covered in rich greenish-brown scales and clutching a silver spear. Flecks of turquoise accented the Amph's face, limbs and tail.

"Call me Xalma," said Xalma.

"I'm Anchor! Did Cato tell you to come here?"

"No," Xalma growled, smoldering. "I ran away from Cato with my friend. And then I ran away from my friend."

"Sounds like a lot of drama," Anchor replied with a smirk, unphased by Xalma's smoldering body or poisonous-looking spines. "You wanna hang out here for a while? This is a drama free zone."

"What *is* this place?" Xalma asked.

"It's Dwarka," Anchor answered. "We also call it the City of Children. Only neo Amphs can live here. We hatch in these pools, and the older neonates raise us. We have no idea who our parents are. When we're old enough to transform, The Resistance gives us jobs, whether we want them or not." Anchor's eyes narrowed. "Are you *really* The Child Queen? Are you here to help us?"

"I guess so," Xalma shrugged, warming to Anchor. "I don't know what I'm supposed to do, though."

"You're going to fit right in," Anchor snickered. She led Xalma back towards the wall of the cavern.

"Hang out with me in the guardhouse," Anchor invited, gesturing towards a clay dwelling that bulged directly from the steep side of the lake. "I'm still on duty, so I have to stay here for a bit longer. I'll take you to my place when I'm done working."

"Working?" Xalma asked.

"Yup, neos have jobs too, but we work for ourselves. My job is to guard that hole you came through," Anchor grinned. "It's usually a great job because nothing *ever* comes through that hole. Except you. Just now. How'd you even find this place?"

"I jumped into a pond and swam around for a while," Xalma replied honestly.

"How can you still breathe, though?" Anchor asked, examining Xalma's stiff neck plate. Before Xalma could answer, Anchor interrupted.

"Wait! Let me tell you everything I learned about The Child Queen, and you can tell me if any of the things I learned are *not* lies, okay? It'll be fun!"

Xalma nodded and sat beside Anchor feeling a little dazed. Everyone else seemed to know a lot more about her than she knew about herself.

"When we're very little, we learn how the universe started," Anchor began. "Everything stopped being nothing all at once, but everything couldn't exist at once in the same space and time, so time and space got bigger." As she spoke, Anchor pressed her hands together and then threw them apart widely, demonstrating the expansion of the universe. "It had to spread apart so everything could fit, you know?"

Xalma nodded.

"After a long time expanding, the universe wanted to learn about itself," Anchor continued. "It got lonely, right? So it made Tsoci, and Tsoci made Insects and sapiens and all the other things. Does any of this sound familiar to you?"

Xalma shook her head. "No, but that doesn't mean it's not true," she said.

"Didn't anyone ever tell you bedtime stories when you were a hatchling?" Anchor asked.

"I can't remember being a hatchling," Xalma replied sadly.

Anchor looked surprised.

"Oh holy cow, you don't know *any* of this stuff, do you?" she exclaimed with surprise. "I'm sorry! I just thought... because you're so old... you know."

"You thought I'd know things?" Xalma laughed. "Nope. Tell me the rest of the story."

Anchor hesitated, but Xalma insisted.

"Sapiens and Insects competed for the best land and food and stuff, and sapiens changed themselves. They became different enough that they weren't competing with the Insects anymore. That's why there are three races of sapiens."

"Oh!" exclaimed Xalma. "I feel like I used to know this! Go on."

"The Amphs ruled the water, so our home was the biggest," Anchor continued, enjoying herself. "We grew more powerful than everyone else. When Amphs found The Grotto, we started living a lot longer than everyone else, too."

"The rest of the sapiens didn't think it was fair that the Amphs lived longer and took up more space, even though Amphs lived in places where other sapiens couldn't live. Eventually, the Insects chased the Amphs away from the Grotto. Without the Grotto, Amphs lose the ability to live underwater after they transform."

"I didn't," Xalma pointed out.

"You're magic or something," Anchor replied dismissively. "Regular adult Amphs can't breathe underwater without exposure to The Grotto, so when the Insects took The Grotto away, a lot of Amphs drowned, and a lot of kids lost their parents. The orphans begged the Insects for mercy, and the Insects allowed them to leave one egg in the Grotto. The Child Queen's egg."

"I've never heard any of this," Xalma admitted. "What am I supposed to be *for*?"

"You're supposed to be like a reset button for the whole thing, in case the Amph children are ever in danger again." Anchor looked at Xalma intently. "You're *sure* no one ever told you *any* of this? No one ever came to see you?"

"The Deejii visited me," Xalma answered. "They didn't tell me any of this, though. Unless I forgot...."

"Holy hobfish! The *Deejii* know about you?" Anchor snorted with surprise. "The Deejii are the richest, most spoiled Amphs in Marrow. There've been rumors about how they stay young for so long! I guess they really *are* visiting The Grotto! It's no *wonder* you didn't come back to Marrow, if the only Amphs you ever met were the Deejii!"

"You know them?" asked Xalma in surprise.

"Not personally," Anchor laughed, "Those stuck up, rich snobs! Everyone from Marrow hates them." Anchor noticed the look on Xalma's face.

"Wow. I'm sorry. They've been your family this whole time, huh? You had a terrible childhood and you didn't even know it until now. That must suck."

"It wasn't *that* bad." Xalma shrugged and tried to look nonchalant. She thought about the beautiful underwater world she'd created for herself. Then she remembered that her home was gone. "I guess I didn't know what I was missing."

"You were missing *us*," Anchor said. "Every Amph has sent you messages. Each year, we send our wishes to The Child Queen. Until we grow old enough to realize... well... until we decide you can't be real. Writing to you is a weird holiday tradition that everyone does and no one really believes in."

"You've been sending me messages?" Xalma exclaimed. "Why didn't I get them?"

"I have no idea." Anchor looked at Xalma intently. "But Amph hatchlings are told that if they ask The Child Queen for help, she'll come. I always assumed it was just a way to break our spirits, you know? Because you never came."

"How could I possibly help, though?" Xalma asked.

"A lot of neos need food and water. Shelter. Education. Stuff like that,"

"Resources," whispered Xalma, remembering Harbeshi's words. "Everyone should have those things."

"The Child Queen can take over and change all the rules, at least according to the stories. I bet the jerks who control Marrow right now won't be very happy to see you," Anchor smirked.

"I don't want to lead The Resistance, though," Xalma objected. "I promised my friend Jessop that I wouldn't help Cato."

"I'm not talking about The Resistance," Anchor said. "You're *The Child Queen*! You don't need Cato's dumb army! You can just march right into Marrow and take over! The Amphs control Marrow, and you're the rightful ruler of the Amphs."

"I only came here to rescue my friend Jessop," Xalma repeated.

"The friend you ran away from?" Anchor asked curiously.

"He's the only one who's always been there for me." Tears leaked from Xalma's eyes. She was grateful to be underwater. "But he doesn't need me anymore. I don't know what to do."

"Whoa, that's rough, sister!" Anchor put her arm around Xalma, but quickly pulled away when she felt the older Amph's body tense and recoil.

"Why do you think your friend doesn't need you anymore?"

"He has Mahali and Edge now," Xalma answered.

Anchor looked up in alarm.

"Uh, did you just say *Mahali*?"

"Yeah, he's Jessop's new friend."

"Round Avian fellow, always looks shocked for no reason?" Anchor pressed.

"Yes…" Xalma watched a complicated set of emotions play across Anchor's face.

"Your friend isn't safe," Anchor said. "Mahali's not what he seems. I've been trying to catch him for years."

"Why?" Xalma asked, alarmed.

"He's the reason all my friends are dead," Anchor answered grimly. Her casual attitude had vanished.

"Is he going to hurt Jessop?" Xalma cried in alarm.

"Every sapien who spends time with Mahali dies or vanishes, so yeah, the odds are pretty good," Anchor replied seriously. "Will you help me capture him?"

"Yes!" Xalma's felt her anger returning.

Anchor grabbed her spear. "Wait here while I get help. If the wrong Amph sees you, they might tell Cato you're here. I'll be right back."

I do *have to rescue Jessop, after all,* thought Xalma as she waited anxiously for Anchor to return. She was worried about Jessop, but she was glad to have a sense of purpose again.

Chapter Thirty

Rescue Party

"If Xalma joins The Resistance, we may not be able to help her," Mahali said.

"She's *not* going to join The Resistance," Jessop insisted. "She promised she wouldn't. She just likes to be alone when she's feeling things. She'll come back."

"We cannot wait for her. We will be discovered."

"What if she can't find her way back?" Jessop stared into the dark pool with concern.

"Then the Insects are our best hope to save her," Mahali replied.

Full of guilt and fear, Jessop followed Mahali back to the hideout. They took turns sleeping and watching the entrance, but dawn came with no sign of Xalma.

When the others woke up and joined them, Mahali explained the events leading up to Xalma's disappearance.

"I have my swimming stuff! I can find her!" Jessop exclaimed, pacing restlessly.

"The ponds are connected by hundreds of underwater tunnels," Mahali pointed out, "and most have no light. Only an Amph can survive there."

"How do *you* know?" Jessop snapped.

"I have a friend who lives in the water," Mahali replied quietly.

"Can we ask your friend to help us? It's my fault Xalma's gone," Jessop said miserably. "I *have* to find her!"

"It's *not* your fault." Edge took Jessop's hands and gently guided him to a chair. "There's nothing wrong with dancing, and you weren't trying to hurt her. You love her. Xalma knows that."

"Regardless, we *must* complete our plan," Mahali insisted. "If The Child Queen does not return before this afternoon, we will have to leave without her."

"We can't just abandon her!" Jessop hollered, jumping to his feet again. "*You* go! I'll come find you when Xalma comes back."

"What if she cannot come back?" Mahali pointed out. "What if she is caught, like you were? If we wait, she may fall deeper into trouble."

"Someone should still stay here," Jessop insisted. "Just in case."

"If she *is* captured, she may lead The Resistance here," Mahali warned. "Then you will *both* be captured."

Edge stood in Jessop's path.

"We won't leave Cowrie without her, Jessop. I promise. Mahali is right. We're safer if we stay together. I'll ask the Insects to help us find her. *Please* come with us."

"Fine," agreed Jessop miserably.

Sole and Mary sat together across the room. They remained silent, but they were moving their hands. Edge suspected that they were whispering.

See? Sole signed to Mary. *Jessop chose the best course of action.*

Sapiens follow feelings they don't understand, Mary signed back. *They are easy to manipulate.*

Anchor returned with a small group of young Amphs. They all seemed much more intimidated by The Child Queen than Anchor was. Xalma led them back to the pond near the hideout.

"I didn't even know about some of those tunnels, and I was born here," Anchor remarked, looking at Xalma with respect. "How did you remember the way back?"

"I don't know if I *remembered* it, exactly," Xalma admitted. "I *felt* my way back."

"*Felt* your way?" Anchor's brows furrowed. "How?"

"Can't you feel the tunnels?" Xalma asked. "I just followed the tunnels with the right shapes."

"I think that might be a Queen thing," Anchor replied. "Or, as I'm going to call it, a QT. But it's useful! It's like you can see in the dark."

"I can only do it underwater," Xalma explained. "It doesn't work in the air."

"It's still a pretty amazing QT, Your Highness," grinned Anchor.

Xalma led them into the hideout through Sole and Mary's secret tunnel, but the hideout was empty.

"They're gone!" Xalma rushed from room to room, checking behind bookshelves and under tables. "They left without me!"

"Do you know where they went?" Anchor asked.

"They were going to rescue the Insects and steal a submarine," Xalma replied. "I can't *believe* they left me behind!"

"Mahali's such a dunderhead!" Anchor fumed. "This is worse than his last plan!"

"The Insects are in the lab," one of the younger Amphs said quietly, looking up at Xalma with concern. "Don't worry, Your Highness, we'll find your friend."

"You *bet* we will," Anchor growled. "I'm not letting Mahali get anyone else killed."

Edge, Sole, Jessop and Mary followed Mahali to a dead grey tree near the lab. It had very few branches, and no leaves. They huddled on the ground around the trunk, and Mahali took out the screamer.

"We are within transmission range," he whispered.

"Couldn't we do this somewhere a little more hidden?" Jessop asked, eyeing the many healthy bushes and trees nearby.

"I picked this place for a reason," Mahali replied. He pressed the screamer into a crack in the dry bark and hit the side of the tree. From inside the lab, they heard a resounding *thud,* amplified through the screamers that Sole had hidden throughout the building.

"The tree is hollow!" Sole exclaimed. "This is *perfect*! Hit it, Mary!"

Mary started beating a rhythm against the side of the tree. Sole and Mahali joined her, and she taught them the pattern. They could hear shouts of surprise from the guards outside the lab, but since the amplified sound was much louder inside the building, no one noticed the small party next to the dead tree.

Mary taught Jessop to clap a counter rhythm while she tapped her feet and shook her thorax and clicked her mandibles. When she was satisfied with the percussion, she joined Edge and they moved through the steps of the egg song.

Edge felt everything melt away except the song as she and Mary's thoughts merged into a larger awareness. They repeated the simple steps over and over again.

One by one, the Insects inside the lab recognized the song from their earliest days. They pulled themselves to their feet and started to dance.

The Insects in active experiments ripped away their wires and tubes, causing the scientists and guards watching them to back away in fright. The Insects didn't pay any attention to the sapiens. Each one of them raised their antennae as though hearing a familiar and comforting voice.

As they joined the dance, their bodies released chemicals into the air in response to the sense of attachment and community activated by the egg song. The chemicals drifted from room to room, and through the soil and cracks in the walls, and out the windows, finally reaching Edge and Mary.

It was not like merging with Tsoci. Edge knew exactly which senses and feelings belonged to her, but she could push her perception up a level, experiencing the combined senses, thoughts and feelings of the Insects. A wave of stories filled with pain, fear, and loneliness washed over her.

Although Edge didn't have the anatomy to participate directly in the chemical conversation, Mary added Edge's story to the emerging Hive Mind's thoughts. The Hive Mind's identity and awareness centered around things each individual had in common with the others, and one thing they all had in common was that The Resistance had hurt them. As she continued to dance, Edge could feel the Insects' relief as their pain was acknowledged. They accepted that something terrible had happened to them, and that it wasn't their fault.

We should free ourselves from The Resistance, thought the Hive Mind. *We're being hurt. It's not okay.*

Harmonies and melodies emerged as each individual contributed a slightly different perspective, but every part of the Hive Mind agreed that they didn't want to be hurt anymore.

The Child Queen needs our help, Edge and Mary danced. They staggered when the Hive Mind replied. Edge felt as though her limbs were being pulled through steps she couldn't control. It wasn't painful, but it still felt awkward and uncomfortable.

The Child Queen is not our responsibility, the Hive Mind thought and danced and sang.

"What's happening?" Jessop asked, watching Edge and Mary falter. "Are they okay?"

"They're trying to change the minds of almost a hundred Insects," Sole replied. "It's not going to be easy."

"Can we help them?" Jessop watched as Edge and Mary staggered, swinging their legs and curling down and up, struggling to carry their own weight.

"Maybe I can." Sole stopped drumming and joined the dance.

The Child Queen is our friend, Edge, Mary and Sole explained together. *We can't leave her behind.*

Mary and Sole translated Edge's memories of Xalma as a child in The Grotto so the Insects inside the lab could experience Edge's affection and fear, but Edge didn't know Xalma very well, and many of her memories made the Insects more cautious about getting involved.

This is for sapiens to handle, thought the Hive Mind.

"Jessop!" Sole cried. "We need your help!"

Jessop left the tree, and Mahali continued to drum on his own. Sole took one of Jessop's hands, and Edge took the other. The rover's soft, glowing antennae touched Jessop's temples.

"Think about Xalma," Sole instructed. "Focus on how you feel about her."

Through Edge and Sole, Jessop shared his memories of Xalma with the Hive Mind. They learned about a child, abandoned and misled, living in a dark cave with no one to guide or care for her for hundreds of years. Jessop described Xalma's creations, her loyalty, and her determination.

We have to get her back, he thought. *We can't abandon her.*

A rich, earth-rumbling harmony resonated around them. Inside the lab, the Insects were droning and buzzing and singing together.

We agree! the Hive Mind rejoiced.

As if from a great distance, Jessop felt his hands start drumming and clapping again. He could feel Edge's mind connected to his own. Without stopping to wonder at what he was doing, Jessop sent tendrils of thought in Mahali's direction.

At the same time, Edge felt her awareness expand, as one by one, the guards and scientists joined the dance. She also felt the Insects recoil as their abusers connected and found herself acting as a bridge between them. The guards and scientists experienced the memory of the Insects' pain, and they felt great remorse.

We were wrong, thought the sapiens. *We're so sorry. Please tell us what we can do to help.*

The doors were thrown open, and the stone walls of the lab started to shake and tumble. Jewel-bright Insects and bewildered sapiens burst from the building. They surrounded the tree, circling it slowly as they droned, clicked, stomped and chirped.

Most of the Insects were terribly hurt, and they all had broken wings. Sapien scientists and guards helped the healthier Insects support those who were too weak or broken to dance on their own.

"We have to leave," said Mahali. "We need to get them to the submarine.

"I won't be able to keep everyone together if the music stops," Edge warned him.

Jessop's awareness shifted from Hive Mind to his individual self when he heard Edge's voice.

"We need to communicate a plan," Jessop replied. "Let's find Xalma and get to the submarine. You told the Hive Mind about the submarine, right?"

In the greater conversation happening in an upper level of her mind, Edge could feel the idea of escaping on a submarine expand from her own mind and spread throughout the Hive Mind.

"They know now," Edge confirmed.

"Let's head to the river," Sole suggested, before flying away and returning a moment later with a hollow log. Mahali removed the screamer from the tree. For a few bars, the only sound was the Insects droning and chirping, and Jessop's claps.

Then Mahali put the screamer into the bark of the wooden log and hit it as hard and as fast as he could.

"To the river!" Edge shouted. The crowd of dancers cheered as the beat dropped. Sole carried the log ahead of the parade of dancers, with Jessop and Mahali drumming and clapping beside them.

As they approached the center of Cowrie, Xalma, Anchor, and the other Amphs had to leave the water.

"All of Cowrie used to be connected by underwater tunnels," Anchor explained, "but they were drained to make new homes for soldiers."

"Why are all the soldiers so young?" Xalma asked, remembering the children who had greeted them when she and Cato arrived at the edge of the rainforest. She tried not to think about the screams of those taken by wild creatures.

"In the early days, Cato ordered the Insects to bring whole families here," Anchor replied. "Until your friend Mahali talked a bunch of other sapiens into trying to escape, and they all died."

"Mahali's *not* my friend," Xalma hissed.

"Sorry… I was being sarcastic," Anchor replied. "Anyway, after that, The Resistance asked the Insects to bring really young children here. They grow fast, and they mostly believe what they're told."

Anchor's face was tight with anger and pain. "I tried to stop my friends from following Mahali. He said the rainforest wasn't dangerous - that the attacks were fake; just a hoax to keep us from returning to Marrow. I *knew* he was wrong, I've seen the jackbears and thornwolves with my own eyes. I lost all my friends, and Mahali never paid for what he did."

"It sounds like he lost his friends too," Xalma pointed out. "And he was trying to escape The Resistance after being taken against his will."

"Here is no different than there," Anchor said bitterly.
"Either way we have to do as we're told. Some sapiens go
hungry while others throw away more food than they eat.
Life's not fair."

"You mean this is what it's like *everywhere*?" Xalma
asked in surprise. "There's no better place to escape to?"

"Cowrie is no different than Marrow," Anchor repeated
firmly. "Mahali led others to their death for nothing. He lied
to them because he couldn't accept the truth."

The other Amphs nodded in agreement.

"The sapiens in charge of everything believe this is
evolution. They think this is just how sapiens *are*," Anchor
continued. "Only the most powerful of us can change the
rules, and most of the powerful sapiens got to where they are
because the rules make things *easier* for them, so they aren't
going to change anything."

"But *you* can, Queen Xalma," whispered the tiniest Amph
in the group.

"I, uh..." Xalma stopped in her tracks and looked into the
hopeful eyes of her companions. "I'm *really* sorry. I *totally*
don't understand what you just said. I've mostly thought
about myself until now. I *want* to help you, I *really* do. But I
have *no idea how*. I don't know how to be a queen."

Anchor grabbed Xalma by the shoulder. Xalma's spines
flared and Anchor withdrew her hand and jumped away
quickly, exclaiming, "Xalma! That's pretty much the best
thing you could have ever said!"

"What?" Xalma asked. "That I'm selfish and clueless?"

"No," one of the younger Amphs replied. "That you don't
know how to be a queen."

"Why is that *good*?" Xalma rolled her eyes in
exasperation. "How am I supposed to do my job if I don't
know *how*?"

Anchor and the other Amphs bowed to Xalma for the first
time.

"We'll teach you," they said, "and you can be *our* Queen."
Xalma looked at the Amphs in disbelief. They looked
back at her pleadingly until Anchor smiled and said, "Okay
you lot, get up, we're making her Highness uncomfortable."
She winked at Xalma as they continued walking.

Xalma felt a confusing mixture of gratitude and absolute
terror. *These Amphs really want me to help them. What if I
can't do it? Will they all hate me?*

"We'll swim to the docks and head towards the lab from
there," Anchor explained as she led them to the bank of the
river. "If the Insects are already free, we'll have to cut off
their retreat. If they're still in the lab, maybe we can stop
Mahali from getting them out. If the Insects escape, Hiro will
punish everyone."

As they approached the docks, Anchor warned them to
move slowly and silently. "We can't let the submarines see
us. If the guns and torpedoes come out, it's all over."

A few guards stood on the docks, but there was no sign of
Mahali or Jessop. Anchor led them through a stone drainpipe
and up into the streets. They ducked into an alley and crept
cautiously towards the lab. Cowrie seemed strangely empty
compared to the bustling forest metropolis Xalma had
encountered when she'd arrived.

"The Resistance is making an announcement tonight,"
Anchor explained. "Neotenous Amphs aren't invited,
though."

"Why not?" asked Xalma.

"We can't be trusted." Anchor grinned. "Life's not fair,
but we can make it a little fairer by fighting back. That's
what Mahali didn't understand. He just wanted to go back to
his comfortable life and forget any of this ever happened."

"Do you hear something?" Xalma asked, cocking her
head.

A crowd of dancing Insects appeared out of the mist.
Music pulsed through the air.

"What the heck kind of escape is *that*?" Anchor exclaimed. "Everyone in the rainforest is going to hear them!" She ran out of the alley and stood directly in front of the crowd of dancers.

"Mahali, you *suck* at escaping!" she screamed.

Hiro stood on a stage overlooking The Resistance and delivered a passionate speech about equality and sustainability and the need for sapiens to restore balance. A thousand pairs of eyes flashed out of the gloom. Huge screens hung from the trees. Like the submarines and the stone buildings, the screens did not feel like they belonged in the rainforest. The mist made the images appear smudgy and unreal.

"As you know by now, Tsoci is real, and they are not our friend," Hiro declared.

The crowd murmured angrily and glanced at one another.

"For too long, sapiens have been confined to the desert of Marrow, cut off from most of the resources and fertile lands of Crescent Island. Tsoci has tried again and again to wipe us out. Over the years, sapiens have been abducted from Marrow to serve Tsoci's irrational goals. Their memories were taken from them, and they were brought here, to Cowrie. The Resistance has liberated them. Now we must liberate Marrow and all other sentient beings from Tsoci's tyranny!"

The young voices of the crowd cheered.

"It is time for us to rise up and take control of the island!" Hiro roared. "With our vision and our technology, we can forge a new future, where sentient life is no longer beholden to a host!"

Sapiens at the very edge of the audience started to hear music. They turned to one another and called out.

"What is that?"

"It's coming from the docks!"

"Should we go see?"

An Avian soldier landed behind the stage as Hiro continued his address and ran towards Cato and Vera. "The Insects have escaped from the lab," the soldier reported breathlessly. "They're dancing towards the river."

"*Dancing*?" Cato asked in surprise. "*How* are they dancing?"

"Um, they're moving their bodies in time to music, Your Holiness," the Avian replied.

Impatience flashed across Cato's face.

"Are they each dancing in their own way or are they all moving together?" asked Vera.

"Oh!" the soldier said. "I didn't notice. One second." She removed a screamer from her belt and spoke to someone on the other end.

"Both," she informed them.

"They've created a Hive Mind," said Cato with a nod of approval. "But not a strong one. The Resistance must go to the river."

"This is *not* what Hiro predicted," Vera said. "He said Edge and Xalma would fight for leadership."

"Yes, and Tsoci will choose a winner for us," Cato confirmed. "Hiro did not say how it would begin, but this makes sense. A Hive Mind can call Tsoci."

"If Tsoci is waking up…" Vera began, looking alarmed.

"They must not reach us," Cato confirmed. "Tsoci is irrational. If they learn that we want to replace them, they will destroy us." He addressed a group of sapiens operating the stage lights. "Cut to the grand finale," he commanded before sending a stagehand to notify Hiro.

The stagehand quickly whispered the news to Hiro and scurried offstage.

"My children! It is time to meet our destiny!" Hiro announced. His amplified voice boomed through Cowrie. His face commanded the attention of thousands of sapiens, and glowed like a beacon from the massive screens.

"We must go to the docks," Hiro commanded. "A miracle waits for us there!"

Pre-recorded music blasted into the crowd, full of triumphant horns and epic strings. Every branch was alight and pulsing to the music. Unlike the soft, organic glow of living things, this light strobed and flashed into the surrounding trees, casting knife-sharp shadows across the leaves. A cacophony of voices drowned out the distant sound of the dancers.

"Summon an Avian patrol," Cato ordered. "We need an escort. Make sure our best soldiers are onboard and ready to depart."

A few moments later, six Avians reported to Cato, ready to carry the leadership of The Resistance to safety.

"Once we get clear, locate The Child Queen and the Forax, and wait until I give the signal. We will extract the winner once the battle is decided," said Cato

"Yes, Master Cato," they replied.

The brand new Hive Mind danced slowly but surely towards the shore of the river. As they moved, the ground around Edge's feet began to glow where she stepped. Then the earth started to shake.

"What's happening?" Mahali wondered.

"Tsoci is coming," said Sole.

"Is Edge going to be buried by plants again?" asked Jessop anxiously.

"Not this time," promised Sole. "She's part of a Hive Mind. She's ready."

The dancers twirled and radiated away from Edge and her friends like ripples in a pond. Concentric circles stepped and bowed, arms and legs contorting through a sequence of complex but absolutely synchronous poses.

A single sapien appeared in the road ahead of them. Yelling, she ran towards them. The dancers barely noticed her.

The Child Queen is coming, the Hive Mind thought. *We feel her. She is almost here.*

As Anchor stood in the road and screamed at the top of her lungs. Xalma and the other Amphs hid in the shadows, urging her to come back. They were terrified of the Insects.

A gap appeared between the dancers and Anchor glimpsed Mahali.

Xalma saw him too. He was dancing with Jessop. In an instant, she took in the hatred in Anchor's eyes and the joy on Jessop's face.

Jessop left me behind to sing and dance with a bunch of Insects! Fury and confusion overwhelmed Xalma. Her scales flared and caught fire. The other Amphs leapt away quickly, squealing in terror.

Xalma stepped into the road and stood next to Anchor, her scales rippling with tiny flames. Every spine from her head to her tail tip spiked out from her body. Her eyes flashed like lightning.

"STOP!" she commanded.

"*That's* what I'm talking about!" Anchor yelled, hopping a comfortable distance away from the furnace of Xalma's rage. "Go Xalma! *Work* those QTs!"

The dancers swayed gently from side to side. The music dropped to a low pulse. The sound of an approaching crowd filled the air. Hundreds of sapiens poured into the streets and lined the sides of the road. They settled on the branches and rooftops overhead. The Resistance had arrived to witness the miracle.

Chapter Thirty One

Sacrifice

"*Y**ou left me behind!*" Xalma screamed, approaching the dancers. A trail of fire licked across the ground where she passed.

"We weren't going to leave you!" Jessop cried, flying towards his friend. "We asked the Insects to help us *find* you."

"*I don't believe you!*" Xalma shrieked. The flames around her blazed brighter and Anchor hopped out of reach, rejoining the other Amphs. A wave of wind and heat blasted Jessop away. His eyes widened in terror as he watched the force of Xalma's rage reduce the surrounding plants to ash. He circled back towards the dancers.

"Sole, what can we do?" Edge asked.

"Tsoci is waking up," Sole informed her. "You can send a message directly to our host letting them know Xalma needs help."

"I'm just going to talk to her, first," Edge decided, remembering her last encounter with Tsoci. Still swaying in time to the beat of the music, Edge approached Xalma. With each step, glowing filaments of light broke through the earth, leaving a shimmering trail behind her.

"Jessop's telling the truth," Edge said gently. "We *were* looking for you. We'd *never* leave you behind."

"LIAR!" Xalma yelled. Flames whirled around her.

Edge raised her awareness to the level of the Hive Mind.

We need to prove she can trust us, she thought.

The dancers rushed forward and surrounded Edge and Xalma. Sole circled above with Jessop and Mahali as Edge faced the intense heat of Xalma's fury.

Anchor led the other Amphs to the top of a building. They joined a crowd of sapiens watching in fascination and wonder as The Child Queen faced Hiro's daughter.

"Is that the Forax that The Child Queen was complaining about?" one of the Amph asked. "How is she getting the Insects to follow her?"

"Maybe Cato *wasn't* lying," Anchor replied. "He said Hiro's kid had power."

The filaments of light blooming around Edge's feet formed a living carpet of intricate geometric patterns beneath the circling dancers. The Insects kneeled, swaying gently in time to the low pulse coming from deep within the earth. The eyes of thousands of witnesses twinkled from the surrounding darkness like stars.

Once Edge pushed her awareness entirely to the Hive Mind, she was barely aware of her smoldering fur and blistering skin. Waves of anger, fear and loss poured from Xalma. As Edge approached her, the furious Amph howled in rage.

"*None* of this would be happening if *you* hadn't come along!"

Xalma struck out at Edge with all the speed and skill she'd learned from Cato. Edge fell back violently, landing among the Insects, who gently passed her back to the center of the circle. Jessop cried out and tried to swoop down, but Xalma's body flared and the heat drove him back again.

"We have to stop this," he cried.

"Edge will be okay," Sole replied, although the rover looked concerned. "She just has to connect with Xalma."

Wherever Edge's feet fell, light and life burst from the ground. Where Xalma passed, flames turned the living light to ash. Over and over again, Xalma lunged towards Edge, ripping at her with claws and teeth and throwing her into the circle of Insects. Each time Edge crashed into the dancers, they lifted her up and pushed her back towards Xalma.

Jessop knew that Edge was not going to be able to endure Xalma's punishment for much longer.

"Stop! Xalma! She's just a kid! She's our friend!"

Xalma directed another blast of searing heat in his direction, forcing him high into the air.

The dancers swayed more quickly as the pulsing rhythm of the earth rose in volume and speed. The Hive Mind felt Tsoci's arrival as a rush of energy rising from the earth. Flowers bloomed and wilted. Vines snaked down from the trees and swallowed up the buildings. Fungus draped the stones and trunks, covering the ground with a multicolored, kaleidoscopic carpet of light.

Tsoci was awake, and was experiencing the world through the first Hive Mind ever to include sapiens.

Just as Xalma was about to lunge at Edge again, roots erupted around her like colorful ribbons of light, securing her arms and legs and pulling her to the ground. The dancers jumped to their feet and started to twirl around Edge and Xalma like planets and moons around binary stars.

"NO!" screamed Xalma, tearing at the glowing roots with her teeth.

Edge knelt in front of her friend. She laid her hands on the Child Queen's burning temples. Smoke rose from her fingertips. Edge opened her eyes and met Xalma's white hot, furious gaze.

"What's happening?" Jessop cried as the watching sapiens gasped collectively.

"Tsoci is here," Sole answered in a loud, clear voice, "They're going to help Edge teach The Child Queen to trust us."

Around them, The Resistance watched the miracle and listened to the words of the rover, their hearts full of wonder.

Xalma stared into Edge's eyes and saw nothing but concern. Slowly, her flames smoldered and died, but her body still glowed red hot. The roots binding her to the ground released her and pushed her to her feet. She and Edge circled one another slowly. Xalma's head bowed low. Edge's hands still holding her temples.

Do you understand? The Hive Mind's message was delivered as a feeling rather than as words, but Xalma sensed the question.

No, Xalma admitted. Her limbs jerked, and the spines of her neck slashed at Edge's arms, but Edge did not let go. *What's happening to me?*

We are teaching you to connect your mind and heart to others, Hive Mind replied. *Follow our steps.*

Xalma?

Distantly, Xalma sensed Jessop.

"Jessop, where are you?" she shouted, struggling to resist the rhythm of the music.

Trust Edge. She's not going to hurt you. No one is going to hurt you or leave you behind.

Xalma felt Jessop's concern for Edge. She also felt his fear, and his guilt. Memories of his time in prison and his anguish at losing her were intertwined with the joy of finding new friends, and his love for Xalma.

One by one, the Insects and sapiens connected to the Hive Mind shared their stories with Xalma. She learned about their pain and fear. The connection to the Hive Mind restored the memories of the sapiens. They remembered Hiro's ceremony, Cato's manipulation, and Vera's terrible experiments. Xalma finally knew, beyond a doubt, that Jessop was her friend, and that Cato had lied to her.

"I'm sorry," whispered Xalma, feeling the music fill an emptiness inside her that had not been filled for hundreds of years. "I didn't know."

Edge released Xalma's head, and Xalma joined the other dancers, her movements free and joyful and wild.

"I don't *believe* this!" hollered a voice. Anchor climbed down from the rooftop where she'd watched everything unfold, and once again stood in their path. The dancers continued to advance. Anchor brandished her spear and hollered at the sapiens still watching from alleys and rooftops.

"Hey! Soldiers! Why aren't you stopping them?" she demanded, pointing at the dancers. "*That's* Mahali! He's helping the Insects *escape!*"

"It's a miracle!" a sapien called back from the top of one of the buildings.

"And it has a really good beat!" called another, who was sitting on a nearby branch.

"*They're taking The Child Queen away*, you dunderheads!" Anchor shrieked.

When the dancers reached Anchor, she struck at them with her spear, leaping around to keep the grasping roots that were erupting from the earth from winding around her legs. The circle of dancers easily and gracefully avoided Anchor's attempted blows.

Anchor lost her balance as the last of the dancers passed by. Her hands connected with the earth. She watched in horror as roots wrapped themselves around her wrists and prevented her from rising again. When the dancers were out of sight, the roots released her, but she didn't pursue Xalma and Mahali. Instead, she ran down a side street and headed towards the river, hoping to head them off at the dock.

Insects and sapiens sang together in sapien tongue, their words incomplete fragments of the Hive Mind's thoughts.

"Uuunnniiittteee," droned the Insects.
"Eeemmmeeerrrgggeee."

The Avians responsible for extracting the winner of the battle ignored the frantic calls from Cato. They dove and twirled above, moving in time to the music, trails of living sparks splashing from their wings. Pollen filled the air as the rainforest responded to Tsoci's waking awareness.

The crowds watching from the rooftops and branches sensed the presence of the Hive Mind. They clapped their hands and joined the dance, raising their voices in song. As more and more individuals joined in, the music rose to a crescendo. For the first time, many of the sapiens experienced a true sense of connection.

When the dancers reached the bank of the river, the web of light swept across the ground. Together, Edge and Xalma stepped into the water. Steam billowed around Xalma, obscuring the glow of her still-smoldering scales. Xalma's rage had not subsided. It was only redirected, and focused on Cato.

They're here, thought Xalma. *I can feel them.* She dove into the water and the red glow of her body disappeared beneath the waves.

The river shimmered brightly around Edge as the microbes and plants in the water became active conduits for Tsoci's waking consciousness. Edge felt her mind stretch as the Hive Mind and Tsoci both channeled their thoughts through her.

I'm fine, Edge thought deliriously, grinding her teeth. *There's thousands of individuals in my head right now, but I'm fine.*

Sole hovered above Edge.

"It's almost over," they said. "It's time to finish our task. Tell Tsoci that the sapiens who designed you are in the submarine that Xalma is about to attack."

Cato, Vera, and Hiro stood anxiously in front of a wall of screens, each showing a different view of the dancers.

"If only the submarine had an external sound system, we could have caused enough confusion to prevent them from coordinating themselves," Cato said. "We'll know better next time."

"*Next* time?" Vera wondered as Edge and Xalma reached the shore.

"We can't let Tsoci have any of them," Cato growled.

"When I suggested the possibility that Tsoci would choose them both, you said the chance was approximately zero." Hiro said mildly. "I'm not saying I told you so, but here we are."

"I was obviously mistaken," Cato admitted dryly. "We still have to cut our losses. We know the variant works."

"This is the first time the anomaly has ever succeeded," Vera insisted. "I need to study her."

"That won't be possible," said Cato.

"You don't mean..." Hiro began.

"We must destroy her, and all those who have been touched by Tsoci," Cato declared.

"Cato, what about The Resistance?" Vera gasped.

"The best soldiers are already aboard the ships," Cato replied. "If we can form a Hive Mind in Marrow, we don't need The Resistance. In fact, they're a liability. Brainwashing is an imperfect way to control a soldier."

"Are you *sure* about this?" Hiro asked. "Destroying the only army we have seems like a bad idea to me. Not to mention you'd be killing thousands of innocent sapiens. You said you wanted to minimize the casualties."

"Don't forget your daughter," Vera added.

"She's *Mana's* daughter, I just donated some genes. But yes, we'd also be destroying Edge. She's just a child, Cato. They are all children."

"We cannot let Tsoci have them," Cato repeated firmly. "We are sacrificing a few thousand sapiens to save billions from Tsoci's madness. It's the only way. I will take full responsibility." His voice trembled. Hiro and Vera saw the tears in his eyes, but they knew better than to offer him comfort.

It was a sense Xalma had always had, so of course she thought everyone else had it, too. Her skin felt energy in the water, and the energy had a shape that her mind turned into a picture. She saw every submarine in the fleet, and she knew which one Cato was in.

The water around her boiled as her body ignited, blasting her forward.

You might be able to hide from Tsoci, but you can't hide from me, *you old liar.*

As Xalma dove towards her target like a molten fireball, a torpedo shot past.

Did that boat just sneeze out a baby? she wondered as her claws and teeth sank into the metal hull of Cato's submarine. Behind her, she felt the river catch fire.

"You're finished blowing things up, you monsters!" Xalma screamed as she tore into the side of the ship. The water around her boiled.

Tsoci analyzed the situation from the perspective of each individual in the Hive Mind, and used this information to react quickly when the first torpedo raced toward the shore. Millions of roots and stones at the bottom of the river lurched at once, throwing a wall of water into the air. The enormous weight of the crashing wave nudged the first torpedo into the soft base of the river. When it exploded, the sapiens near the shore were showered with mud, but no one was hurt.

Through the thoughts and memories of thousands of individuals, Tsoci perceived the full extent of the threat. Weeds and river grass exploded from the water, growing into a massive barrier between the submarine and the dancers. At the top of the barrier, connecting everyone, stood Edge.

Hiro watched these events with growing concern.

"We *must* leave now," Hiro said.

"Not until we end Tsoci's connection," Cato replied firmly.

"How?" Vera asked. "Tsoci tossed that torpedo away like a stick!"

Cato pushed a button and his voice filled the ears of every sapien on every submarine in the fleet.

"Fire all the torpedoes, and all the missiles. All of them. Now."

Xalma felt the attack tear through the river as she breached the hull of the ship. She realized what was happening, but there was nothing she could do to stop it.

Chapter Thirty Two

The Task

Abarrage of missiles and torpedoes blasted towards
Cowrie. Hundreds of huge roots and vines whipped out
of the towering wall of vegetation that stood between
the dancers and the water. They snapped and flailed across
the water towards the shadows of the submerged ships. On
top of the tangled, living shield stood Edge.

"Oh no," Sole whispered, diving towards Edge and pulling her out of the line of fire. Below them, Tsoci and the Hive Mind disconnected, and the protective barrier collapsed. Sapiens and Insects scrambled away from the river as tons of roots and plants crashed back into the water.

Sole streaked through the air, retrieving Mary, Jessop, and Mahali. Each of them went limp in the rover's arms.

As soon as they had their friends, Sole shot straight into the sky. They burst through the canopy moments before everything and everyone below was swallowed by a roaring blast, and the center of Cowrie was reduced to smoke, fire and dust.

Muddy river water poured through the hole that Xalma had ripped into the hull of the submarine, but no matter how deeply she dug her claws into the metal or how desperately she tore with her teeth, the breach was still too small for her to fit through.

The ship started to move.

"No!" Xalma screamed, redoubling her efforts as she sensed the fleet of submarines leaving Cowrie. She tightened her grip, but the ship continued to pick up speed. The water around her rushed past and ripped her claws from the metal hull. She flew back into the water as the submarine cruised away with the rest of the fleet.

Xalma pursued them all the way to the ocean, but she couldn't keep up. Utterly defeated, she swam back up the river. Debris from the attack floated past her. She paid no attention to it until someone called her name.

She cautiously swam towards a raft of flotsam and discovered Anchor, barely conscious and tangled in river grass and pieces of the dock. Xalma hauled her to shore and collapsed beside her. Cowrie was in ruins. The only light she could see was from the still-smoldering fires in the rubble. The air was thick with ash.

"Anchor, can you hear me? Please be okay!" Xalma noticed several deep cuts along Anchor's sides and a jagged gash under her eye.

"Xalma?" Anchor stirred. "You're alive! I tried to reach you..." she coughed and gasped.

"I'm so sorry," Xalma said. "I wasn't strong enough to stop Cato."

"This isn't your fault, Queen Xalma," Anchor rasped between shallow breaths. "It's always been this way."

"Maybe if I'd left The Grotto sooner, this wouldn't have happened," Xalma sobbed, taking Anchor's hands.

"The sapiens who did this are the ones who kept you away from the kids who need you," Anchor struggled to form the words, and her voice fell to a whisper. "They didn't want you to fight for us. I'm sorry I won't be able to help you." Anchor managed a weak smile.

"Stop..." Xalma begged. "You're going to be fine! I just need to get help."

"It's okay," Anchor gasped. "I'm ready. I'm so glad you're real, and that I got to meet you. Take care of the other neos, okay?"

"I will. I won't ever stop fighting for them," Xalma promised, as Anchor's breath grew weaker and her eyes closed for the last time.

Sole found Xalma curled around Anchor's body on the blasted shore of the river.

"Where are Jessop and Edge?" Xalma asked.

"They're safe. I jabbed them with sticklethorn before the city exploded. They're in the hideout. They didn't see..." Sole paused and looked at the dead Amph in Xalma's arms. "They missed the massacre. Are *you* okay?"

"Anchor didn't deserve this," Xalma growled, staggering to her feet. "None of them did. I felt them in my head. They just wanted to live in peace."

"I can carry you back to Jessop and the others," Sole offered. "You should rest."

Xalma shook her head and rose to her feet, pacing restlessly and clutching her spines.

"I need to go back to Dwarka. I promised Anchor I'd look after the neo Amphs."

"You really *should* rest first," Sole pressed. "You did something truly amazing today."

"No I didn't!" Xalma snarled. "I messed *everything* up! *I'm the reason she's dead!*"

Sole and Xalma's eyes locked. Neither moved.

"Xalma..." Sole started.

"Don't," Xalma said, turning away. "I can't talk about this now. Take me to Dwarka."

After Sole dropped Xalma off, the rover looked for survivors, carrying injured sapiens and Insects from the wreckage to a chamber in Ruins. The sapiens who weren't too badly hurt tended to those less fortunate. The survivors struggled to comprehend their leader's sudden betrayal and the massive destruction of their home.

Sole was filled with grief. The emotion was new, and the rover wasn't sure what to do with it. Sole continued to search for survivors long after the last one was found.

Xalma met Sole after nightfall. They built a small fire on the edge of the wasteland that was once Cowrie.

"All the neos are safe," Xalma reported. "Except for the ones who followed me and Anchor. There are only about fifty of them. I thought there'd be a lot more, Dwarka is big enough for thousands."

"Will you stay here with them?" Sole asked.

"I have to," Xalma replied. "They're just kids. Anchor... she was so young." Xalma wiped tears from her eyes. "I'm glad Jessop and Edge didn't see that. Will they be okay?"

"Jessop and Mahali will be fine when they wake up," Sole replied. "I'm worried about Edge, though. I ripped her away from a direct connection with Tsoci. I might have damaged her mind."

"She'd be dead if you hadn't pulled her out of there." Xalma scowled. "How could Cato kill all those sapiens? They were *his* army!"

"As soon as Edge connected everyone to the Hive Mind, they stopped being Cato's army," Sole replied. "The Resistance joined Tsoci."

"Why is this happening?" Xalma asked. "Is it my fault? Is it because I left The Grotto? Or because I didn't leave soon enough?"

"None of this is your fault," Sole replied gently. "Right now, it's as though a bunch of rogue immune cells are trying to take control of their host."

"How do you know?" Xalma asked.

"Tsoci has to be very out of balance for a sapien like Edge to evolve," Sole explained. "It also explains why an entire army was sacrificed. They were contaminated by the enemy. Cato would have had to brainwash and re-train every one of them to make them forget their connection to Tsoci."

"What does any of this have to do with Edge?" Xalma asked.

"Edge makes it possible for individuals to feel a connection to something bigger," Sole explained. "The signs were there from the start. I confirmed that Edge was being trained to lead The Resistance, but I still needed to be sure that her modifications were intentional."

"Not following you," Xalma muttered. "As usual."

"Edge is genetically modified."

"The Resistance *made* Edge?"

"Not exactly," Sole replied. "They designed some of her genes, but her environment determined how they were expressed."

"You lost me," Xalma admitted.

"Edge can see from more perspectives than we can," Sole explained, "but how she chooses to use that power is determined by her environment and upbringing, not by what The Resistance did. She decided that her purpose is to protect us, so Tsoci will protect her. I'm glad I don't have to eliminate her," Sole added. "I like Edge."

"*As if,*" Xalma snorted. "You'd *never* hurt Edge. I can't believe how much punishment she took for us. And *from* us… from *me*. What exactly did The Resistance want to use her for?"

"According to the scientists who survived, they were going to hack Tsoci's memory using Edge's mind."

Xalma stared into the gloom of the wasteland. "So, what's she *actually* for? Do you know?"

"It's not very practical to go through life feeling like a whole tree when your job is to be a leaf on a symbiotic plant," Sole replied. "Edge's purpose is to give the plant and the tree a way to get to know each other so they can work towards a common goal. Hopefully she can stop the plant from over-running the whole tree."

Xalma stared into the fire. Her brow furrowed.

"Sorry," said Sole. "That's probably a bad analogy."

"I get it," Xalma said quickly. "I was just thinking… You knew this stuff the whole time, didn't you?"

"I ran a lot of predictive models," Sole admitted, "but I didn't know anything for sure. I still don't."

"Why didn't you tell Edge that her mutation might destroy Tsoci?"

"Because she's twelve years old," Sole replied. "It would mess her up."

"I think she'd want to know."

"She'll figure it out when she's ready," Sole replied.

"That's exactly what everyone said about me," Xalma said with a frown.

"Edge has teachers who are helping her get ready," Sole said gently. "You didn't have anyone. I'm really glad you stayed with us."

"I must have hurt her so badly." Xalma sighed. "I won't blame her if she hates me now."

"Some of the Insects hate the scientists," Sole admitted. "Even though the scientists were brainwashed, they still could have refused to hurt the Insects. Some did, and they were killed or exiled, like Mahali's friend Sopa."

"What the scientists did is unforgivable." Xalma growled.

"Every one of the scientists accepts that. There hasn't been any violence because all of the scientists have apologized." Sole smiled. "They've all promised to do better, but they don't expect to be forgiven."

"Are you saying Edge might never forgive me?" Xalma asked.

"By the time she faced you, Edge was experiencing too many perspectives for her memory to be able to recreate them." Sole explained. "Tsoci healed her in the river, so she has no injuries. Assuming her mind is intact, she won't recall anything after the Insects left the lab."

"What are we going to tell her? She's going to find out about the attack. So many sapiens died."

"We're not going to tell her anything yet," answered Sole, "and I'm going to take her home as soon as she wakes up. She's going to need a long time to heal."

"Thanks for protecting her."

Sole smiled sadly. "Trauma is not a variable we need to add."

Over the next few days, Jessop and Mahali re-wired the power from the remaining trees, and helped the survivors start to rebuild. Mahali frequently stopped whatever he was doing, staring at nothing for a while. Every sapien he knew from Cowrie was gone. When Mahali finally started crying, he didn't stop for hours. Jessop held his friend and didn't say anything. There was nothing to say.

In the evenings, Jessop read all of Edge's notes to Mahali as they waited for her to recover.

"The pain she endured sounds terrible," Jessop said. "I don't exactly understand what Tsoci *is*, but I don't think they care about Edge. I'm really glad she can just go home now."

Edge woke up a week later. Sole explained that Hiro, Cato, and Vera had departed Cowrie, along with many of the soldiers. As the rover had predicted, Edge couldn't remember anything after meeting Xalma. Her bruises and cuts had been healed in the river. For Edge, it was as if the battle, and the subsequent attack, had never happened.

Sole, Xalma, and Jessop agreed that it was important to keep it that way, although, at first, Jessop resisted hiding anything from her.

"I promised I'd never keep secrets from Edge," he said.

"How do you think she'll feel if she finds out almost everyone in Cowrie was killed after I saved her?" Sole asked. "She needs a chance to decide what she wants to do next, and she should make that decision free of the guilt she's bound to feel when she learns what happened here."

"As long as you promise you'll tell her as soon as she's back home with Mana," Jessop insisted.

"She'll find out when she's ready," Sole said firmly.

Mahali and Mary watched over the survivors so that Jessop and Xalma could meet Sole a long way from the devastation to say their goodbyes. Sole planned to fly through the trees until the great wasteland of ash and dust long behind them.

"Take care of her," Xalma told Sole. "I hope your mom's okay, Edge," she added, giving the small Forax a quick, awkward hug. "Tell her I'm sorry I was such a jerk."

"I'll be back to visit you soon," Edge promised. "I want to see Dwarka! And we should all dance together again, now that the Insects are free! That was so fun! Say goodbye to Mary and Mahali for me!"

Jessop and Xalma continued looking into the trees long after Sole and Edge had vanished. It was the first time they'd been together since the attack. Neither of them knew what to say.

Xalma finally broke the silence.

"I'm so sorry," she said. "I know you probably hate me now. I just..."

"You just can't process emotions very well." Jessop said, rolling his eyes. "Xalma, I *know* you." He smirked at her. "You've been busy learning to be a queen! Don't worry. I'm not going anywhere. We can talk about things when you're ready."

Xalma blinked back tears and wrapped her arms around Jessop. "Thanks, Bird Boy," she whispered.

When Sole and Edge returned to the valley, they found Ashmara and Mana still living in the cave above the canyon river. Harbeshi had moved into a camp nearby.

"I'm so proud of you!" Mana exclaimed when Edge stepped into the cave. "You saved me!"

Edge recounted her adventures as she and her mother flew through the forest looking for a place to build a new home. Mana could not recall the time she'd spent with her memory disconnected.

"I feel like I just woke up in a cave about a week ago," she said. "I don't even remember visiting the Insects. I wish I could! Tell me everything you learned!"

Edge was happy to oblige, speaking long into the night.

"I brought all my notes with me, so you can read them. Uh, Mana?"

"Yes," Mana said softly, leafing through her daughter's notes.

"I met Hiro. He wasn't very nice. Is he really my dad?"

"Yes," Mana sighed. "And you're right, he's not very nice."

"Mahali said Forax can't bear children, and Hiro doesn't look anything like me…" Edge began hopefully.

"He is your biological father," Mana said heavily. "He convinced me that he and I… that our purpose was to bring you into the world. I was devastated when he was taken by the Insects, but I went through with the plan and raised you to be his successor. I wish I could say I questioned the plan, but I didn't. Not until we met Sole and learned that Tsoci is real. I wonder if the Insects who took him were already working with the Resistance."

"Maybe we can ask Mary when we see her," Edge suggested. "Was Hiro nice when you knew him?"

"I thought so," Mana replied, "but I was young and foolish."

"Mana's almost back to her old self," Edge told Sole a few days later when the rover visited her, sitting next to her bed in Ashmara's camp, where she was still recovering from the merge. "At least, as far as I can tell. I don't think I ever really knew my mother."

"You know the parts that matter," Sole assured her.

"I can't wait to show her Cowrie! We've been talking about all the samples we're going to collect when we visit Jessop and Xalma."

Sole nodded but did not reply. The rover had described the devastation of Cowrie to Mana and the Avians, but Edge still didn't know.

Harbeshi visited a few days after Edge returned. He and Ashmara were leaving the valley and travelling to Cowrie with Sole.

"Harbeshi and I will find different places to live when we arrive," Ashmara explained. "We are no longer compatible partners, but we hope to remain friends." She smiled at Harbeshi, and he nodded.

"We will help Jessop and Xalma with whatever they plan to do next," he said.

Mana pulled them both into a long embrace.

"Thank you. For everything. I don't know what I would've done without you."

"We will see each other again," Ashmara promised.

Sole spent the next few weeks carrying survivors to Far Crescent. Mana started rebuilding the treehouse with help from a growing number of new neighbors, who had all agreed not to tell Edge about the massacre in Cowrie.

"So, *is* Edge dangerous?" Mana asked Sole as they sat sipping tea on the deck of the new treehouse a few weeks later. Autumn was in the air.

"Yes," Sole replied, "but she's also our best hope for long term survival."

"Is that why she exists? To save us?"

"I think so, but in the end, it will be up to her."

"I wanted to be a mother so badly.," Mana whispered, tears rolling down her face. "I didn't think about what I was agreeing to until it was too late. I didn't mean to put her in danger."

"Without the danger, she wouldn't be the Edge we know," said Sole. "You did what you thought was best at the time. That's all any of us can do."

"I wish there was an instruction book for being alive," Mana said with a sad smile.

"Being alive is different for everyone, though," Sole replied thoughtfully.

"I don't want Edge to be hurt anymore," Mana whispered, "but I don't like keeping secrets from her."

"We'll tell her soon." Sole promised. "She deserves to know peace and safety for a while, so she understands what she has to sacrifice if she decides to use her power again."

Mana did not reply. Tears streamed down her face as she stared at the building nestled above them, where her daughter slept soundly.

Edge's new home was well-concealed in a sturdy pine tree near the canyon. She missed the sound of the papery leaves, but the pine needles smelled safe and comforting. Edge slept peacefully in the half-built house. She dreamed of visiting her friends and showing Mana all the amazing things in Cowrie.

Epilogue

S ole and Xalma sat next to a campfire at the border of the
  wasteland outside what was left of Cowrie, just as they
had the night after the massacre. Most of the survivors
had left, but Xalma remained, and so did the neo Amphs.
Jessop and Mahali were packing to return to Far Crescent to
visit Edge.

"How's she doing?" Xalma asked.

"She'll be okay. She'll have a lot of new friends when she recovers."

"Does she know what happened here?"

"No. Not yet."

"What are you waiting for?"

Sole picked up a stick and poked the fire. "I'm not sure, honestly. I was created to help Edge complete her task, but she got hurt. She almost got killed. I don't trust my instincts anymore. I don't trust Tsoci, either."

"I don't trust anyone," Xalma admitted. "I'm so angry. I wish I could hunt down Cato and the others. I want them to pay for what they did."

Sole turned and looked at Xalma. "You *did* make them pay."

"I didn't do anything but poke a hole in one of their ships." Xalma snorted.

"You did a lot more than that," Sole insisted. "Sapiens have been cut off from Tsoci for a long time. They've kept themselves hidden. You let something into the ship that will make it easier for Tsoci to deal with what's happening in Marrow."

"What are you talking about? The only thing that got into that ship was some water."

Sole smiled knowingly. "There's an entire world inside a drop of water."

A lot of living matter can collect in a breached submarine before a leak is plugged, and if there's one thing Tsoci is good at, it's producing living matter.

Without Edge to bridge Tsoci directly to their component parts, the Spirit fell back on a more ancient, less dramatic strategy, sending millions of tiny spores through the hole in the damaged ship.

The spores circulated through the submarine. When the sapiens onboard inhaled enough of them, they slowly started to change, but no one would notice for a while.

Cato, Vera, and Hiro returned to Marrow with the rest of the fleet. Soon, Tsoci's fungus spread undetected through the sapien city, quietly adjusting the minds of the population, and waiting for Tsoci to activate the next stage of their evolution.

Please Review This Book

Thank you for reading my book!

It'll make me happy if you leave a review on Goodreads or Amazon (or wherever you bought this book).

I'd love to connect on Facebook, TikTok, or Instagram. I'm @EdgeAnomaly on all three.

Acknowledgements

Lots of people helped with this book.

I'm thankful for my family for making me who I am, especially my Mom and Dad, my son, my partner Alistair, Doreen, Rebecca, and Riley, who cheerfully agreed to be the voice of Xalma in an animated TikTok series.

Curt, Keith, Joss, Rylaan, Jeremy, Jenn, Tannis, and Rachel.

My editor, Kat, who gently nudged me in the right direction without once telling me what to do.

The beta team and sensitivity readers, especially Addis, Inmara, Kayla, Becky, and Eric.

The early access team, who gave me feedback every step of the way, especially Erick, Angela, Aidan, and Shivani.

The Fantasy Writers Critique and Support Group on Facebook, and the many artists and fans who've helped make the characters more real than I could have made them on my own.

Thank you all! If I've forgotten anyone, please know that I'm grateful for you, too. <3

I relied heavily on free educational resources from Complexly, MIT, Standford, Wikipedia, and other sources. If you'd like to learn more about the science, history, and philosophy of Edge Anomaly, visit the Inspiration page at EdgeAnomaly.com.

About Me

I'm a neurodivergent overachiever from a mixed racial family. I grew up running wild in the northern woods of Canada, which is a rare experience for a human person these days. I mainly wrote this book for myself, but I hope you like it. I don't know if you've noticed, but a few people in the world have recently made a lot of money very quickly by creating technology that can make lots of people feel strong feelings about things.

Sometimes technology is amazing. The wheel is pretty cool, for example. Today's technologies can facilitate empathy between people who are different, which makes the whole world a little nicer. Unfortunately, helping people empathize with each other isn't a good way for politicians and companies to make money.

Making people feel angry, confused, scared, or jealous is a really good way to make money. A lot of the technology we rely on is designed to get better at doing this, so we don't always know when our feelings are influenced. We don't know why we feel angry or confused or hopeless. Like Edge, we don't always know whose plan we're following, because the big picture can be hard to see, and even harder to understand.

I'm not done thinking about this, so there will be at least one more book. There will probably be two more.

Made in the USA
Las Vegas, NV
11 January 2022

41154904R00184